HEATH, CLIFFS
&
WANDERING
Hearts

LAURA BARNARD

Tina,

I really hope you enjoy!

All my Love

Laura Barnard

6 6 6

DEDICATION

This book is dedicated to my dear friend Roairy Brown who now watches over me in heaven, cracking up laughing every time I fall over. You were always young at heart and I miss you more than words can say.

Chapter One

Friday 7th October

#FirstTime

'I never imagined I'd have to pay to lose my virginity, but it was well worth it.'

I study my brother's friend, trying to work out if he's joking or not. I've not been paying attention to the conversation as James normally drones on, but now I wish I had. He's looking into the distance as if playing a memory back in his mind.

'You paid a *hooker* for your first time?' I ask in disbelief, a little too loudly.

My brother's ear's prick up from across the room. He

rushes over to be beside his friend.

'Come on, James, I think you've had enough,' he says, looking at me apologetically. 'Maybe you should go to my room and have a nap? Hmm?' He leads him away towards the stairs, rolling his eyes at me.

'Did someone just say hooker?' Heath whispers into my ear, making me jump. I turn to see him grinning at me.

'Shush! My Nan will hear,' I whisper, digging him in the ribs.

'Oh *please*, you know how Judy loves a good gossip.' He smiles and looks over at my Nan, who at this very moment looks like she's locked in gossip with two of her best friends. Can there really be that much to talk about when you're that old?

I've known Heath since we were babies. My Mum has been friends with his mum Karen from way before we were even born. We've lived a road away from each other all our life, so we've basically been raised together, constantly at each other's houses while our mums got drunk on cheap wine and sang Spice Girls songs at the top of their lungs. That and subjecting us to chick flicks. His Mum actually named him after Heath Ledger after watching the film *10 things I hate about you* while pregnant.

He's actually the only one that knows about our situation. Not that he's said a word to me or anyone else about it.

'James is totally smashed,' I explain. 'He started saying that he lost his virginity to a hooker. If you ever get that desperate, tell me and I'll knock some sense into you.' I laugh.

'I told you!' he pleads, suddenly rattled. 'I lost it last summer when I was on holiday with Tyler's family.'

'Yeah, yeah.' I laugh, dismissing this information for the third time since they've returned. We both know that Heath hasn't lost his virginity yet. I've known him all my life, and he can't fool me that easily.

'Whatever.' He snorts, frowning. 'Where's Zahra? She said she was going to get me a drink and then disappeared.'

I scan the room and find her draped around my brother's friend, Shane. She's twirling her long bottle-red hair around her neon pink painted fingers, while pouting her lips and laughing very loudly at everything he says.

He follows my gaze. 'I should have known.' He laughs.

Erin walks through the sitting room door looking hot and bothered, her normal English rose complexion, blotchy. Her cheeks are practically on fire.

'What's up? I ask as soon as she spots us.

She places her hands on her hips. 'Your brother's friend nearly broke the door down wanting to get into the toilet and when he did he threw up everywhere. It only just missed me. What an idiot. I mean, at nineteen you'd think you'd be able to handle your drink, wouldn't you?' She's clearly flustered. She could never tolerate fools. Even back in primary school she never had time for kiss chase.

Heath and I open our mouths to respond but smile at each other when she carries on talking, ignoring us.

'Should I tell your mum? Her light blue eyes grow concerned.

I pause for a moment to see if this is a real question, or if she'll carry on talking. Having known her for so long, I know not to try and interrupt her. She continues to stare at me. Ah, she wants a reply.

'Stop worrying. I'm sure someone will look after him.'

'I'm not so sure.' She frowns, looks around the room and spots my Mum. 'Edith...' she walks off towards her, ignoring my advice. Why am I not surprised?

Heath's eyes suddenly land on my chest. Well, that new gel bra Nan bought me is definitely working wonders.

'Did you spill a drink?'

Huh? What's he going on about?

I frown and follow his eye line down to my boob. He's right. It looks like I've spilt a drink down myself. That's weird. I don't remember doing that. I grab a napkin and start to dab against it, but it seems weird and oily. Could it be...? Oh God, please no! Please don't tell me the gel bra is leaking.

I can't exactly feel myself up and check in front of Heath. I need to distract him.

'Look at that!' I shout with a panicked voice, pointing behind him.

He spins round like the sucker he is.

I turn into the wall and delve my hand into the bra. Yes, it feels slightly oily on the inside, but it's mainly the outside. Shit, the wet patch is getting bigger now.

'I don't see anything.' He shrugs, looking at me quizzically.

'Oh...I thought I saw...a pigeon.'

'A pigeon? Sav, you really need glasses if you think there's a pigeon in your kitchen. That or some kind of Prozac.'

I grimace back at him. Ha ha. Very funny. I need to

get out of here while I can, get to my bedroom and change.

'So, are you going to miss him?' he asks, looking over at my brother who has now returned to the room.

I sigh, my chest feeling tight with emotion.

'More than I originally thought,' I admit. I watch my brother as he grabs hold of his girlfriend and gives her a kiss and squeeze. 'But I have to go and get changed.'

He glances back down at my chest again, a line appearing in between his brows.

'Yeah, is it me or is it spreading? Are you...bleeding or something?'

'I don't know what you're talking about' I shrill with an unnatural laugh, edging as discreetly out of the room as quickly as possible.

'He'll be back before you know it,' he says, his hand on my shoulder to try and console me. Dammit, Heath, stop trying to slow me down. 'A year isn't that long'.

I roll my eyes at him, crossing my arms over the offending leak. It only seems to push the oil out quicker. Shit. I quickly adjust my arms so I'm not applying pressure. I have to keep Heath talking. Stop him from noticing what this leak is.

'Yeah, and I suppose Australia isn't that far away,

right?' I mock sarcastically, edging closer to the door. I feel like a giant bitch, but I can't help but take it out on Heath. He's practically a family member.

He crosses his arms over his chest, clearly offended. 'Alright moody, I'm just trying to make you feel better.'

Can he not see that I'm in the middle of an emergency here? I've started to sweat now. I really hope I don't have sweat patches to match my oily boob.

'I know. Sorry.'

Now. Freedom! Thank God. I can kiss goodbye to this nightmare.

My brother grabs my arm. I look up to him in horror. Why is he delaying me right now?

'You're gonna miss the speech.' He tugs me towards the middle of the room.

'No! I need to go and change,' I protest, trying to get away from him. Dammit, why is he so strong? Sometimes I forget he's a fitness freak that could arm-wrestle Arnie.

'Don't be stupid,' he insists, keeping me next to him with a firm grip. I cover myself as well as I can. 'Excuse me, everyone,' he says, a lot more formally than his normal nature.

This is mortifying. Just pray to God everyone will be

looking at him and not me.

I look up at him as his ginger hair catches the light. I'm worried his pale skin will get him burnt to pieces while away. I keep sending him articles on skin cancer. You know, just in case it changes his mind, and he decides to stay.

The party quietens and turns to look at him. I've always been jealous of the way he can command the attention of an entire room. I can only do that when falling over or making an arse of myself.

Shit, my boob is starting to feel really oily now. This is a disaster. What if someone sees? They'll also probably notice that one of my boobs has completely deflated.

'I'd like to thank everyone for coming here tonight,' he says smiling and looking around at all the faces. He's such a good public speaker, unlike me, the mumbler. 'It means a lot to me and Adrianna that you've come to say goodbye to us before we hit Australia.'

'Wooo! Australia!' Adrianna yells, holding up her beer. She's definitely drunk. Let's hope people are too busy noticing that.

He rolls his eyes discreetly. 'Anyway, we love you all, and we'll miss you.'

'Woooo!' Adrianna yells again.

Everyone raises their glasses and shouts excited encouragement.

'And I want to thank my sister here.'

Shit, why is he turning attention my way? The bastard!

'She may only be little, but she's one of my best friends.'

Where the hell has this come from? I feel my cheeks start to burn. Look away, idiots. I'm not interested in your attention.

'If it weren't for her, I wouldn't have had the guts to decide on this trip. She gave me the kick up the arse I needed to man up and tell Mum and Dad.' His warm eyes meet mine. 'I'm gonna miss you.'

Since when has he become such a soppy bastard? How many beers has he had?

He grabs me and pulls me into a tight hug. Oh no. I'm going to leak all over him. I try to escape, but he just presses me harder into him. Well, this is a disaster. I close my eyes and try to treasure the moment of people not knowing I wear gel bras.

People are still clapping and whopping when he pulls

away from me, his t-shirt now all oily. He looks down in confusion, then back at my top.

'Sav, what the fuck?' he shouts loudly. 'Is your boob...leaking or something?'

Saturday 8th October
#LeavingOnAJetPlane

I was, of course, mortified. It was pretty fucking obvious to anyone with eyes that my bra had exploded. I tried to utter something about a drink, but when I looked down, one side of my chest was completely flat next to the other ample looking bosom. There was nothing else to do but run from the room.

I think Heath's still somewhere, laughing. Bastard.

Added to this embarrassment is a sudden unexpected depression. This will be the last day my brother will be in the UK before he leaves for his travels. I mean, yes, he did *out* me last night as a gel bra wearing flat-chested bitch, but he didn't mean to. Before that, he was too busy telling everyone how much he loves me.

Plus today is the day we have to start packing to move out of our family home. I don't even want to get out of bed.

I eventually stumble out and go downstairs. A cuppa and sausage sandwich will make me feel better.

My brother is sitting at the breakfast bar in his Bart Simpson boxers and dressing gown, laughing along to something funny my Nan is saying while eating rice crispy cakes left over from last night. He's the only fitness freak I know that still eats chocolate.

'Morning, darling,' Mum sings when she sees me.

I grunt in response—not yet ready to talk.

'So you're getting better in the mornings then I see,' my brother says, smiling smugly.

I grunt. 'Yeah well maybe if you weren't at Adrianna's every morning you'd notice,' I snap.

Why am I being so unnecessarily bitchy? This is the last day I'm going to see him for a year.

I sit next to him at the breakfast bar and start helping myself to the remaining cakes.

'Oooh! Saucer of milk, table one,' he mocks. 'Just because your bra leaked, don't take it out on me.'

I stick my tongue out. I can't believe my big brother is abandoning me like this, just when I need intense therapy to get over last night.

'So what time's your flight?' I ask, clearing my throat

15

so I don't show any emotion.

'We're leaving in the next half hour.'

I look at his state of undress. So typical of him to leave it to the last minute.

A text from Zahra pops up. 'Lost my belly piercing ball. Might be on your kitchen floor so if you could have a visual sweep. Love ya!'

God, she's nuts.

I take myself to the toilet to try and get a grip on myself. Pull yourself together Sav. I know you're upset, but Dylan doesn't want you crying all over him.

I open the downstairs toilet door, ready to let loose when I instead stop in my tracks and jump. Dylan's friend Toby is asleep on the toilet, his mouth open, dribbling all the way to his t-shirt. His trousers are around his ankles. Ewww!

I cover my eyes with my hand so as not to see anything gross.

'Toby!' I call, 'wake up!'

He doesn't even stir. Shit, is he dead?

I poke him a few times on his shoulder, hoping for a response. He stirs, but instead of waking, he drops forward onto the floor, smashing his chin on the sink on the way down. He's face-down with his arse out.

That's it. I need help.

'Dylan! Mum!'

They rush in and take over. Dylan lifts Toby off the floor and brings him into the sitting room. His chin is bright red. That's gonna be a bruise and a half.

'I didn't even know you slept here,' Mum says to Toby. 'I'll go and call your Mum. Ask her to collect you.'

'Yeah and I'll get some ice,' Dylan says. He turns to me. 'Look after him.'

Toby smiles sadly up at me.

'Do you think Dylan will be gone long?' he asks, with his puppy eyes. He's so cute. That's the only reason I put up with him.

'Well...they said they were going for a year.' I shrug with a grimace. I don't want to lie to him.

His expression changes to one of a puppy that has just been kicked. Oh God, they say don't kick a guy when he's down.

'But, I mean...I'm sure they'll be back before then,' I quickly reassure, squeezing his arm. 'And he says he's going to start a blog so we can all stay in contact.'

Dylan has been concerned about leaving him behind.

Toby kind of relies on Dylan to organise his life for him, and I don't know how he's going to cope when he goes. Although it makes me feel a bit better that someone else is as miserable as me about this.

It must be the quickest half an hour in history, what with us trying to look after Toby too. Before I know it, he's been picked up by his Mum. Dad's loaded Dylan's bags into the car, and he's kissing goodbye to Mum, Nan and Grandad. We agreed not to go to the airport with him, as we'd no doubt cause an emotional scene.

'Bye, then,' I say, like an idiot, punching him lightly on the arm.

'Are you serious?' he asks, giving me a hard look. He's always been better at showing affection than me.

'Okay.' I lean in for a rare hug. I scrunch my face up to try and stop the tears, but one still manages to escape. I quickly brush it off my cheek and try to pull myself together. 'Ok, bye, miss you. Don't get yourselves killed or anything over there, okay?'

I turn and practically run from the room, knowing after today nothing will ever be the same again.

Sunday 9th October

#HomeSweetShitHole

It took us all day yesterday to pack up the house. Luckily Mum and Dad agreed not to start packing up before the party. I don't want my friends knowing we're poor now thanks to my Mum's business going down the toilet. I did try and tell her a shop selling just candles didn't sound like a moneymaker but did she listen? Of course not.

I look around my new bedroom. New box more like. It's bloody tiny, but a least I have my own room. What with Nana and Grandad moving in to help out my Mum and Dad it's a squeeze, to say the least. Especially as we've had to move from our homely three-bed semi in Burnham-On-Cliffs to a barely three-bedroom maisonette in the dodgy area of Crapstone. Yeah, that's the name of the area. Crapstone. How apt.

It doesn't matter that I've plastered my room walls with posters and fairy lights. It's still a dive. In fact, it was advertised as being a two bed. My room's officially a large cupboard, but it has a small window just under the ceiling, so I've deemed that's good enough. It was either that or share a room with Mum and Dad. No, thanks. I must have the only parents left in the world who still have sex. I've had to plug my earphones in AND sing at the top of my lungs to tune it out. Hopefully with Nan and Grandad here that should stop or at least quieten down.

A Snapchat pings through, showing Heath sticking his tongue out. 'So, what's it like? x'

I send back a scrunched up face. 'Absolute dive.'

Heath's the only one that knows about us having to move. Don't get me wrong, I have a close knit group of friends. But I'd rather they not know how bad things have got for me. No one wants the pity look, do they? I've decided it's just better if I carry on as normal. And why bloody shouldn't I? It's not my fault my Mum's business failed. I bloody told her it was a stupid idea, but nobody would listen. My Dad loves her so much that he just went along with it, telling me it was 'her dream' and we should have to make sacrifices, just like she made for us. Well, losing our bloody home was a step too far.

But now this is my life. You know what they say: adapt or die. I better get used to it quick.

CHAPTER TWO

Monday 10th October

#TripsandTits

    The next morning in assembly, Mr Power is rattling on as normal. Sixth form sure is a lot like year eleven. I had it in my head that it would be like college, but they still treat us like kids. I'm gazing into space when Kate shoves me. 'Did you hear that?'

    'What?' I try to zone in on what he's saying.

    'That's right, for those of you who've just woken up,' he says gruffly with his hands on his hips. 'I did, in fact, say that the remaining payment for the ski trip is due by next Monday at the latest.'

    Shit, the chance of me going skiing is now slim. With

all the drama at home, I'd completely forgotten we'd booked it last year. There's still £150 left to pay! How the hell will I ever get that money? It's not like I can ask my Mum. She's got enough worries right now and is still looking for a job.

Only...well the experience would be amazing and look great on my UCAS application. And what if I manage to get a great job because of it and manage to get us all out of that dump we now call home. Plus, *everyone* is going. It will raise so many questions if I back out now. But where can I get the money?

That's it, my mission. I don't know how, but I'm going on that ski trip if it kills me. After the year I've had, I bloody deserve it.

Me and the besties go shopping after school: Erin, Charlotte, Zahra, and Kate. Well, only window-shopping for poor little me. It's not even like we have a huge selection around here. You see Burnham-On-Cliffs is a small seaside town. It used to be full of holidaymakers coming to marvel at the cliff views, but since the recession, it's gone downhill a lot. Lots of shops on our small high street shut down, along with many B & B's, and still haven't reopened.

'This is gorgeous, Savvy,' Kate says, picking up a black dress in New Look and inspecting it closely.

'Yeah, why don't you wear it to Sarah's party on Saturday?' Erin asks, looking at me hopefully.

Although the original thought of the dress's chiffon material made me want to reach for my jeans, it's actually quite simple; one-shouldered with a fitted waist and fluted short skirt. Shame I can't afford it.

'Come on.' I roll my eyes. 'It's so girly. It's really not me.' I squirm at the feel of the material between my fingers, not to mention the fifty quid price tag. 'Why don't one of you buy it?'

'Just try it on!' Zahra protests. She's always so bloody pushy. 'It would totally suit you!'

I can see Kate holding it up behind her, almost having a seizure from the excitement. Ugh, God. If I know this lot, they won't give up. It's going to be easier just to try it on and show them how I don't suit something so girlie.

'Okay,' I huff, grabbing the dress from them. 'If it will shut you all up, I'll just try it on.' I spin on my heel, heading for the changing rooms.

Once behind the safety of a grotty purple curtain I pull

it on over my head. I begrudgingly turn to look in the mirror and am about to yell how much I hate it when I do a double take. It's not as girly as it first looked when Kate was holding it. I move from side to side and watch as it swishes when I move. It *is* short though and images of me falling and flashing my knickers play through my mind.

Zahra suddenly yanks the curtain open. Thank God I'm not naked. Not that she'd care. That girl has no boundaries.

'You haven't got a choice—you're buying it,' she says forcefully.

'Yeeeeeeehhh!' Kate squeals enthusiastically, clapping her hands.

Charlotte grins. 'The only things you're missing is these.' She opens a box and pulls out two chicken fillets. We don't all have giant knockers like her.

Zahra yanks down the top of the dress and stuffs them in my bra before I even have time to register the horror of the situation. 'These should be a lot sturdier than those cheap gel bras your Nan was buying you.'

'Oh, my God, you're the only friend I know that pimps up her mate,' I shriek unimpressed.

The girls laugh hysterically behind me. I try to ignore

them, desperately wanting to find an excuse not to buy it.

'I'm just trying to help,' she says, looking me up and down like I'm a project.

I look back in the mirror to inspect my new boobs. They do look good, making me look at least a cup size bigger. Far better than the gel bra.

'What if I have to jump?' I ask, trying to get used to the squishy cold feeling on my skin. They hardly feel stable, and with my luck, I'll sneeze, and one will fly out of my top.

'You'll be fine, hun. I wear them all the time,' Zahra chirps in, pushing her boobs together as if to show me their effects. Her tits do always look fab.

'I don't know.' I hesitate.

Come on, Savannah, think of *something*. *You can't afford these.*

'After what happened at the party I don't think I should risk it. And it's just false advertising. What if a guy thought my boobs were this big and then had a huge disappointment?'

Amused faces greet me. It's all a moot point anyway because I'm poor.

'Hunny.' Zahra giggles. 'If you get that far it will be too late for him anyway.' She gives me a cheeky wink.

I'm going to have to just admit it.

'Anyway, I can't afford any of this.' I start pulling it back over my head. 'I really need to find a job if I want to go on that ski trip.'

Charlotte raises her eyebrows, clearly confused. 'Can't you ask your parents to help you out?' I keep forgetting they're all none the wiser to my situation.

Erin studies me with curious eyes. This is the moment I should choose to tell them the truth. Only I don't. Not while I'm wearing a dress and boobs I can't afford. Not when I don't feel strong enough to tell them my life has fallen apart without bursting into tears.

'No. They've said if I want to go on any school trips I have to pay for it myself. So I should be handing out my CV right now rather than trying on stupid dresses with you guys.'

'Ooh, well we're *very* sorry for trying to dress you like a girl.' Kate giggles.

'Don't worry,' Charlotte says, wrapping her arm around me. 'We'll totally help you. Come back to mine, and we'll print off some CV's and then we can hand them around this week after school.'

I smile back at her. This is why I love these girls.

Without them, my life *really* would be up the shitter.

'But even if I get a job between now and next Monday, which in itself is massively unlikely, I'll never earn £150 straight away.'

Erin chews on her lip. 'I've got some money saved up for spending money and driving lessons. If you manage to get a job before Monday and we can work it out that you can pay me back before we go, then the money's yours.'

My eyes nearly pop out of my head. 'You're joking?' I shriek, jumping up and down on the spot.

'Nope,' she grins. 'I'm just that awesome.'

I have such amazing friends. Now I just have to drop my CV into every place available and pray to God I get a job offer.

I get changed back into my uniform and meet the girls back in the shop.

'Ready.'

We make our way out of the shop. I'm already trying to think of what I can put down on a CV. I have zero work experience. All of a sudden a buzzer starts going off, so loud it vibrates all the way down my ear canal and into my chest. What the hell is that?

'Run!' Zahra yells, grabbing Kate and Charlotte.

Run? What the hell is she talking about? Charlotte looks back, eyes wide, before allowing herself to be dragged off.

'Why would they run?' I ask Erin over the noise.

It's then I feel a heavy hand on my right shoulder. Erin's eyeline goes up as she takes in whoever has me their hands on me.

In a split second she turns and legs it away from us.

'Erin!' I squeal.

'I'm sorry!' she shouts back, already at the corner. What a bitch.

I look behind me to see a stern-faced security guard. 'I'm afraid we need to check your bag.'

I'm still so confused. Why did the girls run? This is just a simple misunderstanding.

'Yeah, that's fine,' I shrug, handing it over. 'I have no idea why the alarm went off.'

'Well, your friends didn't look too innocent when they ran for the hills.'

He's telling me.

'I have no idea why they did.'

He fumbles around with my bag, eventually pulling out a pair of chicken fillets. How the fuck did they get in there? I didn't steal them? How mortifying!

'I'm afraid, Miss, that unless you can show me a receipt, you're coming with me.'

Shit.

I'm carted back through the shop for every staff member to tut loudly at me. This is awful.

'I didn't do it,' I try to protest.

'Tell it to the judge,' a snotty manager says. Oh, for God's sakes. Dramatic much?

I'm taken through the back and into a small office with no windows. This is awful. Should I call a lawyer? I'd have to Google one first, but still.

'Look, I really shouldn't even be here. I didn't steal those...' God, I can't even say chicken fillets out loud. 'Those...things. I have no idea how they got into my bag.'

It's only then it dawns on me. One of the girls must have put them in my bag. As a joke maybe? Or did they honestly think we'd get away with it? I bet it was Zahra. She's stupid enough to think it would work. Plus, she was the one shouting run.

'We need to call your parents.'

'My parents?' I shriek in horror. 'Surely you'll just tell me off? Why do you need to get them involved?'

'Its either that, or we'll have to take you straight down to the police station.'

God. All this over a lousy pair of chicken fillets? But who can I call to pretend to be my Mum? Heath's mum, Karen? No, she'd tell her.

'I've...err, I've forgotten their number.'

He narrows his eyes at me. 'Look, young lady, we either do this the hard way or the easy way.'

There's a sudden commotion out front with lots of women arguing.

'I know she's through here!' someone says before barging into the office.

It's my Nan. Why the hell is she here? I haven't even handed over a telephone number yet. Shit, maybe she was telling the truth that time she tried to convince me she had physic powers. Although I really do think envisioning Taylor Swift breaking up with a boyfriend isn't so much physic, just the law of probability.

'There she is,' she says as soon as she sees me, her arms out wide. 'My poor petal. What have they been doing to you?'

I stand up. 'I'm fine Nan,' I insist.

I barely get my words out before she's pushed me into her cleavage. 'Just let me play this,' she whispers into my ear.

Play this? What on earth is she talking about?

'Can someone *please* tell me why my only granddaughter has been dragged back here like an *animal* with absolutely no evidence against her.'

'Actually, we caught her red-handed,' he answers, his arms crossed over his chest.

'Red-handed?' she shrieks. 'How so?'

'We found these in her bag.' He holds up the chicken fillets, waving them floppily in my face. God, this couldn't be more humiliating.

'Everything okay, love?' Grandad asks, appearing in the doorway.

He takes one look at the dangling chicken fillets, pales and walks out. I was wrong, this can be more humiliating.

'In her bag,' Nan repeats. 'So not in her hands. Not red-handed, as you previously implied. I think it's a bit bloody clear to see that she was framed!'

'Framed? That's a bit dramatic isn't it.'

'Really? Coming from the man that marched my

sixteen-year-old granddaughter back into this dungeon. I suggest you apologise and we'll forget all about it.'

'Me apologise?'

'Yes, you! Have you had anyone else here in this room with you?' she asks both of us.

I shake my head.

'Being alone with a teenager like this. You could be a pervert for all we know. Did he touch you dear? Did he?'

'No! Shit, Nan!'

'This is getting out of hand,' the security man says.

'I'll say!' Nan says. 'Come here, my baby. Get away from the creepy man.'

'Nan, he hasn't—' I'm shut up again with her chest in my face.

'We'll be going to the police of course. And the local paper.'

'Wait! I'm sure this is all a misunderstanding,' the security guard says. 'We've got the stolen item back. Why don't we just leave it at that.'

'Very wise,' Nan says with a nod, picking up my bag and guiding me out.

We walk out to Grandad.

'Alright, little one. I bet I've had a worse day than you.'

'Are you joking? Did you not see that in there? They've accused me of stealing chicken fillets.'

'Yeah, well I have an abscess on my tooth and your Nan forces me out to lunch with her today. I've just spent the last hour sucking a steak.'

When I get home, my phone instantly connects to the Wi-Fi and pings with an email. At least this place has a good Internet connection. I open it up to see Dylan's sent me a link to his new blog. No hi or anything. Not even a kiss at the end. Just the URL. Typical.

DYLAN'S BLOG

WE'RE HERE! AUS UPDATE

We decided before boarding the plane that to save money we would buy a bottle of vodka in duty-free. We knew we had more than twenty-four hours travelling to drink it. But as soon as we got on the plane the air hostess told us 'You can't take that off the plane with you. We stop over in Abu Dhabi (what a silly name), and that's a dry country.' So we had around twelve hours to neck the whole bottle. Then she leant in and spoke to me like a five-year-

old and told me all alcohol on this flight was free anyway. That'll teach me for jumping in and not Googling shit.

We got so drunk we couldn't even walk.

We stayed in a place called Kings Cross, which sounds classy, but it's like the red light district of Sydney. It's run by triads and pimps.

The receptionist invited us to a club with her, which we were up for. I ordered a pint of beer and a vodka, lemonade. They were like 'sure, that's $32.' Holy fuck! Our money is worth nothing out here. If we can't afford alcohol, then my money is worthless.

We went to see the opera house the next day, and I couldn't help thinking it's exactly like those millions of photos I've seen online.

We went back to the hostel to find our new roommate. He's from Canada. As soon as he found out we were English, he started blaring out drum and bass. 'You guys are English? You must love drum and bass then?'

'Mmmm, well....'

'Wait, I got a whole DJ set here you will love.'

'Oh, hooray.'

We got horrendously shit faced on five litres of cheap wine. Adrianna and I were both ill—that Canadian must think the English are pussies.

Today we have just checked out and are mulling around. The coach is picking us up at 11 pm (arriving at Bryon Bay at 11 am) from outside an Irish pub. Plan; get drunk in the pub, get picked up and fall asleep. Obviously, there is one big risk there, getting too drunk and missing the coach. A risk I think is worth taking.

Considering we are in Australia, I have barely heard anyone speaking English. The social areas in the hostels are full of Germans, each with a laptop, each surfing Facebook. What a load of wankers.

Saturday 15th October

It's been a week. A week of me ignoring Zahra, and barely speaking to the others. I still can't believe they did that to me. Zahra's argument of *'you only live once'* was pathetic. She bought me a pair as a peace offering, but I've just thrown them into the bottom of my underwear drawer. I can't be bought.

Plus I've had to listen to chatter about the school ski trip from all the bitches getting the trip paid for by their parents. Their parents that haven't flushed their future down the toilet. With just a month to go, it's all anyone can talk about. I want to suffocate them with their own money.

The remaining £150 has to be paid by Monday, and although I managed to drop my CV into practically every shop on earth during the week, I'm yet to hear anything back. That means Erin won't lend me the money, so bye-bye skiing.

I'm sulking in the front seat of Nan's car on the way to Sarah's party, the four girls squashed into the back.

'Right,' Nan announces, 'I think it's time you all got over what happened and made friends.'

'I agree,' Erin nods.

I turn, outraged, to face her. 'Easy for you to say! You weren't the one nearly arrested over it.'

'Hey! It wasn't my fault,' she tries to argue. 'It was Zahra's dickhead idea.'

'That doesn't mean you stopped to ask if I was okay before you ran for the hills.'

She looks down at her lap. 'No. You're right. I'm sorry. I've been saying it all week.'

'I know,' I nod. 'It's fine. I forgive you.'

'Thank God,' Zahra says, with a massive sigh.

'Err, I didn't say I forgave you, Zahra! You have a lot

more sucking up to do.'

'Well...' she looks towards my Nan. What have these two concocted up? 'I bought you those chicken fillets to apologise and you know I've been saving up for months for concert tickets, but instead, I spent it on you.'

I sigh wearily. I know this is as much as an apology as I'm going to get from her.

'Fine. Let's just forget it.'

'Great!' Kate and Charlotte sing. I know they hate atmosphere.

Nan reaches into her handbag. 'So Zahra told me to bring them.' She places the chicken fillets in my lap. 'I think you should wear them.'

'Nan!'

'Why not?' She shrugs. 'If I'd known I could have a boob job without the pain at your age I'd have jumped at the chance.

'Yeah, well I'm not you.'

'You can say that again,' she laughs.

'Anyway, back to the party,' Erin says. 'Apparently her parents have paid for the hall, DJ and food. It should be a laugh.'

'Plus, her parents have told the owners that it's an

37

18th instead of a 16th so it should be easier to get served,' Kate adds, smiling wickedly.

Now that we've cleared the air I am actually excited about it.

'Marvellous,' my Nan responds chirpily. She's the only Nan in the world pleased to hear her underage teenage granddaughter is trying to get served booze. 'Who's birthday is it again?' she asks while turning into the street of the pub it's held in.

'Sarah's,' Zahra answers, attempting to do her lip gloss in the back with just a hand mirror.

'Which one is she again?' Nan asks, her brow creasing up in confusion.

'I think you've met her before,' Charlotte answers, looking up from her phone. 'She's the fruit loop with blonde hair.'

'She's not a fruit loop,' I protest, feeling bad for talking about her. 'I envy how she doesn't give a crap what anyone else thinks.'

'Maybe you should try to be a bit more like her,' Nan says, raising one eyebrow.

I ignore her dig about not telling my friends about our situation and turn to face out of the window. Like I don't feel self-conscious enough. Unlike the others, I couldn't get a new outfit so I'm just in smart skinny jeans and a blue top that luckily brings out my eyes. Or so my Mum tells me.

'You know,' Nan starts, lowering her voice 'mine and Grandad's old flat is empty at the moment. The sale doesn't go through for another couple of days.'

My poor Nan and Grandad had to sell their flat to bail my mum out. She not only ruined our lives but apparently, she had to take them down with us.

'So...' she lowers her voice to a conspirational whisper, 'if you wanted to take some friends back you could.'

She's offering me an empty flat to have a potential party in? She is *so* not a normal Nan.

'Really? Even maybe...some guy friends?' Zahra asks, leaning forward eagerly. How the hell did she even hear her?

She winks. 'Yes, of course, darling. Maybe you should bring quite a few back.' She smiles wickedly at me, her eyes alight with mischief. She knows I'd never take her up on it. I swear the woman thinks I'm a loser. She still slips the key in my bag.

'Enough with the pressure,' I snap.

I must be the only teenager in the world that is being

39

pressurised into getting a boyfriend by her Nan. Most Nan's would be too busy knitting, but mine seems to be far too involved in my lack of a sex life. It's beyond depressing.

'Savannah, shut up talking!' Zahra shouts from the back seat. 'It's a yes! Of *course* it's a yes. But first!' She grabs the chicken fillets and stuffs them down my bra. 'There, so much better!'

The party is in full swing by the time we arrive, having decided we wanted to be fashionably late. That and it gave us a chance to neck a bottle of Lambrini on the way.

Everyone is already half cut and jumping around dancing like maniacs. I wish I'd sunk a few more before leaving, as I'm suddenly very aware of my bare arms. I really wish I could tan rather than freckle like a dot to dot.

We send Charlotte to the bar and watch from the dance floor. With those tits, there's a possibility we could get booze. She saunters over, flicking her blonde hair back, sticking her chest out, and licking her lips. She really can be a minx when she wants to be. We see the young barman clock her and stare at her huge boobs, captivated like a deer in headlights. We're not shocked when she gets served and comes over with two bottles of wine. We start drinking it quickly in case they take it away from us.

I look around to see if anything exciting is happening. Just the usual groups of girls from school. I smile at them politely. They smile back. Unlike a lot of girls, I choose to be friendly with everyone and try to stay out of gossip. It's worked so far.

Our group of guy friends are here: Heath, Tyler, and Ryan. Our mate Tyler's friends, Luke and Robbie are chatting to some guy I've seen around before that goes to our rival school, Leamington's. He's seriously hot with messy blonde hair, sexy stubble and big broad shoulders. I wonder how Sarah even knows him, or if she knows him at all.

Heath waves from across the room and looks me up and down for a second. He always seems shocked when I make an effort. I respond by doing a little sarcastic twirl. I do feel different when I'm wearing heels. I even feel like I'm walking differently. Probably because I'm so desperate not to fall on my face.

The girls and I begin dancing along to the song playing, pretending to be gangsters as we sing along to the rap in the chorus we know so well. I notice that Tia, a girl in our year, is seriously wasted and is grinding not so far away from us. This isn't like her. Normally she wouldn't

41

say boo to a goose, but here she is, dancing like a stripper. Her eyes look a bit weird—they're kind of rolling around in her head. Her dancing starts to slow. Should I ask if she's okay?

I hear what sounds like the start of a cough. My head swings round to see where it's come from. I watch helplessly as Tia projectile vomits everywhere. She's literally spinning around in a circle while vomiting, exorcist style. One by one, everyone in the party stops dancing and jumps out of the way so they don't get hit by the vomit train.

When it finally stops, she looks around wide-eyed before collapsing into a heap on the floor. Shit.

Sarah's mum runs over, signalling the DJ to turn off the music.

'The party is over! Somebody call an ambulance!' She screams at the top of her lungs.

'Bit bloody dramatic,' Erin scoffs next to me.

My stomach tightens as I watch Tia lifeless on the floor. Bit dramatic? This looks serious.

Everyone starts leaving in a hurry. I follow them out onto the high street, not wanting to see anymore. The moment my foot touches the pavement a whoosh of fresh air hits me. Wow, I'm drunker than I thought.

'What are we gonna do? I slur to Kate.

Try and regain normal speech, you idiot.

She looks back at me blankly. It seems she's drunk too.

A lot of people start to walk home, immediately giving up on the night. I look around, crushed with disappointment that the night is ending so early. We've barely got here.

Heath comes running out holding his jacket covered in Tia's vomit.

'Can you believe this?' he shrieks, thrusting it under my nose.

I hold my breath, trying not to inhale the smell, but can already feel myself starting to retch. I clasp my hand over my mouth and try to think nice thoughts.

Robbie and Luke come out holding trays of food.

'Have you stolen the food from the party?' I demand, horrified. They even have the birthday cake!

'Yeah, so what? It's only gonna go to waste now anyway. I'm doing them a service,' Robbie says with a chuckle.

'Whatever.' I roll my eyes, disgusted.

'Give me a sandwich,' Erin says, reaching out. I glare

43

at her. Traitor.

I really don't want the night to end so early. It's barely begun. I could always take my Nan up on her offer and be a rebel for the night. Could I really be so reckless? I know most people would jump at the chance. Plus, it's not like I have a cool ski trip to look forward to.

'Everyone can come back to mine if you want,' I say before I have time to really think it through.

Zahra looks at me in stunned admiration. She clearly thought I'd never go through with it.

'Are you sure, hun? There's a lot of people here,' Erin says looking around anxiously.

'Yeah fuck it! Everyone back to mine!' I slur, punching the air in excitement.

Chapter Three

#LetsPartyBitches

I realise I'm being stupid, but I don't care. A part of me wants to show my Nan that I can be the crazy, rebellious teenager she thinks I'll never be.

We walk the mile to her flat, eating birthday cake and sandwiches. I can't help feeling euphoric from the recklessness of it all.

Only...Is it my imagination or is the group getting bigger? I look behind, and I'm sure that a load of people has tagged along. Oh dear. I think I'm starting to sober up. There are a lot more people than I wanted. We won't all fit in that tiny flat.

I reach into my bag for my phone and ring Jessica,

who I can see further back.

Jessica is my friend from Sociology class. The girls don't really like her because she's a bit of a whore, but I find her hilarious.

'Hey, oh my god, can you believe Tia?' she screeches down the phone without taking a breath. 'She came to my house before and drank a whole litre of vodka. I told her to chill out, but she was hell bent on it. Now I feel really bad. What if her mum blames me? I mean...'

'Jessica!' I shout, knowing it's the only way to interrupt her. She'll go on for days otherwise. 'I need your help'.

'What, babe?' she says, ready to take orders.

That's my girl. Thank God she's not paralytic.

'I need you to hold everyone back. Take them round the block a few times and try and lose them. I can't have everyone in one little flat. My Nan will have a heart attack if she finds out.'

In truth, she'd probably be impressed, but I don't want to tell her that.

'Babes, you don't have to say anymore. Totally get you. Speak soon.' She hangs up.

It seems I don't need to worry as she somehow

manages to get the last crowd to walk slower. Then she shouts something about an off-licence. I smile to myself. Good girl. They start following her in the opposite direction.

I run into the block of flats, unlocking my Nan's door. Everyone piles in within seconds. I stay at the door making sure that no one I don't know tries to sneak in. The girls take care of putting the music on (apparently one of them brought iPhone speakers) and getting my Nan's alcohol stash out of one of the packed up boxes—one of the perks of having an alcoholic Nan. Luckily, the flat backs onto a communal garden so letting everyone know they have to smoke outside isn't much of a problem.

I lock the door behind me and take a deep, shaky breath. Why did I think this was a good idea again? I hope this is everyone.

I ring Jessica, my hands shaking so much it takes longer than normal.

'Hey, babe,' she answers breathlessly. 'I'm still trying to lose them! They're following me like I'm the Pied Piper. I can't get rid of them.'

'Shit.' I can't just leave her out there in the cold. 'Just try anything, but make sure you get in.'

I hang up and wander back through to the lounge, the sound of heavy music vibrating against the walls. My friends are a strange bunch of people—some harmless geeks and some very popular people who seem to be mixing up cocktails in the kitchen. Maybe this will increase my popularity. Damn it, I shouldn't care. But it *is* a bonus.

The girls have gone into Nan's fancy dress box so people have random parts of outfits on. Zahra has a police hat and tie. Ben has a feather boa around his neck and Heath has fairy wings. It looks pretty insane with them jumping around to *Meghan Trainer*.

I finally manage to get Jessica in but have to slam the door behind her. People shout through the letterbox to be let in, making my stomach contract with fear. It's a real shame, but I can't let everyone in. Some of the people I would have loved to have in, but there are too many strangers in the mix now for it to be an option. Probably random gatecrashers.

I lock the door from the inside and put the key in my pocket so that no one can get in by accident. I pray that her neighbours won't call the police, but I try not to care. I'm just acting like a normal teenager. I shouldn't give a shit. I grab someone's shot of Sambuca and down it. Eugh, that's gross.

Within seconds I feel ridiculously pissed. Everyone keeps telling me what an awesome party it is and how pretty I look tonight. I don't know if it's sincerity as some of the people I've barely spoken to before, but I don't care. I'm just enjoying it while I can. Although I really wish Ben would stop swinging on the sitting room door.

After a while I decide I need to check the street from the bedroom, to see if the mob is still out there. There's more chance of the neighbours calling the police if they are. I find Kevin on the way, slumped over the toilet with the door wide open, his forehead sweaty.

'Kevin? Are you ok?' I ask, trying to hide my repulsion. It's hard; he's such a dick.

Of course you're going to get sick when you hog a bottle of Jack Daniels! I tried to find *one* redeeming feature about him, but I just can't.

'Maybe you should go outside and get some fresh air, yeah?' I suggest, suppressing the need to shout *get your life together!*

He nods and slopes off. Frigging idiot. I walk towards my Nan's bedroom, open the handle and walk in, only to be confronted by a bum. A big fat arse almost totally in my

49

face.

'Aaah! What the fuck?' I scream, putting my hands up to try and cover it, but it's too late. My retinas are burning.

'Whoops!' I look up to see it is Robbie, clambering to cover himself with his boxer shorts.

Fuck, what is happening? I look around him to see Jessica's friend, Karen, lying half-naked on the floor, trying to pull her bra back on. I wish she'd chosen her knickers first. It's hard not to look straight at her completely bald vagina. Jesus, she must have been waxed for hours to get it like that.

I don't know where to look. There are naked body parts everywhere. I quickly turn and stumble out of the room, trying to find the door handle in the dark. I manage to bash my leg against the wall instead, but don't stop to react.

I pull the door shut quickly, attempting to hide my embarrassment. I try to erase the memory, but all I can see is the nakedness. My god, how easy is Karen! She only met him tonight, and now she's shagging him at a random party. Jesus, what a total ho-bag!

I force my shaky legs into the tiny spare room, still trying to calm myself down. A gasp causes me to look up and see that hot guy from Leamington shagging a blonde.

'Aaah! Sorry!' I shriek, backing out of the room trying not to look.

Jesus, is *everyone* having sex?

Wait, why am I apologising? They're the ones that should be embarrassed. Imagine fucking in someone else's flat, at a party, on the floor and in a room without a lock. And not just one couple but two. Call me a prude, but I couldn't do it. What if some guy came in, took a picture and posted it all around school? Oh, the potential horror!

I slam the door and take a deep breath trying to compose myself. I crane my head out of the hallway window. The mob seems to have dispersed. Oh, thank God, I can really start to enjoy myself now. I can try to forget what I've seen and enjoy myself.

A deep filthy laugh makes me look out again. Four figures are walking back towards the flat.

'No,' I want to shout at them. 'The party is over. Go away!'

One of them laughs again. This time, I'm sure I recognise the sound. I freeze, my heart missing a beat. That laugh belongs to my Mum. I look closer and yep, my family are walking back from the pub.

What the hell are they doing here? They should be walking back to our own shitty flat in our far rougher area. It can't be kicking out time already. I glance at my watch and see that it's midnight. Shit, that went fast.

I race back into the lounge, ready to tell everyone, but the alarm has already been raised. Someone shouts '*her parents are on their way back.*' Panic is suddenly in the air—people looking around for potential escape plans.

'Don't worry,' I try to shout over the madness. 'My Nan is cool. Anyone that wants to stay, can.'

God, I must be *really* drunk. Where has this defiant attitude come from? But then I remember Nan saying I could bring people back, and she didn't exactly specify how many...So if we're working on technicalities...

A load of people decide to bolt out of the door, regardless of my reassurance. I lock it behind them and look around the room to see that around twenty people are remaining. Panic rises in my throat, but I force it down, joining in with people dancing.

The door slams and my mum's voice carries through. 'Don't worry love, go, get some water, and you'll be fine.'

Stupid fucking, Kevin. Why did he have to hang around outside vomiting? He's such a liability.

The sitting room door is pushed open and as if on cue the door falls off its hinges and onto the floor. Damn Ben, swinging off it earlier. I knew I should have said something.

I'm trying to judge their reactions. Their faces are very different. Dad looks furious, but I can also see that he can't be bothered with the fight. He turns around and walks towards the bedrooms, not saying a word. God, I hope Robbie and Karen are out of the room.

Mum is a different story altogether. She walks straight in and over to the speakers. For a second I'm sure she's going to turn them off. Instead, she looks at Kate with an excited grin.

'Have you got any Spice Girls?' she asks excitedly.

Kate looks back at her baffled. I cringe hard.

'They're a nineties girl band,' I explain apologetically.

'Oh,' she says confused. She flicks through her phone. 'I think I have a nineties album here somewhere. Found it!'

It starts playing and Mum immediately jumps up and down in excitement. Like a bloody teenager herself.

'Let's get this party started!' she yells, grabbing the phone and turning the volume up to the loudest decibel. She is *so* embarrassing.

God, how embarrassing. In a way, I just wish she were a normal strict mum who ends the party, sending everyone home. I mean who says *'let's get the party started'?* She is clearly trying to relive her youth through me.

My Nan and Grandad are the next to come into the sitting room. Grandad's face is almost identical to Dad's, and he also turns to go towards the bedrooms.

Nan's face lights up. This is her idea of heaven. I still can't believe she never seemed to grow up. The real life version of Peter Pan.

Her and Mum start dancing with the girls, doing their usual clap dance, which is basically the chicken dance with a few claps thrown in for good measure.

Please, stop dancing and fuck off home.

If they carry on like this it's possible I'll drop down dead from acute humiliation. Next thing Nan will be getting the spoons out and doing an Irish jig.

I see the Leamington boy, Robbie, and the girls come in from the bedrooms looking sheepish. Ah, Dad and Grandad have obviously gotten to them. Wait, Leamington boy was shagging Amelia from my year? Lucky bitch.

The girls leave straight away, obviously mortified, but the guys come in the sitting room to investigate. As soon

54

as they see my mum is cool, they're grabbing a drink and joining in with the clap dancing.

Is it weird that Tia vomiting could be the best thing to happen to me in a long time?

My Mum dances over to me. 'Sorry about Nan, darling. I know she can be embarrassing sometimes, but I'll drag her home to bed soon enough.' She smiles sympathetically.

I try desperately not to laugh. 'Thanks.' I smile as genuinely as I can, even though she's the one doing the most clap dancing right now.

My Nan dances over to me next, bopping my hip with hers. *How is she now wearing a pink wig and comically huge sunglasses?*

'Hi, sweetheart. I can't believe how many friends you have!' she gushes in shock. 'Don't worry about your Mum. I know she's out of touch. I'll take her home to bed soon enough.' She gives me the same sympathetic smile that my Mum gave me.

I smile back, laughing at how identical they can be sometimes.

We all carry on dancing for a little while, only stopping when a neighbour complains at around 1 am. Mum and

Dad agree to let us stay the night here as long as we turn the music off.

We wave goodnight. Both Mum and Nan turn around to wink at me as if taking the other home to bed is a big favour. Dad and Grandad don't look best pleased about leaving us with the boys, but they're dragged away by them.

I breathe a sigh of relief as soon as the door shuts. I can get back to enjoying myself without their watching eyes.

We turn the music back on but keep it low, conscious of the neighbours. It all continues in a bit of a haze. I'm so happy and drunk that time seems to be running away from me. Every time I look at my phone another hour has passed.

The boys have gone through the fancy dress box and found toy guns, which they've started to use for playing FBI agents. How am I ever going to lose my virginity to a child like that?

Ben is the first one to disappear and falls asleep on the floor of the spare room. We, of course, take this to mean that we can shave one of his eyebrows off. The night starts to wind down slowly, and I offer to get them some blankets so that they can sleep in the lounge.

I go into Nan's old bedroom, ready to root through the remaining boxes in the darkness when I notice that a different song is playing in here. It's Rod Stewart's *Have I Told you Lately*.

I turn the light on and in doing so catch myself in the mirrored wardrobe. God, I look awful. All of my makeup has melted so I look pale enough to be a vampire, and my mascara has run from where I've been crying with laughter. I tug at my tangled hair grimacing at my reflection. Jesus, what a fright.

'Hey,' says a voice out of nowhere. I spin round to where the noise has come from. Leamington boy is sat casually in the corner smiling at me.

'Fuck!' I gasp. 'You scared the crap out of me.'

I try to catch my breath. *Way to sound classy, Savvy.* God, he's good looking.

'What are you doing sitting in the dark listening to music? Who do you think you are, an evil superhero or something?'

God, why do I insist on embarrassing myself? I know I'm drunk. It doesn't stop me cringing though.

His laughter reminds me that I'm still in the room. Stick with the conversation, Savannah.

57

He smiles, bemused. 'I came in here to chill for a bit.' I can understand that. We *are* all loud. 'I love this song.'

He likes Rod Stewart?

'Yeah, me too,' I say a little too enthusiastically. Stop being an eager beaver.

'I'm kind of sleepy,' I admit out loud. God, why am I acting like a three-year-old child?

He laughs and pats the floor next to him. He wants me to sit with him? Why is he being so nice to me? I bound over and make myself comfortable next to him. Well, as comfortable as I can on the thin carpet, which with my bony arse is hard work.

Before I can stop myself, I find I'm resting my head on his shoulder. His big, strong, and broad shoulders. I don't even want to think how inappropriate I'm being. I just want to be cuddled. And he's so warm. I really shouldn't be doing this with a random Leamington guy. He's practically a stranger to me. I don't even know his name.

'I'm Savannah by the way,' I mumble into the material of his t-shirt. Sleep is overriding any sensibilities I have.

He laughs, it vibrates all the way to his shoulders.

'I know exactly who you are, Savannah.'

My eyes widen in alarm. How the hell does he know

me?

'Well, this is awkward,' I admit with a giggle. 'I only know you as Leamington boy.'

He surprises me by wrapping both his arms round me and pulling my body towards him, so that I now sit between his legs, my face nuzzled into his chest. Mmm, he smells like lavender and mint. I wonder what fabric conditioner his mum uses.

'I'm Zach.'

God, even his name is beautiful.

He starts humming along to the music, the vibrations on his chest so soothing that I allow myself to drift off to sleep.

I don't care that I'm cuddling up with Zach, who I know has a girlfriend. A girlfriend that I caught him doing inappropriate things to earlier. I don't care that everyone is in the lounge waiting for me to bring in blankets. I don't care if he thinks I'm coming on to him and just feels pity for me. I just know two things for sure at that moment.

1) I'm incredibly tired and

2) I wouldn't find anywhere more comfortable in the world than in his arms so I'm not going to move.

He starts to talk about something. I think it's

something to do with his girlfriend, but I'm not listening. I'm already starting to go into my dream world. My beautiful colourful dream world...

Chapter Four

I drag my heavy eyelids open and recoil from the sight that confronts me. Kevin's big ugly face is next to mine, his nose almost touching me. It's so close, and he's dribbling. Ugh. I fight back the repulsion and urge to vomit all over him and try to focus. Please god, tell me I didn't go anywhere near that imbecile last night?

I fight back against the headache that is starting to whirl in my brain, trying to recall the last thing I remember from last night. But then the cuddling with Zach appears in my head, and I wince my eyes shut hoping I can forget it again. I don't know what's worse: getting with a fucking idiot like Kevin or being all over Zach. I cringe at the memory. How humiliating.

I turn my head and see Kate asleep next to me. God, she looks like an angel when she sleeps. The sun streams in through the gap in the curtains and shines on her perfect cheekbones. Why couldn't I look like that? I can't see myself yet, but I'm sure I have panda eyes and birds nest hair.

Something cold and squishy is on my neck. Ewww. I tentatively reach and find that it's one of the chicken fillets Charlotte bought me. Fuck. How did that fall out...and not just fall out but jump up onto my neck?

I stand up and throw it into the built-in wardrobe before anyone can see. I automatically reach to remove the other one, but it's not there. Oh no. Where is it? I look round but can't see it anywhere. Please, God, say that it's not in the lounge. I'll *die* if someone's using it as a pillow.

I stumble out to the toilet. The hum of conversation comes through the door. Oh God, people are awake. I follow the sound into the lounge, led by my own curiosity. What if Zach is still here? What if he's seen the chicken fillet? I'll die. *Actually* die.

Heath and Zahra are sat on the floor, laughing away

at something, eating what I know is out of date biscuits from the cupboard. Not that they seem to mind, cackling like a pair of witches. I sit down next to them and help myself to one.

'The others gone?' I ask in a croaky voice. God, I sound like Darth Vader with the flu.

'Yeah, Zach, Ben, and Robbie had football so left at about 08.30 am,' Zahra tells me. 'Most people left last night after you went to bed.'

Flashbacks of me cuddling close to Zach come back to me. I physically cringe. I'm never going to be able to look at him again. God, why do I get so affectionate when I drink? I try to think beyond it. Hopefully, he was too drunk to remember.

'What time did I go to bed?' I ask, still having no recollection. It's like every memory is surrounded by fuzziness.

'You went at about 06.30 am, and Kate and Kevin followed you at about 07.00 am.'

06.30 am in the *morning?* Jesus!

'Oh, my God.' I slump down onto the floor and look at my phone. 'It's only 9.30 now! How can I be surviving on only 3 hours sleep? I feel fine.'

63

That's not a *total* lie. I should have my head stuck down a toilet right now, but I feel strangely wide-awake.

Heath laughs, standing up and grabbing me. 'You're probably still drunk, you lightweight.' He digs me in the ribs and ruffles my hair. 'Imagine how the guys felt going to play football. Especially Ben.' He grimaces, his eyes amused. 'He wasn't best pleased about having no eyebrow.'

I'd forgotten about that.

'Yeah, poor guy,' Zahra says with sympathetic eyes. 'I tried to draw one on with my eyebrow pencil, but I think it ended up looking worse.'

Funny how she feels sorry for him now. She was the one chanting *'brow, brow, brow'* last night before Ryan got the razor.

'I've got to go anyway,' Heath says suddenly. 'My Mum's dragging me out to buy my wedding suit.'

His Mum and her boyfriend are finally tying the knot at the end of the month. They've only been together eight years!

I look towards the bedroom knowing Kevin will be snoring grossly away.

'Do me a favour and take Kevin for me too?' I beg. My hands together clearly pleading.

'Fine,' he huffs rolling his eyes, hands on his hips like a teapot. 'But you owe me.'

I hide out in the toilet until I hear them leave. I don't want to risk seeing Kevin and find out I kissed him or anything equally horrifying.

Zahra and I clean up the empty alcohol bottles. When we're finished, I walk back through into the bedroom checking I've got everything. I need my bed right now.

Something in the middle of the floor catches my eye. I walk closer, my stomach twisting with dread, to see it's my missing chicken fillet with a post-it attached.

I think this is yours. Heath x'

Oh, my God. I sigh and close my eyes. Great. So now Heath knows I wear chicken fillets. There are officially no secrets between us.

When I finally make it home, I'm pleased to see everyone is up already, and the smell of a fry up wafts up my nostrils. Grandad is sat at the table reading the morning paper in his dressing gown, and Dad is sat next to him, already fully dressed, commenting on all of the stories in the paper over his shoulder. I know how much Grandad hates him doing this and can see the annoyance clear in his furrowed features.

My Nan is busy cooking sausages, with Mum helping by organising the toast and tea. It's probably all that she can be trusted with. Despite her enthusiastic efforts, she's a terrible cook. She almost burnt the kitchen down last year trying to cook waffles. We still don't know how she managed that.

'Morning, Savvy,' Mum sings when she sees me, grabbing me by my cheeks and planting a kiss on my lips.

Ugh. I grunt in response, not yet ready to talk. She can be so bloody chirpy sometimes.

'The dirty stop out returns,' Dad says with raised eyebrows, arms crossed over his chest.

I glare at him in response. Anyone wanting to start on me right now is going to regret it.

Nan looks me up and down disapprovingly. 'Darling, have you ever considered getting yourself a bit dressed up before venturing out into the public?'

'Why, what's wrong with me?' I snap looking down at last night's crumpled clothes.

She fumbles in her bag and pulls out a mirror, handing it over to me.

LAURA BARNARD

'Take a look, sweetheart. No guy is ever going to want to wake up to that.' She pouts her glossy pink lips. Why she has lip gloss on when we're just in the house, I don't know.

I ignore Grandad's sniggering and look in the mirror. I have smudged mascara under my bloodshot eyes and hair that looks like it's trying to form dreadlocks. My skin is blotchy, and I have a fresh spot on my chin. Beautiful.

'Leave her alone will you,' Mum snaps to her.

'Yeah, leave me alone,' I groan, covering my face with my hands. 'I'm hungover to hell. And any guy who doesn't want me as I am can go run and jump.'

Nan smiles at me appeasingly like I'm the dumbest girl in the world. 'You say that now, but soon all of that stuff will matter to you. My little caterpillar, soon you will be a butterfly.' She squeezes my shoulders with an affectionate smile.

Her enormous boobs squeeze together with the motion and almost spill out of her vest top. Sometimes I wish she'd dress like a normal Nan. Aren't they supposed to wear frilly dresses and have hair set in tight curls? Not walk around in jeans and uggs like they're still eighteen.

'I agree with you, sweetheart,' my Mum says, glaring

67

at Nan like a rebellious teenager. 'If you find the right person appearances won't matter.'

She snorts. 'Yeah, you keep feeding her that crap. That's really going to help her.' She rolls her eyes with a sigh. 'Just because you found the most laid back man in the world, it doesn't mean she will.'

'Hey!' Dad says, jumping up and wrapping his arms around mum's back. 'You're always the most beautiful girl in the room.'

Gross.

They wonder why I'm so moody in the mornings. Maybe it's because I have to deal with this madness every day.

'Thanks for the confidence everyone,' I snarl sarcastically.

'You sound like you had fun last night,' Grandad says, not looking up from his paper.

'Are you talking to me?' I ask, turning round to face him.

'You talking to me?' Dad repeats, putting on a fake Italian accent and laughing to himself. God, he can be annoying. I ignore him.

'Yeah, were you by any chance laughing again?'

Grandad asks smiling, still reading the paper.

Here we go again. He likes to take the mickey out of me, saying that I laugh too much. Laugh at anything. Well *sorry* for being jolly.

'Yeah, why?' I grunt. 'Were you?'

He looks up, lowering his glasses. 'You did Kung Fu?' he asks seriously. 'What?' I know him too well and realise that he's taking the piss.

'Whatever.' I smile despite myself. Damn him and his hilariously random sense of humour.

I stalk off to my room and throw myself down onto the bed. I check my emails; glad to be back where I have Wi-Fi. There's another email from Dylan.

DYLAN'S BLOG - I CLIMBED A WATERFALL IN THE RAINFOREST. WHAT DID YOU DO TODAY?

Ok, since the last update:

We travelled an epic 14-hours from Sydney to Byron Bay. We got to the bus station early and got chatting to someone who has travelled Australia tons, and he took us to a pub. We spent an hour drinking while he told us how Byron Bay is easily the best place in Aus and he was going there to spend his last three months in Aus. Man, that was good to hear.

Eleven hours into the trip they found out someone had snuck on board the bus, and we had to wait for ages while they called the police. We did not need that in our tired state. Selfish bastards.

Then we got to Byron Bay. Man, I fucking love this place. It's probably the best place I have ever been. Also, the hostel is soooooo nice. Spacious, clean, quiet. We have a balcony, a volleyball court, a pool, and it is right on the beach.

To get to the beach, you just have to go out of a gate in the garden and over some disused railway tracks (they needed repair six years ago and have never bothered so instead they just stopped the trains, typical Aussies).

The next day was possibly the best day I've ever had. I got up quite early and nobody was up so like only I would do, I went for a run. There is truly nothing like running along the beach with your feet just in the water during a sunrise, listening to Yellowcard and playing with people's dogs. Obviously, I got carried away (lost) and couldn't find how to get back to the hostel.

Then we went on a walking tour through the rainforest. Like proper rainforest, not just the woods we have at home.

We went to the top of a 100m waterfall and then walked to the bottom, climbing over rocks and under trees. The stuff we saw was like nothing else. We will have pictures that we will hopefully put up soon.

You know how they say you learn something new every day? Well, that day we learnt that it's leech season. Also that they can JUMP. Adrianna got one on her leg, but it was fine

Side note: while we were walking we heard this noise from the mountain. The woman told us it was a 'red eyed tree frog'. It's funny how you can put some words in front of the least scary creature in the world, and they automatically become a little bit more intimidating. For example, ants are fine, but nobody wants to mess with the red ant. Like cats aren't scary, but if I were to say there was a 'jumping red claw cat' outside your room, you would probably shit yourself.

Another side note: we did see some fucking huge red ants

After the walk, there was a BBQ at the hostel so we got a slab (crate) of beer and headed down. It was cool to be sociable with everyone there, and we've got to know the Aussie we share the balcony with quite well.

71

Then there was a 'fire show'. It was shit. Everyone was amazed, going OOOOOWWWWWW and WWWWWOOOOOOOOWWWW, but with our friends being able to do much better we were not impressed.

They had the cheek to ask us for tips because this is 'actually our job' and they have three kids. How about this, instead of me tipping you, you either wear a fucking condom, get a fucking job, or learn how to do some decent tricks with all of the spare time that you have while you aren't working to support your kids. As you may have noticed, I still haven't settled into the chilled Aussie way of thinking.

Everyone is soooo chilled here. Nobody locks anything. Farms leave their fruit in their shed at the end of their driveway with a price list and people just leave the money in a box, and people actually do!

Today we are looking for some farm work to extend our visa—we will update soon.

Last side note: when spell check gave me the suggested spellings for Aussies it came up with pussies, hussies, and wussies before Aussies. LOL

Trust my brother to rub it in. I can't even afford a ski

trip, and he's off having the time of his life. Oh well, I'm too tired to drown in my own self-pity now. Maybe later.

There's another email with the subject *Job Interview*. I open it, hoping it's not a joke.

Dear Miss Franks,

I'd love you to come in for a chat today if you have time? Morning would be preferable.

Thanks, Katie.

A job interview! I can't believe I got one. I jump up and do a little skip to myself. I might still get a job after all! But wait, I'd have to shower and go straight away. I rush back out into the kitchen.

'Can one of you give me a lift into town today?' I ask looking around desperately.

'Yeah, sure,' Mum smiles. 'I'll take you. Me and your Dad are going out for the day anyway.' She squeezes his shoulders. 'He's back on night shifts next week, so I'm making the most of my baby while I can.'

Ugh, these two!

He smiles, but I can't help but feel sorry for him. All of that attention from mum must be exhausting.

When breakfast has been eaten, I have a quick shower and get changed into my smartest jeans and white shirt. I look at the email again. *Pet Emporium,* so I'm guessing a pet shop? I applied for so many I really can't remember which one it is. Luckily the address is printed under her name.

I tell Mum the road it's on and try to answer her incessant questions as vaguely as I can.

'When did you apply for the job? Why do you need a job? Will it affect your schoolwork? What's it doing? How much does it pay?' *So* bloody annoying.

'Look, I really don't know anything about it. I just know that it's a pet store.'

She glances out of the window. 'Not Pet Emporium?' she asks with her nose turned up.

'Yes, *actually,* that's it,' I retort. I could really do without her judging right now. 'You should be bloody glad that I'm going for a job at all. Something you should be doing yourself.'

Her eyes widen in shock. 'That's not what I meant. And you know I'm looking for a job.'

Too late. I'm already getting out of the car and slamming it in her face, not giving her a chance for a witty comeback. I stare up at the pink and blue sign. It looks modern and cool. I could totally work here.

I walk in, and the smell of dried dog food jumps up my nostrils. Ugh, gross. I walk up to the glass counter with no one behind it. What do I do here? No wonder they need staff. Is there a bell or something I can ring? I rock on my heels, looking around for any help. There's a window behind it. I look through to see a woman grooming a dog on a table. That's weird. Why would they want people to see them?

She catches my eye and waves. She walks out of a door I hadn't noticed before, wiping her hands on a tea towel. She's got short red hair with electric blue streaks through it, a pierced lip and eyebrow, and her entire arms covered with tattoos. Wow, she looks cool. She can't be the boss, can she?

'Hi. Can I help you?' she asks cheerily.

'Err, yeah. I'm Savannah.' She looks back at me blankly. 'I sent in my CV, and someone emailed and told me to pop in.'

'Oh, of course!' she laughs, throwing her head back at how silly she is not to have remembered. 'I'm Katie.'

No way! She's the boss?

'So do you have any experience with working with dogs?' she asks with an expectant smile.

Working with dogs? I'm confused here.

I look back blankly. 'Err...no. No, I haven't.'

'That's no bother. We'll obviously train you up.' She smiles cheerfully.

Okay. I'm going to have to say something. This is getting weird. Train me up in what? Serving dogs?

'Sorry? Train me up...in what?' I smile as politely as I can.

She raises her eyebrows. 'In the job.' Her eyes crease suspiciously. 'You...do remember which job you applied for, don't you?'

Shit, she's onto me.

'Of course I do!' I shrill, attempting to laugh it off.

She raises her eyebrows, seeing straight through me. 'Well, just in case you don't—you applied to be a trainee dog groomer here.'

My stomach drops. 'Dog groomer? As in...cutting dog's hair?'

'Yep, that's generally the definition,' she grins, clearly finding me hilarious. 'Follow me, and I'll show you.'

I force my jelly legs to follow her through the door into the back. I find three tables with dogs attached to them by their leads. There's another girl in there, who I'm told is Yasmin.

'We've been let down by our other girl, Ava today. So today is as good a day as any.'

God, I'm sleepy. What is she going on about?

'Good enough day for what?'

'To start. No time like the present. Here's your apron.'

She wants me to start washing smelly dogs *today?* Today of all bloody days when I'm feeling like the walking dead?

'Come on. You'll love it.'

Chapter Five

Monday 17th October

#MysticMeg

I still can't believe I spent my hangover-Sunday washing mutts. Well, it was only two hours, but it may as well have been a week for all the hard work I did. Lugging those dogs into the bath and trying to shampoo them while they wailed and shook their spray all over me. And after all that, she gave me £8. Eight measly pounds. What the hell can I buy with that?

Luckily my Monday perked up when Erin brought in the money for me to settle the ski trip payment. This bitch is going skiing!! I worked out with my set hours of 9-5pm on Saturdays and 10-12 on Sunday I'll have enough to pay her back by the time we go.

Plus, everyone is talking about my awesome party. It seems over the weekend my social status has gone from practically invisible to popular party queen. Everyone who didn't attend has been kissing my arse, begging me to invite them the next time. Yeah, like I have them all the time.

Poor Tia isn't in. According to school gossip, she had to have her stomach pumped, and her heart stopped twice. Who knew alcohol could do that to someone?

Plus, my brother's blog is keeping me entertained. It's so funny, and at the moment I'm hearing from him more than when he's at home.

DYLAN'S BLOG - SLAP THE GOON!!!!

We've mainly been chilling out. Although things keep happening which are really surreal. Perfect example: Me and Adrianna were sitting in a hammock for two hours staring at the small jungle at the back of our hostel. Really relaxing and then all of a sudden, Flash Gordon, a drag queen, and a king walked past and gave us a beer for no reason at all. See what I mean? Relaxing and then surreal.

I had my first encounter with the wildlife here (not counting the cockroaches in the fridges in one of the hostels we stayed in). Adrianna pushed me into a bin (as you do) and when I went to put it back up, a lizard ran up my arm. Obviously, I totally shit myself for about ten minutes.

I can't decide whether I like Australian people. I'm in two minds.

On one hand: they are friendly, generous, energetic, and considerate.

On the other hand; they don't stop telling you how they're friendly, generous, energetic, and considerate. As soon as they find out you're foreign, they have to tell you how good this place and the people are, instead of just letting us see it for ourselves.

Germans, on the other hand, I fucking love the Germans here. Although because I am a moron, I keep mistaking their accents for Americans. I have no idea why.

The other night we went to a bar, and they were having a wet t-shirt competition (SWEET) when they revealed the ten contestants. Number one was our very quiet German roommate, and the bitch went fucking crazy when it was her turn. She was gyrating like a stripper, whooping and hollering. Someone's been watching too much Coyote Ugly. She should have won, but obviously, the girl who got her tits out won.

I was sitting in the TV room the other day, and I thought, man, living in a hostel is a lot like prison. You don't have a choice who you share your room with—you have to share a toilet and shower, and you have an exercise courtyard. And this is our fucking holiday.

Last night I sat in the kitchen with six Americans who were all from different parts of America, but all go to Uni in Australia. We played ring of fire for hours as everyone plays different rules. We played it so whoever picked up the card played the card by the rules they know. Man, I've got some new rules for everyone when I get home.

Then me and Adrianna went to a bar to see some live music, but we got there far too late, and I just got there to see them packing their gear away, whoops. We are going to try again tonight.

I will explain the GOON comment in the title now. Goon is a drink here that is massively popular with students and backpackers. It is essentially like a box of really shitty wine, but without the box, just the bag. You can get litres for $10. That's really cheap when you remember that a slab (crate) of bottles here is $40. Everyone goes through the same cycle here. You get totally shitfaced on it one night.

81

Then for the next week, you can't even look at it without feeling ill. Then you forget about it and get shitfaced on it, and the cycle repeats.

On Friday we went to the bank to open an account. We were making idle chit chat when the bank teller asked us where we'd stayed in Sydney. When we told her, she burst out laughing, right in our FACES, for like five minutes. I love that about Oz.

I am starting to get quite hippyish. I haven't worn a watch in three days and now prefer walking around barefoot. It's quite strange. I might just come back as a hippy.

Anyway, I will update again soon. Hopefully with more interesting stuff.

By the time I'm walking out of school, I'm knackered and looking forward to my bed. It might be in a cupboard, but I've quickly come to rely on that small piece of privacy.

I see that Nan's decided to pick me up. It's hard to miss her in her pink mini convertible. Again, she's so far from a normal Nan. She's stood outside the car in pink jogging bottoms, Uggs, and a black vest top chatting to a young man walking his dog. I cringe at the sight of her trying to flirt. She's flicking her short blonde hair over her shoulder and laughing, her boobs shaking with the action.

I roll my eyes and cross to her side of the road.

'Oh, there you are, my sweetheart,' she says, winking at the man like they're sharing an inside joke.

'Yeah, I'm ready,' I say a little rudely. I smile, to try and apologise, but I feel knackered and want to get the hell out of here before she can embarrass me further. Just when people were starting to think I was cool.

She unlocks the car, and I jump in quickly, hoping hard that no one notices me. I hate this car. Everything about it screams 'look at me', a little like my Nan herself. I, myself, would prefer something a little more discreet. Not the girls, they love this car.

I take the scrunchie out of my bag in anticipation of the car ride. My hair's big enough thanks. I don't need it wind swept to Oz.

She starts the engine—S Club Seven blasting out of the speakers. I sink a little lower in my seat.

'Well that young man's a bit of a dish isn't he?' she says with a wink.

'Is he?' I ask unenthusiastically, staring out of the

window at the crowd of people openly laughing at us.

'Of course!' she shrills. 'If I were twenty years younger...'

I turn to stare at her with narrowed brows.

She shrugs. 'Okay, maybe forty years younger. I *am* only 65 you know. You shouldn't write me off yet. Anyway, that's the kind of boy you should be going after,' she adds, trying to sound casual.

I can see where this is headed.

'I'm not interested in a random bloke that just walks by. And he looks old enough to be married with kids.'

She shakes her head with a tut. 'Well maybe if you *pretended* you were interested and just had some fun, maybe you'd end up *being* interested.'

'That makes no sense.' I turn to stare out of the window again.

'All I'm saying is that you need to cut loose every now and again. Have more wild parties.'

'Yeah, because we can fit people in our flat, right? I'm sure Grandad would crack open his tin of biscuits, and we'd all have a right riot.'

She sighs heavily. 'All you seem to do is go to school and do homework. And now you have this job. You're so serious for someone your age. I know we always say that you were born a forty-year-old, but maybe it's time to start acting your age?'

I sigh heavily, annoyed that we're having the same conversation as always. And act my age? She needs to have a word with herself.

'I'm sorry my life is so boring to you,' I snap, attempting to hide my hurt, 'but someone in that house has to be the adult.' I know it's harsh, but I want to hurt her feelings right now. I try to pretend it doesn't, but it hurts to hear your Nan thinks you're such a loser.

'Oh, you're adult enough for all of us.' She laughs, catching my eye and winking.

I can't keep in the laugh that spills out of my throat. This is typical Nan. She can totally slate me to my face, make me feel like shit and then do something silly which makes me forgive her instantly. I know she means well, but the last thing I need is my Nan giving me advice on how to live my life.

I turn back to looking out of the window, but no longer recognise the road. I frown, trying to work out where we are.

'Where are we going?' I demand.

She smiles wickedly. 'Ah, that's the surprise I was telling you about.'

'What surprise? You never mentioned a surprise?' I say wearily, feeling a thrill of excitement despite myself.

'Oh, didn't I?' She seems confused. That'll be dementia setting in early. 'Well, you'll just have to wait and see.'

Knowing Nan, it could be absolutely anything. She could take me to a strip club, and I wouldn't be that shocked.

Almost five minutes later we pull up outside a parade of shops. We're in some kind of rural farm with about seven shops, all unique. No chain stores here.

'So where are we going?' I ask as I get out of the car, my legs heavy. I really need sleep.

The smell of raw meat from the butchers catches my nose. I force myself to stop inhaling, so as not to vomit. I hope we're not going there.

'We're going here,' she says, pointing to a tiny old door wedged in between a florist and a gift shop.

She seems to relish the fact that I don't know where we're going. Crazy old bat. I follow her to the door and watch her press the buzzer.

'Hello?' a voice says in a Spanish accent.

'Hello, my darling. It's Judy Bree,' Nan says into the speaker.

'Ah, come up'.

A buzz sounds through the door, and Nan turns to me smiling and hunching her shoulders up at me excitedly, before dragging me through the door.

A dimly lit staircase with a grubby carpet greets me. I try to fight every sensible feeling in my body to allow myself to follow her up the stairs. This is weird. I don't like it.

She leads me into a tiny room, the strong smell of smoke shocking me. I look around the room, trying to make sense of it.

There's a large old sofa with blankets thrown over it, probably to hide the stains from the last one hundred years. It has hundreds of scatter cushions, each a different brightly coloured pattern.

There's a small coffee table next to it with some sticks that seem to be on fire. I assume it's burning incense, as it would explain the smell. Even though it's still daylight outside the blinds are down. The only light supplied is from several small lamps around the room.

'Where the hell are we?' I whisper to her, feeling on

edge.

Before she has time to answer me, a Spanish lady with a particularly long face walks into the room. She wears a long pink summer dress, and her hair is plaited into at least seven individual plaits. Very strange behaviour for a woman who looks at least 55.

'Hello, Judy, darling,' she says, grabbing her hands and air kissing her on both cheeks. 'This must be your granddaughter, Savannah.' She looks me up and down before grabbing me into a tight hug. Okay, this is getting weirder by the minute. I don't hug my own friends this tight.

'Sorry.' I pull back from her. 'But who are you? And what the hell am I doing here?'

She throws her head back, laughing hysterically. So hysterically, I wonder if this woman is crazy. Is Nan trying to show me that this is what I will turn into if I don't start 'letting loose'? Some mental hippy woman.

'Judy, you bad woman. You didn't tell her.' She crosses her arms over her chest and pretends to be cross.

'I know, but I knew if I did she wouldn't have come,' Nan answers, looking at me nervously.

'And?' I demand, frustration clear in my voice. This is

getting ridiculous.

'Ok, well try not to over-react,' Nan says, fidgeting with her bag, avoiding my quizzical gaze. 'But I've booked you in to get your tarot cards read.'

My eyes widen to twice the size.

'What?' I squeal in horror.

'I've booked you in—'

'I heard you the first time,' I snap, ready to throttle her. *Remember she's an old lady. You can't physically attack her.* 'I'm just horrified that you thought I would want this.' I lower my voice to a whisper, so I don't hurt the crazy woman's feelings. 'You know I don't believe in any of this stuff.'

'I know, but that's why I brought you. You need to stop taking everything so seriously. Can't you just be a little more open-minded?' She puts on her puppy dog eyes, her baby blues attempting to hypnotise me.

I glare at her for a long time, furious that she's put me in this situation. Just because she's old, she thinks she can get away with anything. It's so annoying.

'Okay,' I say giving up easily, with a big sigh. 'What do I have to do?'

'Great,' she beams back. 'I'll just leave you with Sasha.

Come to the car when you're finished.'

Before I have time to object she's running down the stairs and the sound of the door slamming echoes around the room. I'm alone with crazy Sasha. I could end up cut up in her freezer.

'I'm pleased she's left us,' she says, her voice now eerily calm. 'This way I can talk to you openly. Please.' She gestures to the other corner of the room where there's a dining room table with two mismatched chairs. The table is covered in a pink cloth with heavy yellow fringing around it.

I sit down feeling extremely vulnerable. I gulp a little too loudly, my palms beginning to sweat.

'Please don't be nervous,' she smiles kindly. 'I want you to be relaxed and open.'

I smile back politely. Easy for her to say. If I got paid to sit in my dining room talking crap over cards, I'd be pretty calm too.

She pulls a set of cards out of a glittery pink scarf and starts to shuffle them.

'Tell me, Savannah, do you have any questions you would like the universe to help you with?'

I try desperately not to roll my eyes. 'No.' I don't want

to be rude, but I just want to get this over and done with as quickly as possible. I'm humouring her for Nan's sake.

She eyes me suspiciously, a wicked smile on her lips.

'Please, there must be *something* you would like to know about. Perhaps a boy?' She leans forward looking closely at my face. Talk about invading my personal space.

I sigh, realising she's not going to let this go.

'Well, I suppose you could ask if there is ever going to be a boy.' I feel ridiculous even saying it out loud, but it seems to appease her. And I would like to hear I'm not going to die alone and a virgin.

'Okay, we can do that.'

She spreads all of the cards on the table and shuffles them another three times.

'I will pull four cards for you and then describe what I think they mean to you.'

I nod to show my understanding.

She parts the deck in half and puts them down. She lifts the first card from the top of the deck. I curse myself for being so curious as to what it will be.

She places down a card with a lady on it who looks like a queen.

'The High Priestess,' she says, pausing for dramatic

effect.

I look at her expectantly, wishing she wouldn't drag this out so long. I've got homework to do.

'This card was facing the opposite way to me. This shows a lack of personal harmony and problems resulting from suppression of the feminine or intuitive side of your personality. There is some repression and ignorance of true feelings.'

Has Nan told her I need to dress more like a girl?

'What does that mean? And do you mean for the future or right now?' I ask, sounding a lot more inquiring than I mean to. I'm not hiding my feelings. Am I?

'Only you will know the true meaning of these cards.'

Well that helps. Not.

She pulls out another card and puts it down in front of me. This card is upside down to me. I crane my neck to see two naked people underneath an angel.

'The Lovers'

I feel myself get excited. This is more like it! This bitch is gonna lose her virginity this year.

'This card shows that there are choices to be made using your intuition and not your intellect that will result in harmony and union. Sometimes this decision is not based on love, but I get the feeling that in your case it is. There is some kind of test or consideration about commitment for you. Possibly a struggle between two paths.' She smiles knowingly. 'I get the feeling this will be very interesting for you.'

I smile self-consciously, trying to take it all in. I wish I could have brought a notepad so I can remember it all. Struggle between two paths?

She pulls the next card, but her brows quickly knit together. She unwillingly places the card down facing her. I crane my neck to see a giant creature with wings towering above two naked people.

'The Devil?' I ask, reading out loud. A shiver runs down my spine. The fucking devil? I *knew* this was a bad idea.

'Yes,' she nods with a strained smile. 'But please don't worry. The card is upright'.

'And??' I ask, terrified. 'What does that mean?'

'It means that you desire physical or material things. In your case, I think it is physical. There will be a lot of lust and sexual obsession in your future. Possibly a decision between safe security or the temptation of lust.'

What? That sounds nothing like me!

'I thought you said you couldn't know if the cards were for the present or the future?' Ha ha. I've caught her out. She's surely a fake.

She nods gravely. 'I did say that, but it is clear that these sexual feelings are in the future. You are a virgin, no?'

My eyes widen in shock and humiliation. How the hell does she know that?

'Yes,' I whisper, hanging my head in shame. I must be walking round with a massive virgin sign on my head.

'This will be the last card,' she says, dramatically hovering her hand over the deck. God, she's a drama queen.

She lays down a picture of a woman next to a lake with a big star above her head.

'The Star. This is reversed so shows self-doubt and stubbornness.' She looks at me quickly, as if to remind me how stubborn I am and then continues. 'There is an unwillingness or inability to adapt to changing circumstances. You should learn to do this as these changes may bring opportunities with them. There is a lack of trust and some self-doubt. You will have many obstacles to happiness.'

Oh great. *Many obstacles.* That sounds like a very

long time away. And difficult adapting? Yeah, I'm finding it hard living in a shitty flat in Crapstone. Who wouldn't? That's not stubbornness—that's normal bloody behaviour.

'Are you pleased with your reading, my dear?' she asks, straightening up and smiling as if she didn't just tell me my life's about to go down the shitter.

I'm more confused than ever.

'Yeah, thanks.' I nod, already on my feet, ready to leave. 'My Nan will be waiting for me.'

I start walking quickly from the room, but stop when she grabs hold of my arm, a little roughly.

'Please remember what I have told you today.'

Just as I thought. Poor woman must have a mental health problem.

'I will,' I nod, feeling her eyes hypnotise me. She let's go of my arm, but I still feel like I can't move. Her face is beautiful up close. Her eyes are warm, with little wrinkles underneath them. I want to reach out and touch them.

'Goodbye, then,' she says abruptly, reminding me that I'm in the room.

God, I must look mental, staring at her.

'Bye,' I mumble before bolting out of the door.

As soon as I'm outside, I run for the car. Nan runs

after me, apparently having waited for me outside. She really is quick for a pensioner.

'There's no need to be so spooked, sweetheart.'

I roll my eyes. 'Whatever.' She didn't just get the devil card. 'I just want to go home.'

'But we're going in here now,' she says, pointing to a hairdresser's called *Cuts and Curls*.

'Why?' I ask, eyeing her dyed blonde hair. 'You don't have roots yet, do you?'

'It's not for me.' She grins excitedly, practically bouncing up and down.

I look at her puzzled and quickly realise that this is intended for me. Haven't I suffered enough today?

'No! I don't need my hair doing.' I touch my brown hair protectively. It might not be the most exciting hair, but I like it.

'I just think you need a change, sweetheart. I was thinking maybe you should go blonde.' Her face lights up in excitement.

'Blonde? Are you crazy?' I ask, unable to hide the horror from my voice. She's trying to turn me into a Barbie doll.

'No, I'm not.' She looks hurt. 'I don't know why you're

doubting me now. This weekend you dressed up like a girl and look at the positive effects it had on you. You had a household full of people round. You behaved like a teenager, and you were popular!'

'Nan! Shouldn't you be telling me how popularity doesn't matter and it's what's inside that counts?' I ask with a hand on my hip.

She rolls her eyes. 'I'm sorry if, unlike your mother, I don't insist on feeding you that crap. You need to get into the real world. You'll never get a boyfriend unless you start caring about what you look like.'

'What's wrong with what I look like?' I ask, gazing down at myself. I mean, yeah, in this school uniform I hardly look sexy, but I'm hardly ugly either.

'Need I say it out loud?' she says, eyeing me up sadly.

I sigh heavily. Clearly, I'm not going to win this argument.

'Do I even have a choice?' I ask defeated.

'No.' She grins, dragging me into the purple salon.

When we arrive back at the flat, I run into the bathroom before anyone can comment on my new hair. I run myself a bath adding lots of Mum's bubble bath and take a deep breath before looking in the mirror at my new hair. It's just *so* bright. They assured me that it would eventually tone itself down, but until then I look like a sunflower.

Ok, I'm being dramatic. It's only highlights, but it still feels so weird. It doesn't look like me. It's like it's changed my whole face. It's going to get people to notice me, and I hate drawing attention to myself.

When I'm out of the bath, I put on my fleecy pyjamas, tidy up my bedroom a little bit and curl into bed. It feels like ages since I've been alone with my own thoughts. I'm so used to my life now being chaotic, all of us crammed into this flat.

I curl in the foetal position and try to think nice thoughts to drift me off to sleep. I know it's awful but I replay the cuddling with Zach over in my head. I try to work it out. Do I suddenly fancy Zach or is it just nice to have someone show me any kind of affection? Am I that starved of it? Anyway, there's no point even considering it as he has a girlfriend.

BEEP BEEP my phone demands loudly at me. Damn it. I should have put it on silent. Why is it always when I'm going to sleep that someone texts me.

I reach begrudgingly for it, curiosity getting the better of me. I swear if it's a network message I *will* launch it. But it isn't. It's a number I don't recognise.

```
Hey,   thanks   for   listening   Saturday.
Had  a  great  time.   Ended  up  dumping
girlfriend.  C u soon I hope.   Zach x
```

Well, what the hell does that mean? This could make things *very* confusing for me.

Chapter Six

Tuesday 18th October

#NewHair

'Oh, my God! Your hair!' Zahra shrieks, her face lighting up as I walk into the common room the next morning.

'Isn't it lovely?' Erin says, having already gushed all over me the minute we met outside. 'I keep telling her I love it, but she's not sure.'

'I love it.' Zahra reassures me with an excited nod. 'I can't believe you were brave enough to do it.' She dyes her hair a different shade of red every month.

I look round from under my hair and notice a few people turn to stare at me. This is exactly why I didn't want my hair done—all this attention is excruciating.

'So, you going to Jessica's house party on Saturday?' Heath asks as he slides into the chair next to me. Well, at least he hasn't seemed to notice.

Jessica's parents are going away for the weekend, and she's never had a party before so obviously she's having a party inspired by mine. Not that she'd ever admit that.

'Course she is, fool,' Kate says with a giggle, trying to tame her wild red curls into a ponytail. 'You know we wouldn't miss it'.

'Ok, cool. Savvy, can I bum a lift?' He smiles, fluttering his lashes in an attempt to be cute.

I bark a laugh. 'You cheeky bastard, I'm not even sure how I'm getting there yet.' I pretend to be surprised at his boldness. When in truth I expected nothing less.

'Oh come on, Savvy, Edie will take you won't she?' He puts on his best puppy dog eyes. 'And of course she'll want to take me, she thinks I'm a delight.' He does a cheeky wink.

I burst out laughing but roll my eyes. My Mum *does* love Heath.

'I'll check,' I shrug, not promising anything.

'You can't anyway,' Erin interrupts. 'We're getting

there earlier remember? Her mum thinks we're just going over for a sleepover.'

'Oh yeah.'

Thank God for Erin. She always remembers the small details when I'm too scatty to remember if I have PE today.

'And her parents still have no idea?' Charlotte asks biting her nails nervously. She hates any form of lying.

'Apparently not,' I shrug. 'It's their own fault for going to Devon for the weekend and expecting a teenager not to get up to anything. How naive are they?' I laugh.

I find Heath staring at me, puzzled. 'Have you done something different with your hair?

Typical.

'Anyway,' he shifts uncomfortably in his chair. 'I need your advice.' He suddenly looks serious, pointing out to the hallway.

I nod and follow him, intrigued. Has he got a rash or something? Ewww. I'm not sure I want to hear about that.

'So what's up?' I ask, completely intrigued as he guides us into an empty classroom.

A stupid smile spreads on his face. 'Well, I met this girl the other day in McDonald's when I was with Tyler.'

'A girl after my own heart,' I interrupt smiling. I could

really do with a cheeseburger right now.

'Yeah, well anyway.' He cracks his knuckles, which always makes me cringe. 'She was really nice, and she gave me her number.'

Woah. He wants *dating* advice?

'But I don't know if I should ring her. I mean, what would I say? It's alright when I'm with Tyler, I have a bit of backup, but on my own, I'd be worried I'll just come across like a dick.'

Wow. This really is a revelation. I had no idea Heath even had the ability to pull girls. I immediately look at him in a new light, as if I were a stranger. I suppose if I were seeing him for the first time I'd notice how his shoulders are broad, and he does have stunning big brown eyes. Always has. His rounded jaw is actually very chiselled now with a slight smattering of stubble. When did this happen?

He's still staring at me, waiting for an answer. Pull yourself together, Savvy.

'Yeah, course you should ring her. Just go for it. What's the worst thing that can happen?'

A Dr Pepper advert pops into my head, and I find myself giggling.

His face suddenly drains of colour. 'Yeah, I suppose,

I just feel really nervous about it,' he admits with a sigh.

Bless him. He's still my little friend, Heathy. The same one that played Lego with me when we were younger.

'Why don't we do it quickly now? Get it out of the way?' I suggest with an encouraging smile. 'Otherwise, you'll just keep thinking about it.'

'Okay,' he nods, his brows knitted together. I've never seen him so worried.

He gets his phone out and pulls up her number, pacing around the room.

'You know you have to press dial, yeah?' I mock with a teasing grin. 'Remember, out of the way. Like a plaster. Just do it.'

He nods seriously and presses dial. I feel his nerves spreading onto me. God, all of this stuff really is excruciating, even when it's not you. I'm never going to be able to do this.

'Hi, Mercedes?' He looks at me nervously.

Her name is *Mercedes*? Oh my God, she must be awful. Where did he find her? Jeremy Kyle?

'Yeah, it's Heath,' he says smiling back at me, his shoulders relaxing slightly. 'Yeah, well I thought that we could...yeah, that's what I was thinking...hang on a minute.'

He comes across all shy and then walks to the other side of the classroom, still on the phone.

Well, what the hell is that all about? He drags me in here to give him moral support and all of a sudden he's so confident he's out on his own, probably whispering sweet nothings to her. I feel a bit cheated, to be honest.

He finally comes back towards me after what seems like forever, a big obnoxious grin on his face.

'Went well then?' I ask, more curious than I let on.

'Yeah.' His smile is getting bigger by the second. Goofy fool. 'She's really up for meeting. She's invited me back to hers tomorrow after school.'

Back to hers? Hello! Slag alert!

'What?' I utter in disbelief. 'Jesus, she's keen! You've only just met her, and she's already inviting you back to her house. She's a bit forward, isn't she? I mean you could be a nutter for all she knows.'

'Yeah, she's cool,' he says dreamily looking away, clearly imagining her naked. What a shit. Not that he'd have any idea what to do with her anyway. He's still a virgin, just like me.

'Aren't you a bit scared?' I can't help but ask. He scowls, clearly perplexed. 'I mean, what if she's a massive slut and wants to jump your bones?'

He rolls his eyes. 'I *told* you. I'm not a virgin anymore. Me and Tyler told you about the holiday girls.'

Wait, that was serious? I just assumed it was a story they made up.

'Yeah, but I just assumed that you'd made it up. I mean...you've *actually* had sex?' I ask, disbelief colouring my tone.

'Yeah,' he nods adamantly. 'Don't get me wrong, like I said, it was nothing special. But she was up for it and so...you know.' He shrugs. That poor girl.

I sit in disbelief. I mean, this changes the whole dynamic of our friendship. I suddenly feel like a giant loser for still being a virgin. Even Heath has lost it. What is wrong with me?

Like Heath said, that girl on holiday was just up for it. She wasn't anything special either. Girls are supposed to be able to just demand sex with any guy and get it. What's wrong with *me?*

'Sav, you okay? he asks, jolting me out of my destructive thoughts.

I try to pull myself together, realising that I must have a strange look on my face.

'Yeah, I'm fine. I'm just shocked that's all.' I shake my head, realising I should sound happy for him, not bitter. 'Anyway, congrats and good luck tomorrow.'

I get up to walk back into the common room but divert to the bathroom instead. I look at myself in the mirror. I look closely. This is the face of a virgin.

My eyes are blue or green; they seem to change daily. My nose and ears are too big for my face, and I have tiny pencil lips. Maybe Mum and Nan *are* right. Maybe I will have to change myself to get noticed. Plus, that psychic said I was suppressing my feminine side. I just don't know if I can be bothered. I already dyed my hair and look at the attention that drew.

I go back down to the gang and sit back down next to Heath.

'You okay?' he asks.

'Yeah, just tired,' I shrug.

He always normally gives me a cuddle when I'm a bit down. Will that change if he gets a girlfriend?

I often think that he treats me like a teddy bear, using me for comfort every now and again. Luckily, I use him just the same, but today he doesn't, and I feel very, very alone.

DYLAN'S BLOG - AUS Update

On Monday, Adrianna and I went to a place called Nimbin. Everyone round here talks about it. Basically, they had a hippy festival there twenty-odd years ago, and none of the hippies left. There are loads of shuttle buses that go there every day, and everyone said it was awesome. We hopped on a bus and headed down.

When we got there, it was just like ten really dirty shops and a few places to eat. The shops all sold things like hemp clothing, but mainly they all sold bongs, pipes, grinders and every other thing that has to do with smoking weed. On top of that, every ten feet you walked you had someone offering you drugs. They were easily the politest dealers in the world.

'Do you want some weed or cookies?'

'Nah, Man. I'm good.'

'Ok, no worries. Have a good day. Check out the candle factory if you have a chance, it's really nice.'

There was one dealer that was mental and started talking to us about drunken mud wrestling or something like that. Also, all the shop owners were soooo fucking high they didn't have a clue what was going on. Part of me thought that you could replace the whole shop with cardboard cut outs of the things that were normally there and they wouldn't notice. We didn't really see people showing us how you can live in peace and be self-sufficient. They were only really worried about smoking weed. There was loads of protest stuff about trying to legalise weed, but not a single one about going vegan or anything like that.

That night our friend, Chilli, was leaving, so we went to a place called Cheeky Monkeys.

Side note: His name isn't Chilli. We have just started calling people where they come from by name, so at the moment our friends are German, Chilli, Yorkshire and so on and so forth.

We went to Cheeky Monkeys, and they started playing games for jugs of beer, and man, we cleared up. I won the rock, paper, scissors game. Adrianna won the basketball and the flag game, and our friend Blondie won the joint rolling game. Needless to say, we got a lot of free booze.

Then we went on to have loads of drinks and dance the night away on the tables.

Tuesday we spent the whole day sitting in a hammock

staring into the bush. That night everyone came to our balcony with drums and guitars. After we got kicked out of the hostel, we took the party to the beach. Then we sat around the campfire with a load of people from all over the world taking turns to play music together while drinking stupid amounts of goon.

Wednesday we just had a BBQ and a lot of goon (again)

Friday 21st October

'Tell me again. Why are you going to the park?' Mum probes, frowning down at me as she makes cheese on toast. Someone's feeling brave in the kitchen.

God, she's annoying. Playing the concerned Mum card when she fancies. It's not like I'm asking to go travelling round Australia. It's the park for God's sakes.

'I don't know,' I shrug. 'Everyone is going to just hang out.' I wish she'd stop interrogating me and concentrate on not burning the kitchen down.

'But I don't get it. Why not just have everyone round here?'

Is she *serious?* This flat? This flat my friends don't

even know about yet?

'Maybe because I don't want them to know what a complete hovel we're living in!' I shout. 'It's not like I'd be able to fit more than two people in anyway.' How does she not understand that?

'Okay,' she says, putting her hands up defensively. 'If you want to act like the stereotypical teenager you see on the news, then go ahead. Go, do heroin in the park for all I care.' She storms off leaving the cheese on toast to potentially burn the flat down.

Trust my mother to out-do me with a teenage hissy fit.

I walk to the park and meet the usual crowd. Robbie and Luke join us tonight. I have no idea why. They're a bit too popular for us, but we bump into them loads because they've been friends with Tyler since primary school. I'm tempted to ask where Zach is tonight, but don't want to act like a crazy psycho obsessed with him. Which, you know, I totally am.

I sit on the swings and watch Robbie entertaining everyone with an impression of our biology teacher Mr Plank.

Cold hands suddenly creep up my coat resting on my waist. The swing is pushed slowly. I look round to see it's

Luke. I hadn't even noticed he was there until now. A bit intimate isn't he? But maybe I'm being a bit too prudish. Maybe that's how some people are pushed on swings, and it's no big deal.

Except the swing starts to slow instead of increase in speed. His arms wrap around my waist, hugging me into him. I freeze. Does he not realise it's me on the swing? Could he have got me confused with one of the others? Maybe Charlotte because of my blonder hair.

One of his hands leaves my waist and starts to caress my lower back like he's writing numbers on it. Okay, this is definitely not how you get pushed on the swing. My skin feels tingly from his cold touch, but my vagina clamps shut in fear. This is weird.

I don't know what to do but can't help feeling flattered by the attention. That is until he moves his hand and shoves it down the back of my jeans, grasping onto my knicker-clad arse. My eyes nearly bulge out of my sockets.

Panic races through my veins, numbing me so much I can't move or make a sound. His hand finds his way under my knickers and starts to caress my arse cheek. Dear God! What the hell is happening?

I continue to look forward as I can't bear to turn and

look at him. Who does this player who enjoys forcing himself, or at least his hands, on unsuspecting victims, think he is? But what the hell can I do without causing a scene? Maybe this isn't even a big deal.

I try to think rationally. Could I just say 'no, thank you'? I doubt it. No one around me seems to notice my desperate eyes as I plead with them to help me. I thought us girls had a built in sensor for these things?

Right, the only way to escape this is to physically move. I have no idea how else to deal with it. So, without looking back, I get up and spring over to Heath and Tyler on the roundabout. I casually join in on the conversation of rating the girls in our year, hoping no one has noticed. Thank God it's dark here. No one should notice my flamed cheeks.

I still can't believe he had the cheek to do that. Cheek being the word. God, I'm hilarious.

I can tell my skin is still flushed from the whole experience, I feel like I'm literally on fire. I try to slow down my breathing hoping it will help me to calm down. Deep breath in, calm breath out.

After a few minutes of pretending to listen to Heath's conversation, I finally feel brave enough to look back at

Luke. But he's moved. Where is he? I spot him and nearly swallow my tongue in shock when I see he's moved on to Kate!

He's doing the same move on her, and unlike me, she isn't hiding it so well. Her skin is bright red, and she's developing a rash on her neck. Her nervous rash—it must be bad. She catches my eye, and the pleading in them is clear.

'Kate,' I call, trying to sound casual. 'Come here a sec. We want your help'. She practically sprints over.

'Thank you,' she mouths as soon as she's next to me.

I put my cold hands on her cheeks to try to calm them down. Bless her; she can never hide her feelings. Her blushes always give her away.

'Guys, we're just going to go for a wander,' I say to the boys, taking her by the hand. We have loads to talk about.

'No, you're not,' Heath argues, his face twisted as if in anger. 'It's pitch black out. Knowing your luck, Sav, you'll end up getting attacked by a fox.'

'Oh, shut up,' I snap, trying to dismiss him. I hate when he tries to big brother me. I already have one, even if he is currently on the other side of the world.

But maybe he is right. I look out into the dark fields.

God knows I'm scared shitless of wildlife. I mean you never know how *wild* they're gonna be do you?

I can see Kate practically gagging to talk. I suppose we can talk in front of Heath. I know he can be trusted, especially since he hasn't revealed my chicken fillet incident or the fact I'm poor to the rest of the group. Plus, he's a bit like a girl with gossip anyway.

'Come with us then,' I reason, seeing that he isn't going to let us go without an argument. Once he's got an idea in his head nothing will stop him. 'That way at least there'll be three girls to fight off the foxes.'

He jumps up, looking pleased with himself, and starts walking through the field with us. The minute we're out of earshot from the others, we start gossiping.

'Did Luke try it on with you?'

'Yeah, can you believe it?' she shrieks, her eyes wide in disbelief.

'Yeah, he tried it on with me too.'

Heath's eyes nearly bulge out of their sockets.

'I can't believe how forward he is, he was so pushy,' she says, her shaky hand tucking a curl behind her ear.

'I know,' I grimace. 'Total perv or what?'

'Wait a minute,' Heath interrupts, rubbing his

forehead. 'Are you seriously telling me that Luke tried it on with both of you?'

'Yeah,' I nod, confused by his reaction. Why does he have that strange scrunched up expression on his face? 'What, don't you believe us or something?'

He turns towards me. A faint glare of a distant streetlight makes it possible for me to make out his anger. His forehead has a wrinkle between his eyebrows. Even when we were children he always had that crease in his brow line when I stole his action man and threatened to flush it down the toilet.

'I told that prick to keep his hands to himself. I told Robbie not to bring him. I knew he couldn't be trusted. Tell me exactly what happened,' he demands, one hand on his hip like a teapot. God, he's a drama queen.

I tell him what happened, but manage to play it down as I can tell that he's getting more and more pissed off—his eyes harder by the second. I know that if he goes storming over to Luke for a fight, he'll no doubt lose. I feel sick at the thought of him getting hurt. Especially over me.

'I just can't stand guys like that. Into anything that moves for three minutes and then moving on.' He seems irrationally annoyed over this. Take a chill pill, dickhead.

Do I notice a hint of jealousy in his tone? Wait...That's it. That's why he's so upset; he fancies Kate. Of course he does. I can't believe I haven't seen it before now. He's protective of her because he likes her. Who wouldn't? With those cheekbones, she could pass for a model.

'Ah, you big softie' I mutter, secretly planning what hat I'll buy for the wedding. How did I not see this sooner?

We walk back, joining the park again, with a huge grin on my face. Luke is now standing against Zahra, face to face. Maybe he's finally pulled, but then I notice he's talking to Robbie and Tyler, arching his neck to comment on whether he agrees that Nessie Stevens is fit enough to be in the top ten. How romantic.

It's only when we start on our walk home later that Zahra says it.

'So guess what?' she grins, waggling her eyebrows excitedly. 'I got fingered tonight.'

'What?' I gasp in disbelief. She got *fingered?* In the *park?*

'Yeah,' she grins, 'by Luke.'

Kate and I exchange a worried look. It seems he did get lucky.

'Sorry,' Erin interrupts, 'but when on earth did this

happen? You didn't leave the park once.'

She rolls her eyes, still smiling dreamily. 'That's because it happened *in* the park.' She laughs, carefree, tossing her long red hair behind her.

I'm *so* confused.

'Sorry?' Erin clarifies. 'So while we were all there you were getting *fingered?*' she exclaims, still in disbelief.

'Look, it's no big deal.' She attempts to shrug it off. 'It's all experience, isn't it. And Luke's hot anyway.'

I look to Kate. We have to tell her.

'He's not a nice guy,' I warn. 'He tried it on with Kate and me tonight too, but we turned him down.'

Her face drops with disappointment. There's nothing worse than hearing you're not a guy's first choice. Especially when said guy just had his fingers inside you.

'Well, I don't care,' she snaps stubbornly, speeding up her pace.

'Are you not scared that he'll tell everyone at school?' Kate asks, nibbling on her bottom lip.

'I don't care. He can say whatever he wants,' she snorts becoming more defiant by the minute.

'We're not having a go,' Charlotte reasons, always a calming influence.

'I kind of am,' Erin interrupts. Charlotte gives her a warning look.

'We're just worried about you,' Charlotte says sympathetically. 'I mean, did you even kiss first?'

'No,' she admits reluctantly, her gaze falling to the floor. 'It just kind of happened. And I enjoyed it until you lot pissed all over my fun.'

'Well, we're *very* sorry that we ruined your fun,' Erin growls sarcastically.

'Look,' I try to reason, 'Why don't we just try and forget about it. It was a mistake, right? I mean, you're not going to do anything like this with him again are you?'

'Maybe, maybe not,' she shrugs, a wide grin spreading on her face.

Jesus, she's a liability. We all roll our eyes. I take a deep breath to try and calm myself down. Typical Zahra, letting her vagina make her decisions.

'It's *my* reputation, so you shouldn't even care,' she snaps. Does she not realise she reflects on all of us? She runs ahead to catch up with the boys.

'Can you believe that?' Kate gasps, still seeming in disbelief.

Erin folds her arms across her chest. 'I think she just

wants everyone to think she's badass. It's pathetic,' she hisses, thoroughly pissed off. She always takes things to heart.

I can't get over it myself. She's only met him a few times before tonight and has never uttered more than three words to him. She doesn't even have his phone number. I mean, how can you get fingered by someone that you haven't even kissed? And doesn't she care that he might tell the entire school? Maybe Erin was right, and she wants everyone to find out. Wants them to know how up for it, she is. I'll never understand her.

We walk to the point where there's only me, Kate and Heath left. Everyone else has gone their separate ways towards home. Kate wanted to sleep at mine tonight, but I instead convinced her it would be better for us to stay at hers.

Heath only lives two roads away from her, so I'm sure he'll offer to walk us home.

'So I take it you ladies are escorting me home?' he says out of nowhere, catching me off guard.

'Err, no, love,' I snort. '*You're* walking *us* home. Like you said, *we* are the ladies. *You* are supposed to be the man. And it's like what you said back in the park—it's not safe.'

He rolls his eyes. 'Oh please. There are two of you. It only makes *good* sense for you to walk me home and then you have each other. It's not safe for a pretty boy like me. There are lots of freaky guys out there waiting to take advantage of me. I can only imagine.' He fakes a shudder at the thought. 'Plus,' he adds, 'the scariest thing to happen in our neighbourhood in the last ten years is that cat found dead a month ago.'

'They still don't know who did it!' I whisper, suddenly aware of how dark it is.

He rolls his eyes. 'They say it died of natural causes. You know this, you drama queen.'

Damn it – why does he have to pull the drama queen card? Now anything I say is going to sound melodramatic. I give up.

When we finally trek to his house, I insist that we go inside for a drink. We're parched. After all, we have just walked...okay only about four streets, but still, I want to make the magic happen between Kate and Heath. I'm already imagining what their babies will look like.

I say hello to his mum, Karen, who is on the computer with a bottle of wine next to her. No doubt she's talking to my mum on Facebook, not wanting to break a habit of a lifetime.

We head to the kitchen and once in there I lie and say that I need the loo. As I leave the room, I try to give Kate a look that says *'he's into you – go for it.'* She just seems baffled. She's never been very good at mind reading.

I fool around in the toilet, not really needing to go. I count how many tiles are in the bathroom, put on his mum's perfume and then decide that enough time has passed. They've probably had enough time to chat, flirt and maybe even a kiss? Am I being too hopeful?

I slowly walk downstairs, expecting to hear them flirting, but only silence greets me. Oh my God, I must be right. They must be getting off with each other. I creep to the door, and peer inside but all that greets me is Heath giving me an odd look.

'You took your time. You ill or something?' he asks, looking me up and down suspiciously.

'No!' I shout, my cheeks hot. God, I really hope he doesn't think I have the shits.

'Shall we set off then?' Kate says, seeming eager to leave. Is she not into him? Why wouldn't she be?

Once we're out of the door, I start to interrogate her.

'*Soooooo?* Did anything happen between you two?' I ask, jumping up and down excitedly.

'Happen?' She looks back at me blankly. God, she can be so slow and innocent sometimes.

'Yes, happen. You know...you and Heath. Did anything happen? I'm sure he fancies you.' I can't help a big smile breaking over my face.

She bursts out laughing. She's hysterical actually. Whenever she turns her head to look at my confused face, she crumples over in a new bout of giggles.

'What is so funny?' I ask, annoyed that I'm not in on the joke.

'Me and Heath?' she laughs. 'There is more chance of me getting together with Jamie Puggent from Year 11.

'Why?' I ask, offended. 'What the hell is wrong with Heath?' I feel protective of my friend.

'No, nothing.' She tries to look serious. 'It's just that we're not into each other. I mean, we're barely even good friends. He's your friend, not mine.'

'But, he's always flirting with you' I say, more to myself than to her. I don't get it.

'God, you really are blind,' she laughs, creasing up again. 'We've always thought you two would end up together.'

I stop walking and turn to stare at her. Is she serious? Me and Heath?

'What? And what do you mean *we?*'

She sighs and rolls her eyes. 'Don't worry about it.'

How can I not think about it now she's said it? Me and Heath? It's bloody ridiculous.

'Anyway, he was too busy telling me about this new girl, Mercedes. Apparently, he's bringing her to Jessica's party tomorrow.'

Mercedes? Has he already met with her? That's a bit cosy, isn't it? Going to a party together. Why the hell didn't he tell me that? And why do I feel so insanely pissed off?

CHAPTER SEVEN

Saturday 22nd October

#JessicasParty

It turns out that work isn't so bad. They're actually a really nice bunch, and we manage to have a laugh in between getting soaking wet and stinking of dog.

Especially today as my boss Katie has ordered us a pizza for lunch to thank us for our hard work. Apparently, we've just come out of a particularly busy period. Thank God. At least that means it will be calmer from now on.

I run out to the delivery driver as soon as I spot him pulling up. I'm bloody starving.

'Pizza's here,' I announce as I go round the back with it.

'Yummy,' Yasmin squeals, rushing over to wash her hands.

When we're all washed up, we leave the dogs tied to the top of the table and move to the side so we can tuck in.

Katie's dog, Liv, sits comfortably in her basket. It's the most chilled out I've ever seen the Yorkshire terrier. She's normally a neurotic barking nutter.

Ava frowns. 'Benny's looking a bit strange.'

I glance over. The golden retriever does look weird. He's pulling the strangest face, curling his lip. Then he jumps up.

'Oh no, I bet he needs the toilet,' Katie says with a heavy sigh. 'We never get to eat around here.'

'I'll take him,' I offer, putting my slice down and wiping my hands on a tea towel.

It's then I hear the noise. A loud, long, disgruntled fart. We all turn in horror to see Benny not just pooing but having what seems like projectile diarrhoea. It's barely missing us.

'Cover the food! Cover the food!' Yasmin yells, leaning over it protectively.

'Liv!' Katie screams looking helplessly at the dog. 'She's going to get sprayed. Get over here now!'

'Liv!' we all scream. 'Here girl, now!'

The poor thing looks terrified from us shouting and gets up—barking back at us. She's almost... Oh no, she's walking straight into the spray of the poo!

'Nooooo!'

Brown slush hits her in the face. She squeals and falls down, clearly in shock with what's happened.

'Jesus!' I scream. 'Someone grab a cloth or something!'

'You can!' Ava shouts back, horrified. 'I'm not going anywhere near that shit!'

'My baby!' Katie screams.

Benny is still going. It's like he's fucking possessed! We shield ourselves and the pizza, as it sprays closer towards us. The dog finally seems to calm down, and the poo spray stops.

We all turn to look at each other, out of breath from screaming.

'Err...suddenly I'm not so hungry.'

We all burst out laughing, clutching our stomachs from the aches. What a fucking disaster.

BANG BANG.

We all turn towards the banging on the window. It's

Jessica's bloody Mum. Waving like a total lunatic. How the hell does she know I work here?

I check myself for poo and then go out front to greet her. God knows she won't leave until I do.

'Hi, Mrs Sheridan.'

'Savannah,' she smiles engulfing me in a huge hug. I stiffen in her arms. We're really not close enough for a hug. 'I didn't know you worked here.'

She's lying. Jessica would have definitely told her even though limited people know and I've sworn them to secrecy. She's never been good at keeping secrets.

'Anyway, I'm glad I bumped into you.' She guides me over to a corner. 'Savannah, you would tell me if Jessica was planning on having a party tonight, wouldn't you?' she probes, accusation in the tone of her voice.

Shit, she's onto us. I thought we'd been discreet as fuck. How can she know?

'Of course I would,' I mumble, lying through my teeth and avoiding her gaze. I've never been good at lying.

Her eyes narrow beneath her perfectly drawn on eyebrows.

'It's just that I get the feeling she's planning something...but maybe I'm just being paranoid.' She stares at me expectantly, awaiting my answer.

'Yeah, I think you're just paranoid,' I agree, nodding like a maniac. I try to busy myself by straightening some dog collars.

I've already had enough drama for one day. For one year actually. Now I have to face this interrogation. Is the whole thing a trap or something?

'Well, as long as you're sure.' She nods, her voice deeply sceptical.

'Yeah, I'm sure.' I nod back, forcing a sweet smile.

After another hard glare, she finally turns to leave.

As soon as I see her car leave, I ask Yasmin to cover me as I go into the toilets with my phone. I ring Jessica, jittery as a druggie at the thought of being caught out.

'She's on to you,' I announce as soon as she's answered.

'Err, hi to you, too,' she chuckles. How can she be so calm about this? 'How can she be? I've been so careful.'

Not careful enough, clearly.

'Well, she came into my work today and pretended like she'd forgotten I work here. It's miles away from your house, and your dog wasn't even with her. She asked me if you were planning a party, and I had to lie through my teeth. I feel terrible. She looked really worried.' My breathing speeds and my stomach becomes unsettled at just the thought of us being caught.

'Savannah, calm down! You're ranting again.' I can imagine her rolling her eyes. 'There's no need to feel terrible, you idiot. This party is gonna be amazing. Don't chicken out on me now.'

I try to take a deep breath. She's right.

'I know, I know.' I look at my white face in the toilet mirror.

I really have to pull myself together. I just have to forget about her mum and any loyalty I feel towards her. I pinch my cheeks to try and bring some colour back into them and go back to work. Those mutts won't wash themselves.

Later on, after much scrubbing of my skin in the shower and spraying of perfume, I'm round at Jessica's smelling fresh as a daisy. Her parents think we're just here for a girly sleepover so we have to keep the ruse up. I kind of wish it *was* just a girly sleepover. I'm actually dreading it.

I can't help but worry that her Mum's setting her up, but she won't listen to me. Whenever I think about everyone arriving my throat tightens and a sickening feeling rises in my stomach. Her Mum's disapproving face pops into my head causing me to physically shudder. I hate letting people down.

As soon as we watch their car pull out of the drive, we start to change clothes and do our makeup. Girly chatter fills the room and the same nervous energy I always feel before a big night makes itself present in my stomach. I suddenly want to pee every thirty seconds.

It doesn't help when Jessica tells me that she's invited her cousin and some of their friends from Brixton. I have a bad feeling about them, as all of the stories I've heard containing her cousin seem to end with the police getting called or someone getting pregnant.

I open my overnight bag and frown when I find a denim mini skirt in there. I haven't packed this. I don't even own a denim mini. Maybe I have someone else's bag. I pull it out and find a post-it stuck to it with my Nan's scrawl.

Please listen to me for once and wear this. You will look fab. Love u xxx

I'm instantly annoyed. Why does Nan feel the need to keep dressing me up like a Barbie doll? She knows I'm much more comfortable in jeans. I throw it back in the bag, determined to stay in my current jeans just to spite her, but then I think about it. I know I'm being stubborn and getting in the way of possible new opportunities. If that psychic was right, I could have the love of my life coming round tonight.

Will it be too dressed up for a house party? I look around at the other's outfits. They're all wearing short dresses apart from Erin who prefers to cover herself up a bit more. I slip off my jeans and try it on, ignoring the sideways glances from Erin and Charlotte. I feel a bit self-conscious and naked with my legs on show. Not that my legs aren't nice. I've always got good compliments about them, but that doesn't mean I want to flaunt them. Thank God I shaved.

I glance round at the others glamorous outfits and decide that I should try to be more like a girl. It's decided. I'm going to wear the skirt. I wonder if Heath will like it? Woah! Where did that come from? I don't even like Heath. Right?

I mean Heath? Bloody Heath? They always expected

me to end up with him? Since when? Are they all having private conversations about how perfect we are for each other while the whole time we're both completely oblivious? I mean, of course I'd never date Heath! He's my best mate. I don't even think of him like that. It's just...well it's weird to try and think of him in any other sense than a good friend.

The first few eager beavers arrive at 7 pm on the dot. We put the stereo on high and show people where the fridge is. I fluster unnecessarily round the house, awaiting the Brixton cousin.

At about 8 pm Tyler, Heath, and Ryan arrive. I feel my shoulders relax just knowing they're here. That is until I see, who I can only imagine is Mercedes, with Heath. In my panic I'd forgotten about her.

She's short. I'd guess about five-foot-two, with a curvy hourglass figure shown off in a tight, navy bodycon dress. Her hair is raven red and falls in long curls down her back. Her lips have so much red lip gloss on them I'm expecting them to start dripping.

Heath has a weird look on his face. I watch as his eyes

travel lazily up my body. My skin heats as if he's scorched me. This is weird. Heath never checks me out, and he really shouldn't be doing it in front of his girlfriend. Even if she is a classless tramp. I can't help but grin like a bloody idiot. What is happening to me?

'Wow, look at you in a skirt!' Tyler says, looking at me in awe.

I roll my eyes. Yeah, yeah, I'm in a skirt.

When I look back at Heath, the weird look is gone, and his huge goofy grin is back. That's more like it.

Robbie and Luke follow them in. Great. Now I have to add avoiding Luke for the entirety of the night to my list. I do my best to avoid his gaze, remembering his hand on my arse cheek only last night. I get the feeling he knows I'm uneasy at his presence, smirking away like he likes it.

I nearly lose my breath when behind them walks in Zach. Oh, my God. They brought Zach.

I can already feel myself blushing which I realise is pathetic. Apart from that text I'm sure he's completely forgotten I even exist. I prepare myself for him not to remember me. He meets my eyes, and I'm shocked that he not only remembers me, but he smiles as if he's pleased to see me. Swoon!

134

He nods from across the room as if to say hello. I smile back, although I'm so nervous I'm sure it looks more like a grimace. God, I'm bad in situations like this.

I turn around and head straight for the front door. I need some air. Awkwardness is just so cringey. I really don't need it in my life, but at least this will take my mind off Heath and my weird new feelings.

I take a few deep breaths to try and calm myself, my thoughts whirling around in my head, but there are so many people smoking out here it instead causes me almost to cough up a lung. Sexy.

I'm distracted when Jessica's cousin arrives with her crew. I've met her cousin, briefly, once before, about a year ago. She hadn't been very friendly and to be frank scared the shit out of me. Something about her let you know that she wasn't to be messed with. I remember how she'd made me and Jessica shoplift some earrings for her. I'd cried for weeks about it, which is quite funny now.

She doesn't seem to have changed much. She walks past me as bold as brass, chewing gum, in a grey velour tracksuit and dripping in gold jewellery, from Argos no doubt. She's surrounded by about ten big, broad guys.

My body tenses up, immediately on guard, as I try to

look at their faces behind their raised hoods. They're like grim reapers. I follow them back into the party and watch as most people in the room look over and immediately look away, scared to catch their eye line.

They descend on the room, splitting off into little groups. Well, it's going to be harder to keep an eye on them now. My stomach does a little nervous flip. Get a hold of yourself, Savannah. I should probably try to break the ice and talk to one of them. It'll probably put my mind at ease. I'm sure they're lovely guys.

I walk over to one of the hoodies, reminding myself to act confident. They can probably smell fear. I square my shoulders, standing tall. I try to smile and not look intimidated.

'Hi, I'm Savannah, Jessica's friend. You came with her cousin, right?'

I practically *feel* Kate tense from across the room. I turn to see her staring at me, eyes wide in horror, clearly thinking I'm mad to try and talk to them.

'Yeah, we came with Nell,' he says not smiling and looking a bit bored. Well *sorry* if I'm boring.

Wait, who the hell is Nell?

'Oh right.' I rock on my heels. Well, he's chatty. 'Do

you...want a drink or anything?'

He yawns. Actually yawns. How bloody rude can you be?

'Nah, thanks for the offer but I've got some weed with me.'

Weed? Shit, they're all going to get stoned out of their heads. I didn't even consider people might bring drugs.

'Oh, okay,' I utter, a bit taken aback. I'm surprised by how well spoken he is, even though he's clearly a druggie. Trust me to think of that right now.

I leave him, much to Kate's relief, to find the others and start drinking my vodka, which by now I really need. I can't see Zach anywhere, and I'm glad. I can really do without the added stress tonight.

It's 9 pm when I hear their house phone ring. I meet Jessica's eyes from across the room, my stomach a ball of nerves. We both run upstairs to her mum and dad's bedroom so we can answer it away from the loud music. She answers it trying to sound as calm as possible.

Her face drains of all colour within seconds. 'No, mum, it's just me and the girls.' She's desperately trying to hold her hand close to the phone to block out the background noise, but she must still be worried her mum can hear it because she's looking more panicked by the second.

'No, I swear. I don't know what the neighbours can hear, but it's not us.'

Shit, the neighbours grassed us up. I have to sit down—I'm going to get sick. I perch on the bed and put my head between my legs. I saw once in a film that it can help. It only makes me feel dizzier.

She hangs up and looks down at the floor.

'My neighbours grassed on me.'

'Duh,' I retort not feeling very helpful.

She looks sick to her stomach. 'Yeah, well I told her they couldn't be hearing us but that we would turn the TV down anyway.'

'And do you think they believed you?' I can't hide the doubt in my voice.

'Yeah,' she shrugs. I can tell she's lying for my sake. We're dead girls walking.

'We were so stupid to think we could get away with this,' I whine, biting my lip. 'Who do we think we are? One of the Kardashians?' I can't help but feel hysterical.

'Savannah, calm down!' Jessica snaps, having no patience for my nervous breakdown. She grabs me by the shoulders. 'We're going to be fine.'

We walk back downstairs on shaky legs. I'm going to cope by getting *very* drunk. I switch from vodka to wine and started glugging. Before long I feel the usual calming effects: I feel confident and happy, and my face feels a little bit numb.

I can still see Jessica fussing around, asking people to use coasters and not dance on the furniture. It's a bit late now. And I'm too drunk to help or even care anymore.

'Ryan, why the hell are you eating that whole tub of ice cream?' she screeches at him.

'Heath dared me,' he admits, sighing heavily and looking like he might barf at any given moment.

'Where's Zahra?' Kate asks me, a line appearing between her brows.

'Don't know,' I say dismissively. I'm too busy looking over at Heath's new girlfriend. At her drippy lips laughing at everything Heath says. He's really not that funny.

Her concerned face and the way that Charlotte and Erin look at each other makes me take an interest. It's like they know something I don't.

'What?' I look between them, 'What?' I press, my own forehead creased.

139

Charlotte stares at the floor, avoiding my gaze. I eye their faces, growing impatient. Erin is the first to speak.

'Well...' she says with a big sigh. I can tell she's annoyed that Zahra being absent is causing a fuss. Yet again. 'Charlotte told me that she went off with Luke...and that was about half an hour ago.' She rolls her eyes, chewing her thumbnail, agitated.

'Luke?' I repeat, confused. 'Don't tell me she's getting with him again? That girl is a serious fool if she thinks she's special. I mean he's tried it on with all of us before.'

I know my words are mean and unnecessary, but I don't care. This is *so* Zahra. Craving attention and not thinking about the rest of us before she acts irresponsibly. God, I feel like that girl's mother sometimes. I'm totally feeling sober again from worry.

'Well, I'm sure she'll be back soon,' Charlotte says trying to sound confident. 'Let me call her.' She pulls out her phone.

'I've already tried,' Erin chimes in. 'It keeps going to voicemail.'

Perfect. It's nearly 11 pm, and she's pissed off to god knows where.

'Maybe try one more time?' I plead. I look at my watch

again in the hope time has stopped.

Erin lets out a loud exasperated huff and then tries again. We all wait, expecting a miracle. I'm starting to worry about what trouble she might have got herself into.

'Zahra. Thank God!' she shouts into the phone. Oh, thank God. 'Where the hell are you? Okay, okay, we'll meet you in the toilets.' She snaps her phone shut.

'Where is she?' Kate sighs, rolling her eyes.

'I don't even know,' Erin tuts, a flash of anger passing across her face. 'Let's just go to the toilet and see what she says.'

I wave to Heath and Tyler from across the garden, and mouth to them that we're going to the loo and will be back soon. I don't even know if they're listening, as they're clearly too interested in what Mercedes is saying. She must be talking about boobs or Fifa. Most likely boobs. Why does that make me feel insanely jealous? Probably just because I'm used to their undivided attention.

By the time we get to the toilet Zahra is already waiting there, leaning casually against the wall. We push the waiting line out of the way and rush her into the tiny toilet, desperate for an explanation.

Once we've locked the door shut we turn to stare at

her expectantly. Well, all of us apart from Kate who apparently has to wee so desperately it's 'like her bladder is gonna explode'.

'SO???' We all seem to ask at the same time. 'Where the hell have you been?' Erin demands.

'And why the hell do you have a leaf in your hair?' I say noticing it.

'It's no big deal,' she smiles, brushing it out with her fingers. 'Move over, Kate. I'm bursting.'

Erin looks like she might burst into flames from the fury. 'Will everyone *please* stop pissing and tell me what the fuck has happened?'

I know she's sick of Zahra's attention-seeking games, but her tone still startles me.

Zahra ignores her, pulling her jeans and knickers down to sit on the toilet. My jaw drops open as more leaves fall out. It's then that I notice a spot of blood in her knickers. What the fuck?

'*Please* tell me you've come on your period, and you used leaves to stop it!' Erin squeals in disbelief. 'Please tell me you didn't just lose your virginity to Luke fucking Jeffries!'

She rolls her eyes like we're overreacting.

'Oh, calm down, you big drama queen! It's no big deal. Just a bit of fun on the cliff,' Zahra says casually, avoiding our judging gazes.

I can't quite believe this. Zahra, our Zahra, has slept with Luke—the biggest player around. On the top of makeout cliff.

Her very first time—the thing we've all always talked about. The thing that should have been special. We had all agreed it would be with someone we were going out with. We weren't naive enough to think that we had to be in love with this guy. We even agreed that there didn't have to be a time limit that you were going out for, but we had all agreed that it would be with a guy that was ours exclusively, and who we would feel comfortable with.

But this is so out of touch it's unreal. Luke fucking Jeffries. I mean this isn't something that someone in our group does. This is something other slutty girls did. But here she is, Zahra, my friend, the slut.

I look around at the others. They have the same horrified expression on their faces I imagine is on mine. I guess they're thinking the same thing. We're all so involved in each other's lives that when someone does something we all feel like we have too. I feel violated—like I'm dirty.

'Did he push you into it?' I ask, before thinking.

'Of course not!' she snaps defensively. 'I just went with the moment.' She shrugs. How can she be so casual about this?

Erin is the next to speak up. I can see the anger rising in her, her face red and blotchy. *'Calm down'* I think as I look at her, trying to make her read my thoughts.

'What about the way we had all talked about? What about finding a guy that actually likes you? I mean—Luke Jeffries! What were you thinking! You know he's probably telling the whole world right now! I mean, since when did you start behaving like a slut?'

Zahra's expression changes, first to hurt and then to anger. Erin has gone too far.

'How fucking dare you call me a slut!' she shouts, arms crossed over her chest. 'I'm sorry I'm not a frigid bitch like you, and I actually enjoy guy's company.'

Ouch. This isn't going well.

'Hey, fuck you, Zahra,' is Erin's quick response. She folds her arms across her chest defensively. I can tell she's hurt, not that she'd ever let on.

'Okay, let's all just calm down,' Charlotte attempts, looking at Kate and me in desperation.

144

'Oh, shut up, Charlotte!' Zahra barks aggressively.

'Hey, don't start on Charlotte!' I shout, quick to defend her honour.

'Yeah, don't start on Charlotte,' Erin agrees with a snarl. 'She's only trying to help.' This must be the maddest I've ever seen her.

Zahra and Erin lock eyes, scowling at each other. It's hard to know who the first one to break will be— it's like a battle of wills.

'Please just tell me you used a condom?' Kate asks quietly, touching her temples like she's trying to calm herself down.

I'm shocked Kate feels the need to ask such a stupid question. Of course she would have. I've barely finished thinking this when I notice the silence. I look at Zahra, expecting her to answer and reassure us, but her expression is one of shame. I try to reassure myself that Zahra isn't your average thick bitch. She's clued up and knows about all of the risks. I look at her now crimson face, puzzled.

'WHAT?!' Charlotte explodes, suddenly finding her voice.

Zahra looks at the floor, ignoring the questions. I know I have to take control of this situation before it gets out of hand.

'Okay, don't worry,' I shout, placing my hands up in what I hope is a calming way. 'This is what we're gonna do. Tomorrow morning we'll take you to the chemist and get you the morning after pill.' I inhale deep breaths to try and calm myself down. 'I only hope that Luke normally uses a condom and isn't riddled with disease...' I add before realising that this probably isn't helping. 'Although I'm sure everything will be fine.' I smile as brightly at her as I can. 'Zahra had sex—that's it. It's not the end of the world. We all just need to adjust to it.' I look round the tiny toilet at their faces, each different in expression.

Erin is still angry with Zahra, and it shows the way she's scowling at her. Charlotte looks hurt and worried, probably scared about a possible pregnancy scare and Kate just looks disgusted.

I look at Zahra, trying to find some regret on her face, but nothing is showing at the moment. Instead, I think she looks triumphant, and I wonder if I could possibly be right. Maybe it is too soon for her to realise what a giant mistake she's made. Maybe it will take him to spread it round the school before she realises. Am I imagining it or is she truly looking smug?

'Okay, fine,' Erin agrees on a deep sigh.

'Fine,' Zahra huffs unlocking the door and storming out.

The phone rings again as we walk down the stairs. Jessica passes us, making a run for it. I should follow her, but I'm feeling far too drunk and selfish right now. We have our own drama. Instead, I follow the girls into the sitting room.

'Your arse looks good in that skirt, Sav,' Tyler says as soon as we're back in the kitchen. He brings back his hand and whacks my arse so hard it makes my eyes water. It's the sort of pain that debilitates you, and you can't even make a noise—you just freeze in agony.

'Oh my god, you fucker! That hurt.' I rub my bum, but even the touch stings. He whacks it again, laughing hysterically.

'Leave me alone,' I shout, anger rising in my body. I'm still trying to process Zahra losing her V plates, and this idiot is trying to put me in hospital.

'What you gonna do?' he says playfully, his eyes alight with mischief. He stands up and waves the hand at me menacingly.

I put my hands up in defence, backing away. 'I'm

147

warning you. Leave me alone.'

He smiles menacingly, so menacingly that I turn and run out of the room. It's no use as he chases me, laughing so hard he's almost crying. I run as fast as my little legs can take me, through the living room, back into the kitchen again and then into the garden.

He chases me back into the house and throws me over the couch, onto two of Jessica's cousin's friends' laps.

'Sorry,' I apologise as I try to get up, embarrassed at having basically crutch dived them.

I've barely said the words before Tyler has me bent over it, attacking my arse like it's the bongo drums. My head is thrust into one of the guy's laps. I squirm at how close I am to his penis. Ewww.

Tyler laughs so hard I think he might wet himself. The pain is immense, burning so bright I fear I'll pass out, but I quickly realise that he'll only stop if I just stop squirming and let him grow bored.

After what seems like ages he does. I get up, tears almost falling from my eyes and try with all my force and anger to hit him in the face. He's too quick for me and grabs my arm before I touch him. His features contort into concern.

'Shit, Sav, are you okay? I was only joking around.'

'No, I'm not, you shit head!' I cry in frustration. 'My arse is on fucking fire!'

His eyes turn mischievous again, a smile playing on his lips. 'Calling me a shit head? Do you really want me to have to smack your bottom again?' He smirks playfully.

'You must have known you were hurting her,' Heath snaps at Tyler, a murderous look on his face. 'Too far man, too far.'

'Alright!' Tyler laughs, arms crossed over his chest defensively. 'We were only messing.'

'It doesn't look like she had much choice over it,' he snaps back.

It's nice to have someone stick up for me.

'Just all of you leave me alone!' I huff, trying to pull my hair back into place while walking into the kitchen.

Heath runs after me. 'Sav, wait!' I turn, bad tempered to face him. 'Are you okay? Did he really hurt you?'

'Yes, he bloody did!' I attempt to shout. It comes out more of a whimper and before I have time to stop myself I can feel tears tightening my throat.

His eyes droop. 'Oh Sav, he didn't mean it.' He wraps his arm around me and pulls me into his chest. I sniff, a tear falling straight onto his t-shirt. He rubs my back affectionately. 'I'll get you some paracetamol.'

I nod, accidently smelling him. Since when did he smell so good? I tense, now desperate to be out of his arms. It's bloody confusing me. I let him leave me to find some.

Zahra appears, smiling. 'Have you two composed yourselves now then?'

Like she's in any place to judge right now.

'Don't ask me. Ask the punisher over there.' I glare back over at Tyler. He must have borrowed his sister's copy of Fifty Shades of Grey.

'Oh please, you're both as bad as each other,' Erin snaps, irritated by both of us.

Goose pimples rise on my arm, and I shiver. Shit, it's so cold out, and people keep leaving the back doors open so they can go in and out to smoke. Plus, I'm not wearing many clothes.

Heath appears with two paracetamol and a glass of water. I smile back gratefully as I take them. He takes such good care of me. I shiver again. He rubs my arms.

'You cold?' I nod. He looks around and grabs Jessica's younger brother's jumper. 'Here, put this on.'

It seems to look more like a crop top on me.

Whatever, it still warms my shoulders.

I've barely put it over my head when I notice Heath's body language change. He actively takes a step away from me and moves closer to Mercedes. Is she giving him shit for helping me out?

He takes a bottle of vodka and guides her out into the garden. Moody bitch.

Two hours later and I'm starting to feel better about the whole thing. We've got away with it. It's a great party, and everyone is having a blast. That's when something changes in the atmosphere. The people in the sitting room turn quiet and then I feel the bodies next to me freeze. I look up to see Mrs Sheridan staring at me so hard I'm surprised I don't burst into flames.

'Savannah, where the FUCK is Jessica!?'

CHAPTER EIGHT

#ShitTheBed

My stomach drops as if on a roller coaster. I think I might vomit. I feel like a child, ridiculous for ever thinking we could get away with this.

She's still staring at me, with anger filled eyes, almost growling like a dog, expecting an explanation.

'I don't know,' I mumble looking at the floor, admitting defeat.

She huffs and walks back into the sitting room. Everyone turns back towards me, their eyes wide with panic.

'Fuck,' Erin whispers, her chest rising and falling rapidly. 'What are we gonna do?'

Most people have already made their decision and are trying to bolt for it, bodies piling out into the living room. Just having to walk past her is giving me palpitations. I grasp the sides of the jumper, desperately trying to take it off. In the panic, I manage to get it stuck with my arms over my head.

'HELP, HELP!' I yell, spinning around in a frantic circle. I'm going to be found dead, suffocated by a child's jumper. What a way to go. I'd expect no less from my idiot self.

Someone's hands wrap around it and help me pull it over my head. When I'm fully out it I see it's Kate, thank god.

'Come on', she yells over the hysteria, grabbing my hand.

We run into the living room where all hell is breaking loose. Jessica's dad is standing at the door grabbing people and literally throwing them out. People too scared to go near him are jumping on the sofa and flinging themselves out of the window onto the flower beds outside.

Her cousin comes running down the stairs with one of her 'friends', both flinging their tops back on. Well, that doesn't look good. Her Dad grabs them both, his face as purple as beetroot, and throws them out.

'GET OUT, GET OUT!' he screams in his thick Irish accent. It makes it seem scarier. Like a seriously pissed off leprechaun. Who stole his pot of gold?

Kate and I walk as quickly and inconspicuously to the door as possible. We make a run for the door, hiding my face with my hair. He grabs hold of my arm, seemingly unaware of who I am and before I have time to reason with him he flings me out of the door. I feel the night air whoosh through my hair, my feet completely leaving the ground before landing on my side. I gasp with the pain of being winded, pain so overwhelming I can't even answer Kate asking me if I'm okay.

Shit. He's a fucking nutter. At least I haven't fallen on my already bruised arse from Tyler I suppose. Silver linings and all that.

Kate and Charlotte drag me up quickly so that I avoid being crushed by the bodies that are still being thrown out with wild abandon.

I look towards the green outside. There's a small mob of people obviously wondering what to do. We wander over to them looking for familiar faces. Shit, how many gatecrashers got in? There must be two hundred people here.

I spot Tyler, Heath, and Mercedes in the crowd and drag the girls towards them. Heath is chewing his tongue. He does this when he's wasted. How has he got drunk without me noticing? Or maybe I was as drunk as that five minutes ago, and I've suddenly sobered up with all of the drama.

'Where's Jessica?' I ask Tyler, deciding I'm not going to get any sense from Heath. He's now too busy snogging Mercedes' face off anyway. I have no idea why I feel so irrationally angry about it.

'Savannah,' a voice calls out behind me. I turn towards it, but can't find anyone.

'Savannah!' someone calls again. This time, I see Erin and Zahra weaving through the crowds.

'Have you seen Jessica?' Erin asks, concern etched into her forehead.

I sigh. 'No, I was going to ask you the same thing.' I'm a terrible friend.

I glance up at the house and notice her through the front bedroom window. The main light is on so she can clearly be seen sitting on the bed, chewing her nails. The poor thing must be shitting herself. Her parents are going

155

to kill her. And I mean he might actually kill her. Shall I go in to save her?

Her Dad has stopped throwing people out now and slams the door so hard the doorframe trembles. He'll be with her in a few seconds. Bile rises in my throat. This is bad. Really bad. Am I about to watch her be murdered? Surely they can't be that angry. It's only a party. No one died. Yet.

Most of the party watch from the green—captivated, nervous chatter filling the cold night air. Her Dad enters the room with her mum behind him. I can almost feel the tension in the room from here. It's as if everyone in this crowd holds their breath in nervous anticipation.

He shouts something at her so angrily I can make out a burst blood vessel on his cheek. She jumps up, putting her arms up defensively, clearly begging him to calm down.

Before any of us have time to react, he picks her up and launches her across the room. She flies through the air like a rag doll, hitting the wardrobe with what I imagine is an almighty thud.

I gulp back the vomit. This is fucking awful. He's going to kill her.

I can't look anymore. I push my hands up to cover my

eyes. Should we call the police?

'We have to go back in there to help her,' Tyler says frantically before trying to break through the crowds.

Is he serious? Does he want to get us *all* killed?

'No!' I shout, grabbing his arm and trying to pull him back.

I'm far too weak to make any impact and only seem to get dragged along with him. I look back at the others in desperation. We can't let him go in there. I get that he wants to be her white knight, but with her Dad's mood he could end up dead. Ryan and Erin grab hold of him too and try to reason with him.

'He'll just get even madder if you go storming in there, and that won't help her,' Ryan reasons, trying to get through to him.

The front door slams and we look up to see Jessica come out already. Thank God. She walks straight to her cousin who gives her a fag. Her trembling hands light it as she walks with them towards the station. She's gone in a second.

I feel a bit hurt that she didn't even acknowledge us, but I have to remember that she isn't thinking straight right now.

Now I have to get back to the present—being stranded in High Pill. High Pill is even rougher than Crapstone and located just outside of Burnham-On-Cliffs. It's easily the roughest area within twenty miles. People joke that it's called High Pill because everyone's always high on pills.

Okay, try not to panic. My arms cling onto Tyler and Erin. I could just call my mum and ask her to pick us up, but then I remember that she's out tonight for a friend's 40th. Okay, I can call a taxi. Where's my phone?

Then it dawns on me. My phone is with my bag and everything else, upstairs in Jessica's bedroom.

'Oh no, I haven't got a phone,' I mutter out loud.

'Neither do I,' Erin says, looking at the other girls, hoping that one of them will say they have theirs.

'Don't look at me,' Zahra shrugs, 'my stuff's upstairs too'.

'Don't worry.' Heath giggles stumbling over to me. 'Stick with me kid—you'll be fine.' He slaps my wrist with a handcuff.

I push him off, annoyed at how drunk and stupid he can be at a time like this. He flies back a few steps, but I find I'm dragged along with him. I look down at the handcuff strapped to my wrist and realise that the other cuff is strapped to him.

'Well done, you idiot,' I shout, trying to pick it. It feels easier to be angry with him right now.

He hiccups in response. Dammit, he's cute.

'Where is the key?' I demand, scratching at it with my nails.

'I don't know,' he says, pulling his pockets inside out, an innocent stare in his eyes. How much has he had?

'You don't have the key?' Mercedes asks looking at me with contempt.

Err, hello? I didn't handcuff *myself* to him. I do smile internally though. Haha, bitch, I'm attached to your boyfriend.

Erin and Charlotte start to laugh hysterically.

'Are you *seriously* laughing?' I ask, my lip curling up in anger. 'This isn't funny! Help me get this off!'

The others join in chuckling. Yeah, yeah, bloody hilarious. I'm glad my unfortunate situation can bring some comedic relief to our situation. Not.

When they've stopped laughing, they try twisting and pulling the handcuffs, attempting to help me out of them. Every time they yank it chafes my wrist.

'Ouch! Be careful! It hurts,' I whine like a toddler. I

suddenly feel claustrophobic, like the walls are closing in around me.

Erin tries to hide her smile. 'Sorry babe, but I can't get them off.'

'Where did you even get these from anyway?' Charlotte asks Heath, hand on her hip with a questioning stare.

He points to Mercedes. 'We found them in her parent's room, didn't we?' He smiles smugly.

Ewww! He was in Mercedes' parents' bedroom with her. When was this? Did they have sex? Are they having sex now?

'Ugh! That's gross,' Charlotte responds in clear disgust. 'Why the hell do old people insist on having sex?'

I look down at the offending sex cuffs and try to block out images of Jessica's parents doing freaky stuff together. I mean, these are *real* metal handcuffs. Where on earth did they get them anyway? Do they also have matching gimp masks? Ewww. Just the thought has me shuddering.

The crowd starts to disperse, everyone going in different directions. I can feel myself start to panic, my stomach lurching violently. We're in the middle of High Pill with no phone, no money, and I'm dressed like a slut.

I remember the story I read about a gang that attacked a woman walking home around here. They snatched her into their car, gang raped her and threw her out. I'm starting to lose my breath a bit as I look around at the rough estate we're in. It makes Crapstone look like Buckingham Palace. I'm suddenly pleased that I'm handcuffed to Heath if I have to be handcuffed to anyone at all.

'Savannah.' I turn round to see Zach. I smile. He's just *so* beautiful. 'Hey, I was gonna say my Mum's picking a few of us up round the corner.' He looks down and spots my handcuffed arm. 'Ah...but there's only one spare seat. I can see you're...' he raises his eyebrows, 'occupied.'

Wait, does he think I'm with Heath or something?

'No, he just...' I try to explain, pointing towards Mercedes.

'No worries,' he smiles backing away, clearly unimpressed. 'See you around.'

Well fuck. That went well. Not.

'Let's start walking,' Tyler says, looking suspiciously at a group of hoodies on the corner.

How could the night end in such a disaster?

161

#LongWalkHome

We start to walk, although it takes me a while to realise how to achieve this, what with being handcuffed to Heath. My right hand is cuffed to his right hand so we can't walk side by side. In the end, he has to walk with his arm stretched across his body. It serves him right.

'Does anyone have a phone?' I ask the small group of us. I already know that the girls don't, but one of the guys must have. I look from face to face. There are numerous excuses ranging from them leaving it back at the house, to a dead battery, to no credit.

'Well, thank God for me, hey?' Nick, a guy in our year, says holding up his phone.

We all sigh in massive relief. Thank God *one* of us has some sense.

'Thanks.' I reach for the phone.

Heath reaches out to get it too and manages to get to it before me. He pulls his arm back to hand it to me, but it slips. I watch helplessly as he drops it on to the floor, the outside case smashing into pieces.

I fall to my knees, grazing them on the gravel. I scoop up the pieces and still attempt to type a number into the smashed screen, but nothing comes up. Of course it doesn't. I can't believe the one phone we had is now broken, and it's all Heath's fault. I smash the remaining pieces onto the floor in a tantrum and burst into ugly tears.

'I'm so sorry, Sav,' Heath says, seeming to sober up quite a bit.

'How could you be so stupid?' I sob, snot already falling down onto my lip. 'If you'd just have let me take the phone myself we would have been okay. Why fuck it all up?'

'I was trying to be helpful!' he snaps back, jaw clenched. He turns to Nick. 'I'm so sorry, Dude. I'll buy you a new one.'

'We'll be okay,' Erin says reassuringly patting me on the shoulder. 'Look at us, we haven't been murdered yet.' She laughs nervously. Around here I wouldn't speak so soon.

'Yeah, let's just walk home,' Charlotte says cheerily. 'We'll be there before we know it.'

I really can't stand her eternal optimism right now. Kate passes me a tissue from her stuffed bra. I attempt to pull myself together. This isn't the end of the world, Savvy.

I look around for Zahra. Where the hell has she got to? I try to look over people's heads and spot her long red hair swishing against her black top. She's got an arm wrapped round her waist. Oh, my God. I recoil when I see it's Luke. He's got his nasty paws on her again. Obviously wanting round two.

I shiver, not just from the sight of Luke coming onto Zahra again, but also from the cold. It's bloody freezing. I feel completely naked in my little top without a jacket, and stupid mini skirt. Damn Nan making me dress like this. I'll give her a piece of my mind when I see her. If I ever see her again and don't get eaten by coyotes. I can feel my shoes digging into my skin and the soles burning.

'My feet are killing me,' I whine. I really am being a cry baby.

The girls ignore me and carry on walking up ahead. I'm probably annoying them.

That's it. I'm taking my shoes off and walking barefoot. There's no point trying to look good now.

It's hard work dodging all the broken glass that seems to be on the ground. God, it's rough around here.

After a while, I demand that Heath gives me a piggyback. He pulls me over his back, no problem, Mercedes glaring at me the whole time. I'm tempted to stick my tongue out.

After about 20 minutes he's wavering.

'Are you still ok to carry me?' I ask, finding it hard to believe he's tired. I'm not even heavy. Am I? 'You seem knackered.'

'Don't be stupid, I'm fine' he says, trying to be a big strong man. The way he keeps wavering to the right tells me different.

'Yeah, I think you should have a break,' Mercedes says, her hand possessively on his shoulder.

'Yeah, honestly,' I insist, squirming down. 'I can walk the rest of the way'.

I pause while I attempt to put my shoes back on. Ow, ow, ow! The straps go over my already cut feet, and I grimace.

'You don't *look* fine,' he smirks.

I can feel the hatred emanating from Mercedes.

'Just leave me alone will you,' I snap.

I hate when he baby's me. Especially in front of his girlfriend who already looks like she wants to kill me. I know I'm being mean and should just be grateful, but he annoys me so much sometimes. It doesn't help that I'm handcuffed to the idiot.

We turn the corner to Tesco's, and Tyler grabs a loose

trolley. Heath grabs me under the arms and throws me into it. I just glare at him, imagining the sorts of tramps that have used this earlier on today. I'll probably catch Hepatitis B.

Then I realise just how practical it is. All I care is that the pressure is off my burning feet.

The petrol station is still open, so I call the others. Only the guys have money and even when it's all clubbed together we can only afford two packets of mini cheddars. What a bunch of poor bastards we are.

We make our way down the long A road that connects High Pill to Burnham-On-Cliffs. Kevin starts chasing Nick, throwing mini cheddars at him. That's it. Waste the limited food we have. Idiot. Bear Grylls would be furious. Kevin wouldn't last two minutes in the jungle.

'Run, run from the cheddar man,' everyone shouts after him.

It makes me laugh despite myself. For the first time since we started walking, I let it all out. Yes, we're in a shit situation, but if you can't beat them, join them.

There isn't long now until we get back to Heath's house. He told everyone they could crash at his. It was either that or they'd have to sleep in the park. They knew they couldn't stroll into their houses at 2 am in the morning and not get interrogated, especially when most of them had lied saying they were sleeping at a friend's house.

I don't actually have a choice about staying with him—what with me being chained to him. I'm hoping his Mum will have some kind of master key, which can get me out of this.

I doze in the trolley for a little while, the overhead streetlights lulling me. Might as well. It's the longest journey home ever!

It can't have been long, when Heath wakes me, slapping me gently on the face. What a gentleman. Zahra calls my name. I stretch, forgetting I'm chained to him.

'Babe, we're nearly at Heath's road. We're gonna have to abandon the trolley and walk the rest of the way.'

Ugh, walking again. I swear I'm never wearing heels again. Ever. Heath steadies the trolley so I can climb out, and I jump on his shoulders before he has time to ask.

We walk the last few streets to his house, the feeling of relief intense. I can see it on everyone's faces. We just want warmth and sleep. I actually really want a cup of tea and a hundred biscuits.

'I'm bursting for the loo,' Erin complains, doing a

167

strange sort of walking dance. 'I have been for the past half hour. If anyone gets in my way, I swear to God.' She glares at all of us in warning before upping her pace towards the door. She looks like a penguin trying to skip.

Heath gets his keys out. I remember when he was able to put his arm through the letterbox to let us in. His arms have definitely bulked up since then. I look over his lean muscles. The boy's gym sessions are seriously paying off.

Once it's open I fall to my knees in relief, the soft carpet comforting me like a giant pillow. Everyone tramples over me into the sitting room. They turn on the TV quietly, although most people are ready for sleep anyway. Erin pushes past me towards the downstairs loo, knocking me face down into the carpet. Thank God Karen keeps it so clean.

I know my way around, so I grab as many blankets and pillows as I can from around the house, all the time dragging Heath with me, and pass them out to everyone. They all plan on sleeping down here. For the first time tonight I'm glad I'm handcuffed to him. Means I'll have a bed at least. But what are we gonna do about Mercedes?

'Come on then, Miss Limps-a-lot,' Heath says with a wicked grin.

I punch him on the arm. 'I'm never wearing high heels again.'

Mercedes follows us up the stairs. This is so weird.

We bump into his mum on the upstairs landing as she's headed for the toilet.

'Hi, Mum,' Heath whispers. She looks from me to Mercedes. 'Listen, don't panic or anything, but there's about fifteen of my closest friend's downstairs.'

'What?' she rubs her eyes, obviously checking to see if she's still dreaming.

'Jessica's parents came home, and her dad kicked everyone out.' I explain. Luckily, I'd already told my parents about the intended house party as I know with Karen knowing it will definitely get back to Mum.

Her face reddens in fury. 'I can't believe that! The bloody cheek of him!' she explodes.

Why is she so angry? We're the ones in the wrong.

'Anyway, so now there are some people downstairs,' I explain, so tired I can barely keep my eyes open.

She folds her arms over her chest, shaking her head. 'What a silly man. To throw all you girls out in the middle of High Pill! I might even call him tomorrow and give him a piece of my mind!'

'No, please just leave it,' Heath pleads.

She sighs and takes a deep breath. 'Oh, and who is your friend, Savannah?' she asks looking at Mercedes suspiciously.

I smile, happy in the knowledge he hasn't told his mum about her. 'Oh, this is Heath's girlfriend Mercedes.'

'Girlfriend?' she repeats in shock.

I secretly hope she hates her too.

'Yep,' Heath nods, his cheeks growing red.

Mercedes smiles shyly at her.

'Wait, why are you two tied together?'

'Your genius son,' I retort snarkily.

'Well, you two have always been tied at the hip.' She laughs as if this is hilarious. 'I don't mind you two sharing a bed, but not you,' she says to Mercedes. 'I don't want any babies made under my roof.'

'Mum!' Heath shouts, mortified.

Heath looks apologetically at Mercedes before we make our way to his bedroom. I hear her walking down towards the living room and then Karen's loud voice bellowing. 'Right everyone, who wants cheese on toast?'

Heath and I laugh uncontrollably. She's never changed, and I hope she never does.

'She never likes to miss out on anything, does she?' Heath laughs, covering his face with his hands.

I laugh but quickly change it to angry again when I remember our situation. I drag him into the bedroom, not having the patience to try and break the handcuffs off with a screwdriver or a knife. I just need a bed.

Heath doesn't seem to have the energy to argue with me. I lie down on the bed and pull the quilt over us. Heath still has to sleep awkwardly because of the position, but it serves him right.

God, he smells good. Has he always smelt like this? I fall asleep the moment my head hits the pillow, smiling as I think of Mercedes downstairs.

Chapter Nine

Sunday 23rd October

I wake up to find Heath's face squished against me, and his loud snores almost bursting my eardrums. Instead of pushing him away, I find my body drawn to the warmth of his. It's so cold this morning, and Heath always seems to be running hot. He presses against me in his sleep, the warmth of his body forcing back the cold.

I look up at his lips. He really does have the most perfect Cupid's bow in the world. I'd die for lips like that. Shame about the snores coming out of them. I wonder what they'd be like to kiss? Woah, where the hell did that come from? I shrink back, hoping to God no one can read my thoughts. Just thinking them has me almost purple with embarrassment.

Time for him to wake up. Apparently, I'm still drunk and forgot that Heath is the idiot that handcuffed himself to me last night.

A loud snore escapes from his mouth. That's it. I sit up and punch him on the shoulder.

He wakes up with a start.

'What, what?' He looks around panicked as if expecting a burglar.

'You! Snoring your head off. I can't bear it.' It's because of him I'm in this ridiculous situation.

He smiles lazily clearly amused that I find him annoying. He pulls the cover up over his chest, his eyelids still heavy.

'Come back,' he whines, beckoning me with his finger. 'It's freezing without your body heat.'

He wants to cuddle me again? Is he still drunk? Not that I don't want to. Right now all I want to do is snuggle up under this duvet and sleep the day away, but I can't. Not only that, I shouldn't. He has a girlfriend downstairs. We have to start building some boundaries in our friendship, otherwise, it will upset Mercedes and totally fucking confuse me.

'Come on. Let's check on your girlfriend.'

He groans as I stand up and force him to follow. He trails after me, tripping down the stairs.

The sound of laughter coming from the sitting room leads me to the door. I open it to find Ryan, Tyler, and the girls rolling around hysterically laughing. Mercedes meets my eyes, a nasty, smug smile on her lips.

'What's so funny?' I ask, still in a bad mood.

'This,' Ryan says holding up the handcuff keys.

I was, of course, furious, but tried desperately to find it funny. I didn't want them to think I was a total grouch. It also seemed too much energy to be mad, and I was already aching all over.

My feet are in the worst state they've ever been. I have blisters on the balls of both of my feet, the size of half a golf ball, and cuts where the straps have rubbed. I'm worried that I've picked up a disease from walking barefoot on those horrible streets.

My legs ache from all of the walking, and my wrist is red raw and marked from where the handcuffs have rubbed.

However, the worst and possibly most embarrassing part is my bum. Tyler's attack has left me black and blue. It's only just starting to bruise up, but I can tell it's going to be a big one.

I have to go to work, even if it's only for two hours. It's still an absolute bitch. Heath has invited a few of us round his to chill later and watch a DVD, as way of an apology to me. We all agreed that it would be nice to relax after such a traumatic night. I really hope we order a Chinese. I really fancy a sweet and sour chicken. It's the only thing keeping me going with these mutts.

When I get home, I have a bath and apply plasters over the cuts on my feet, wincing as they sting. Why high heels? Why? I dress in just my jeans and a blue jumper, reasoning that trainers will probably hurt my feet the least.

Charlotte offers to take Zahra to the family planning centre, and we let her. I can't be bothered to deal with it, especially when Zahra is acting so pleased with herself. If she had lost it any other way, we would have stayed up all night asking questions, but we weren't even curious. The thought of it repulses us. It's not something any of us desire. We'd rather remain spinsters than harm ourselves that way. That's how I see it, a form of self-harm. I grab my iPad and quickly check my email. There's another blog update from Dylan.

DYLAN'S BLOG - OZ UPDATE

Yeah, I was in a rush when I finished the last note so I forgot a few things. On Wednesday, Adrianna and I took a walk to the lighthouse. Everyone told us it was a 'nice walk'. Unfortunately, none of them mentioned it was a fucking 18km four-hour walk with a shit load of massive steps. Most of the steps were up to Adrianna's knees.

Apart from that, it was cool. We saw a snake, two big fuck off lizards, a wallaby, and some dolphins. We do have pictures of these, but I'm starting to fear that we will never put the pics from this camera up. The next day Adrianna had (somehow) injured her leg just from walking. Like a massive bruise. She does not like me taking the piss.

Last night we just sat around playing drinking games. Man, we have a lot to teach you guys when we get back.

Today we took a walk up the beach, saw some more dolphins and then just sat around in the garden while about thirty rugby players took over and arsed around and got drunk all day.

For me, however, the highlight of the day was being

there when two American surfers met in the kitchen and
had a conversation that genuinely consisted of:

> *'dude'*
>
> *'sweet'*
>
> *'rad'*
>
> *'awesome'*

At least I can always rely on him cheering me up. I ask Mum drop me at Heath's. She's still horrified that Jessica's dad threw all of us out, without even our bags. She's promised to have a word with him when she next sees him. I begged her not to, but I know nothing will stop her. I pity him having to deal with her and Karen tag team attacking.

Without my phone, I feel a bit lost. How did people ever survive without them? What if someone's WhatsApped me? I quickly check Instagram and Snapchat before I leave for a bit of damage control. There are a few awful tags, but nothing too horrific.

When my mum pulls up outside his house, I ask if she can collect me later. I realise that I'll have to use Heath's house phone to do it. I hate not having my independence. Well, my Mum pays my bill, but still...

I limp up to the door trying to balance the pain

between my two feet. Nothing seems to help—they hurt equally.

I ring the doorbell and wave back to Mum for her to leave. She seems to be laughing at me. Does she think this is funny? I scowl at her and turn back to the door. What a cruel Mother I have. I should call Childline.

He takes what seems like forever to answer the door. Hurry up you imbecile!

When he finally does, I throw myself to the hallway floor, glad for the relief.

'Ouch, ouch, ouch.'

'Hi, to you too,' he laughs.

'Thank God for your mum's rule about taking your shoes off. I'm in agony.'

I crawl while kicking off my trainers. Even releasing my feet from the shoes is a mission. I crawl on my hands and knees into the sitting room with Heath watching me amused.

Everyone else is already there curled up, so it looks like I have the floor, but I don't mind. I grab a cushion from the sofa and lay down placing it under my chin. Mercedes isn't here, thank God.

'Come and sit up here, Sav,' Kate says, shuffling up

towards Ryan. He has his arm casually around her. Is it just a comforting thing? I mean we're all tired, maybe everyone just feels cuddly. Or maybe they're into each other.

Either way, I'm not giving up on a sofa place. I crawl over and climb up.

'Aaah,' I moan out loud in ecstasy, the soft plush couch comforting my sore bottom.

'You okay there?' Erin asks, amusement dancing in her eyes.

I nod. 'Yeah, I'm fine, just a bit sore,' I whisper.

Tyler seems to wake up suddenly, his eyes full of recognition.

'Is your bum sore?' he says, seeming proud.

'Yes, you bastard,' I snap. 'Its proper bruised up. I can't believe how much you've damaged me.'

I'm half tempted to report it to the police. Really scare the shit out of him.

Zahra giggles. 'Oh, my God. Really? Can we see?'

'You perv,' Heath laughs, nudging her. 'Go on then, give us all a look.' He rolls his eyes in fake exasperation as if having to stare at my bum would be such a chore.

I raise my eyebrows. 'Ok, the *GIRLS* can come to the

179

toilet with me to have a look.' I wonder how it's looking by now.

The girls are already up, racing up the stairs.

'Hey wait for me, I'm a cripple remember,' I shout, crawling after them. Heath chuckles with the boys.

Charlotte and Kate come back to help me up the upstairs. Why am I always the butt of the joke? Oh God, I am *literally* the butt of the joke.

Once we're in the toilet I yank down my jeans and the big cotton knickers I'm wearing. I didn't even attempt to be sexy today. Look what that did to me.

I crane my neck to see if I've got it out enough for them to see when I hear a collective gasp.

'Oh, my God,' Zahra shrieks with a giggle. 'You've got a handprint on your ass.'

'Don't laugh,' Kate reprimands her, eyeing me sympathetically. 'It looks really sore.'

'It is,' I whine, taking any sympathy I can get. 'I don't know how I'm gonna walk around school tomorrow with injuries like this'.

'Bunk then?' Zahra suggests with a shrug as if it's no big deal.

'I can't. They take that all into consideration when we

apply for university.'

She rolls her eyes, but I know she hasn't even decided if she wants to go yet.

We walk back downstairs to the guys.

'So is it bruised?' Tyler asks, smiling proudly.

'She's literally got a hand print on her arse,' Erin laughs, so loudly she's almost spitting.

Tyler chuckles. 'What can I say? I'm *very* strong.'

'*Anyway,* changing the subject,' Ryan interrupts. I shoot him a warm smile, pleased with the interruption. 'Thank your Mum for last night. Did you know she made us all cheese on toast?'

'No, but I could have guessed as much,' Heath says, rolling his eyes, giving me a knowing smile.

'Yeah, good old Karen,' Zahra says with a smile. 'She was telling us some of her old stories again. There is seriously nothing that you could ever do that would shock that woman.' It's like she's in awe of her.

Thank God his family is just as embarrassing as mine.

'Yeah, she's cool,' Tyler agrees. 'Plus she's a total MILF.'

'Tyler!' we all shriek throwing pillows at him.

'So...' Heath says, clasping his hands together. 'What

did you guys think of Mercedes?'

'Loved her,' Tyler says. 'She has the best tits. I'm almost jealous.'

Heath laughs and looks round at us girls.

'She seemed sweet,' Charlotte says. 'But I didn't really get much time to talk to her.'

'What about you, Sav?'

Everyone turns to look at me, awaiting my reaction.

'She's...nice.'

Heath stares intently at me. Everyone watches on, obviously wondering if he's going to buy it.

'Okay,' he shrugs, turning back to look at the TV.

People start to get back to the film, a comfortable silence settling over us. It's only about 2 pm, but last night's events are showing on everyone.

I have to change plasters on my feet as they've started to ooze through my socks. It really makes me sick, but I just have to suck it up and peel my socks off and clean them up. I try to do it as discreetly as I can, but still get a few grossed out looks. Only me.

I try to watch the film. It's a teen action romance that easily pleases everyone, but my mind starts to wonder. I'm starting to worry about Jessica. Where is she? Still at her cousin's? And will she be in school tomorrow?

Plus, she still has all of my stuff, I think selfishly. I've had to borrow my mum's makeup this morning, and I feel lost without my mobile.

'You thinking about Jessica?' Heath asks, interrupting my thoughts.

'Sssssh!' people hiss.

'You reading my mind now?' I whisper back. 'Yeah, I'm just worried about her.'

He shrugs. 'Don't worry about it. I'm sure her cousin will look after her and it will all work out.'

'I love your eternal optimism,' I tease.

I turn towards Zahra, who still seems completely un-bothered that she lost her virginity last night on a cliff. Has she got the morning after pill yet? 'Don't you and Charlotte have that thing you have to do?'

'What thing?' Charlotte asks, clearly clueless. Bless her—she can be so dumb sometimes.

'You know.' I raise my eyebrows at her. 'Weren't you two going to Boots to collect your *prescriptions.'*

'*Ohhh,*' she nods, finally catching on. 'Yeah, we should go now,' she says to Zahra.

Zahra looks like she might sink into the sofa from

humiliation. I'm glad she's at least showing *some* remorse.

'Okay,' she sighs, begrudgingly getting up.

I roll my eyes. Don't go thanking me or anything. I'm only trying to ensure you don't have Luke's bastard child growing in your stomach. Some girls can be *so* ungrateful.

CHAPTER TEN

Monday 24th October

#EmergencyInterception

I bump into Charlotte on the way into school the next day.

'Hey hun,' I beam, even though my feet and arse are still killing me. She smiles back. 'Get everything sorted yesterday?'

A normal person wouldn't notice it, but I've known Charlotte too long. I see how her eyes bulge in the slightest way before she quickly recovers.

'Err, yeah. All sorted.' She forces a smile, avoiding my eye line. It looks more like a grimace. She's always been a shit liar. Which can only mean one thing—they didn't get the morning after pill.

'You have to be fucking kidding me!' I shout, so loud a few people turn around and look at me weird. I lower my voice to a whisper. 'What the fuck happened?'

She fiddles with her school bag. 'Ugh, my mum made us babysit the brats when we got to mine and then by the time she got back it was closed.'

I can't believe these girls.

'Did you at least *attempt* to find a twenty-four hour one?'

Her eyes hit the floor. 'It's just...well, we were really tired so...we ended up falling asleep.'

Asleep? Their excuse for not getting it is they were tired? Fucking *tired?*

'Well, I hope she got a good night's rest, because if she's pregnant that will be the last one for a long time!'

'Calm down, will you!' she whisper-hisses, looking around us to make sure no one heard. 'Don't go mad at Zahra for this. It was my fault.'

'What was your fault?' Zahra grins appearing from nowhere. Her smile drops when she looks from Charlotte's face to mine. 'Oh God, you told her?' she whines, stamping her foot.

'Yes, she fucking told me, and I'm glad she did.' I glare at her. 'Now I can take you myself.'

She rolls her eyes as if I'm being dramatic. 'Don't you have that maths test?'

Oh yeah, I do. Not that I remembered to revise for it.

'I have no fucking choice but to bunk. This is far more important or in a couple of weeks you'll be taking a far more important test.'

We bump into Jessica on the way through the gates. She hands over our bags with our phones, rushing off to class before we can interrogate her.

We Google the nearest family planning clinic, and it turns out there's one just round the corner from school. Handy, seeing as this school is full of sluts.

When we get there, I'm shocked to see it's just a normal looking building. Yeah, the sign does say *Family Planning Clinic* but if you didn't know it was here it wouldn't stand out. There isn't a queue of skanks rolling out of the door alerting you to their bad decisions.

'I don't think I even need it anyway,' Zahra shrugs, hopping from foot to foot. 'No one gets pregnant the first time they have sex.'

I roll my eyes. 'That's *so* something a girl says before

falling pregnant. Don't be that dumb girl.'

She sighs, rolls her eyes and storms in ahead of me. By the time I catch up with her, she's already whispering to a receptionist what she's there for. She's trying to brass it out, but I can see the delicate hint of a blush on her olive skin.

'If you just take a seat, someone will call your name soon.'

'Thanks,' I smile, appreciating that she doesn't seem judgmental.

I link arms with her and lead her towards the seating area. The room's decorated in a God awful peach colour with a green runner making it even uglier. I can't imagine a year this was *ever* fashionable.

We're just sitting down on the matching peach-coloured chairs when I spot Rachel Bloomsbury from the year above. Shit! Zahra's already flicking through a magazine, and I dig her in the ribs to get her attention.

'Owww! What was that for?' she asks loudly, causing the whole room to turn and stare at us.

I glare at her. *Way to cause a scene, Zahra.* It's not like I can tell her Rachel's over there now, can I?

An older woman comes out of a room with a clipboard.

'Rachel Bloomsbury?'

This is enough to get Zahra's attention. Finally. She looks up at the same time as me. Poor Rachel looks mortified. She walks past us with her head bowed, trying to hide behind her hair. I politely smile.

Another woman with a clipboard comes out. 'Zahra Taylor?'

Zahra gasps next to me. That was bloody quick. I hope Zahra's about to move, but she looks frozen in shock.

'That's us.' I wave, dragging Zahra to her feet.

The woman forces a smile, but it's obvious what she's thinking. Another young girl, having reckless sex. She really shouldn't work here if she's going to insist on being a judgemental bitch. It seems only the receptionist is non-judgy.

She sits down on her fancy swivel chair and asks us what the problem is without even looking up from her clipboard.

'Err...I need the morning after pill,' Zahra blurts out, twirling her hair manically.

'Please,' I add. My mum always said manners cost nothing.

She ticks something off her clipboard. 'Okay. And

when did you last have unprotected sex?'

Zahra has the grace to look embarrassed, her cheeks turning pink. 'Um...it was Saturday night.'

'Saturday night?' she repeats in horror, finally looking up.

Why is she so horrified about Saturday night? Do people not have sex on Saturday nights? Surely it's the most popular night?

'Err...yeah,' Zahra nods, chancing a glance at me. 'What's the big deal?'

She sighs heavily—like she's so sick of her job. 'The morning after pill is much more effective if taken within twenty-four hours of unprotected intercourse.'

'Can you please not call it unprotected intercourse?' Zahra says with a grimace. 'It makes it sound gross.'

'Anyway,' she interrupts, ignoring her. 'If taken within twelve hours it has a 95% effective rate. Within twenty-four hours it's 85% effective. Now it will only be 75% effective.'

'Shit,' I mutter out loud. 'Are you saying she could still get pregnant from this?'

I never actually imagined it would get that far.

'It's still possible,' she nods. 'But don't worry. If that

does happen there are options available to you.'

She means abortion. I shudder just thinking about Zahra having to go through that. I might think she's a stupid bitch, but no one deserves that.

'I won't get pregnant,' Zahra declares, almost to herself. At least she's remaining positive.

'Now we also need to do an STD check.'

'What?' she shrieks. 'I don't need that. I'm fine.' She wraps her arms around herself as if creating a protective barrier.

'Really?' she asks, raising her eyebrows in amusement. 'Was the boy you slept with a virgin?'

I burst out laughing. Luke? Biggest man-whore in school.

'Sorry.' I use my hand to muffle my laughter.

'No, but I'm sure he's fine,' Zahra insists.

'I'm afraid I'd have to insist,' she says sternly. 'It's for your own safety.'

God, I didn't even consider any of this. By the look of Zahra's face, I'd say she didn't either.

The woman turns around, pulling plastic gloves on. 'If you could please lie down on the bed. I'll make this as quick and painless as possible.'

I suddenly feel lightheaded. Do not pass out on your friend. Not when she needs you.

'So, there will be *some* pain?' Zahra asks with an audible gulp.

'More discomfort.'

I smile encouragingly to Zahra. 'You can do this. It's for the best.'

'Okay,' she nods, her brows furrowed. 'But stay with me.'

Ewww. I don't want to see her vagina, but I guess that disappearing wouldn't be the supportive thing to do right now. So instead I follow her onto the bed and look away when she lowers her red and navy spotty knickers.

The woman comes towards her with what looks like a glass dildo.

'What the hell is that?' I shout in horror.

'What?' Zahra yells, opening her eyes and lifting her head to see.

'Please don't worry girls. This is a speculum. I'm going to place it into your vagina so that I can take some swabs. Don't worry though, I've covered it in lube.'

Don't worry. Is she *insane?* I haven't stopped worrying since this morning.

'Slight bit of discomfort,' she says as she lowers the speculum to beneath the blanket.

Zahra grabs my hand and squeezes it so hard it's painful.

'Aaagh!' she cries, scrunching her eyes together and turning her head into our hands.

Oh, my god, this is awful.

'What are you doing to her? Can't you be a bit gentler?' I ask the woman. If I could take the pain as my own, I would.

'All done,' she smiles, removing it quickly. I suppose she must do this several times a day. 'I can't see any evidence of herpes.'

Ewww.

'Great,' Zahra snarls sarcastically, sitting up and pulling her knickers back into place.

'Now, I just need you to give me a urine sample and some blood.'

My poor, Zahra. What the hell have I forced her to go through?

Twenty minutes later we're walking out.

'At least this way it's all over and done with,' I say, trying to find a positive from this.

'I suppose.' She shrugs like a petulant child.

Sat leaning on her car is Rachel Bloomsbury. Has she been waiting for us? Is she going to beat us up?

'Hey, Savannah! Zahra!' she calls—all friendly smiles.

Shit, what is she going to say to us? Zahra looks at me questioningly.

'You guys want a lift back to school?'

'Err...yeah, thanks,' Zahra answers, smiling awkwardly.

We get into the car, both of us choosing to sit in the back. She turns round to face us.

'Look, I know this is majorly awkward, but I'm assuming we're not going to tell anyone that we saw each other here today, right?'

'Of course not!' Zahra shouts. 'You honestly think I want anyone to know about the lowest day of my life?'

'Thank God,' she smiles, clearly relieved. 'It's just...well, I'm mortified.'

'Snap,' Zahra snorts. 'Can we just get out of here?'

She smiles brightly. God, she's beautiful. I wonder who she slept with. She starts the engine, but it makes a weird kind of strangled noise.

'Oh crap. Not again.' She sighs, hitting her head against the steering wheel.

'What's up?' I ask, raising my eyebrows to Zahra.

'It's this stupid car. It does this sometimes. It needs someone to push it while I keep starting the engine.'

'We'll help,' I find myself offering.

Zahra glares at me like I've lost my mind.

We get out of the car and stand behind it, placing our hands on the top of the car, ready to push.

'It's only small. It should be fairly easy,' I say to Zahra reassuringly.

'You guys ready?' Rachel calls out the window.

'Yep, go!' I call back cheerily.

She starts trying to turn the engine but before we even have a chance to get some power behind us and push the car forward it starts rolling back. Onto us! What the fuck is happening here?

'Push!' I shout frantically to Zahra.

The car's rolling closer to us now. And we're against a fence. Shit. We're going to be crushed! Crushed to death by a car in a family planning clinic! And everyone will know we were here. God, the shame. They'll probably slut shame me at my funeral, even though it wasn't even me!

Zahra looks back at me, pale as a ghost.

'STOP!' I shout. 'STOOOOOPP!!' I scream at the top of her lungs.

'What?' she shouts back. 'What?'

'STOOOOOOOPPPP!!!!' I scream scrunching my eyes shut. I cover my face, accepting my awful fate.

Except...nothing happens. I open one eye to see that the car has stopped and Zahra is panting hard, her face as white as a ghost.

Rachel jumps out of the car. 'I'm so sorry girls! I didn't realise it had an incline, and I took the handbrake off. My bad.'

Understatement of the fucking year.

Chapter Eleven

I've just about recovered from my near death experience by later that night. Honest to God, only I could get myself in this shit. But the main thing is that I can now sleep at night knowing Zahra's not pregnant.

I'm just settled into bed with a book when I hear my phone beep. I nearly jump for joy when I realise it's Zach.

'Hey, you going to Jake's party on Sat? x'

He put a kiss. Don't panic. Think of something cool and witty to say.

'Maybe, just got to see if I can find an outfit. U?x'

I wait, tapping my fingers nervously on the screen.

'Same. Well maybe I'll c u there then, hope so x'

Hope so? Wow. Is he leading me on deliberately? Does he enjoy making my heart stop? Should I reply? What should I say?

'Well, maybe I'll be persuaded then x'

Perfect. I sound cool and mysterious. Not at all like the hysterical bumbling idiot I truly am. This is just what I need—to concentrate on my obsession with Zach and forget about Kate's comment about me and Heath. There is no me and Heath.

Saturday 29th October
#ItsHalloweenWitches

The whole rest of the week has been filled with daydreaming about the party, enjoying the fantasies where he'll sweep me off my feet and kiss me to within an inch of my life. And the reality that it's probably just all a wind-up. 'Get the minger to believe you're interested' or something.

I leave work on Saturday, exhausted. With it being Halloween weekend, all of the dog owner's took up Katie's offer of them being 'Halloweenified.' Yeah, like that's even a word.

It basically meant I had to make sure the dogs were

ready with a big skull handkerchief on and ghost antlers when they were being collected. Yeah, that's a lot easier *said* than actually done. Shocker; dogs don't actually like wearing stupid outfits so I have some scratches on my arms that I'm hoping I can pass off as part of my Halloween outfit for tonight's party.

I run a bath and check my emails. Another blog entry is waiting for me.

DYLAN'S BLOG - AUS Update

Sunday we went to the local market here. It was so cool. They have live music everywhere. It was more like a festival with some shops. Mainly there were two guys who played drum and bass with a didgeridoo. The stalls were all filled with crazy crap, none of which you could haggle for. In the end Adrianna ground me down, and she got a nice dress. I was thrilled (insert sarcasm where applicable).

Monday we spent the whole day on the beach. We found out there is a massive 'brown snake' living in the path between our hostel and the beach. We saw it. It was cool though. As soon as it saw us coming, it slithered away. Hooray for being higher in the food chain.

Last night we went to Cheeky Monkeys again. We won LOADS of free stuff in the games. It turns out me and Adrianna are equally competitive. We won: four jugs of beer, a $300 trip to Frasier Island, a 2-night hostel stay in Rainbow Beach and a kayaking safari with dolphins which I am going on in an hour. Fair enough Adrianna did need to take off her bra twice for us to win these, but the less said about that, the better.

So the next update will tell you all about the kayaking hopefully. Speak soon xxx

When we arrive at Jake's Halloween party, we're greeted by Tyler and Ryan, who are outside the front, smoking.

'Hey, biatches,' Tyler shouts over. His eyes roam up and down our bodies. 'Looking hot tonight. You do scrub up well.'

I notice Ryan linger his glance on Kate, who has come dressed as a policewoman, her red curls spilling out of the hat. I'm sure that he fancies her. Why does she seem so oblivious to it?

'Hey, Zahra, take off that scary mask. It's terrifying,' he adds, blowing smoke towards her as we walk towards them.

Zahra smiles and sticks her tongue out at him, confident that she looks stunning dressed as a Cat woman in an all-in-one PVC catsuit. I have no idea how she got it on or how she intends to use the toilet. Especially with the stick on nails she applied earlier.

I walk into the house before they can start on me, too freezing cold to be polite. Kate hangs back to chat to them. I smile to myself. Maybe she's not as oblivious as I thought. I hope that her and Ryan get it on.

The minute I get into the hallway I'm dumping my leather jacket in the pile and scanning the room for him.

'You want a drink?' Zahra asks, holding up the bottle of vodka she brought.

'Yeah, whatever,' I nod, not listening properly. I'm too pre-occupied with having an anxiety attack.

'Love your pompoms, Sav,' Tyler says, suddenly at my side with a cheeky grin. He follows it with a pinch on my arse.

After much deliberation, I chose a cheerleading outfit. I think it's the right mix of innocent and sexy.

I smile absentmindedly while craning my neck to look around.

'Scary contacts though. You really went for shit scary, didn't you?'

Wait, he thinks I look terrifying? Well, that's not the look I was going for. I mean yes, I decided to wear the white coloured contact lenses Nan bought me that make me look like a zombie, but I thought they looked cool. And okay, the girls said I should have stopped with just the fake bloody coming out of my mouth and not go with it also tumbling from my eyes. But what can I say? I love Halloween!

'Who are you looking for? he asks, clearly annoyed by me ignoring him. He's always been an attention whore.

'No one,' I snap quickly, desperate for my cheeks not to be on fire.

The girls roll their eyes, already sick of me going on about Zach.

'Well, if you're looking for Heath he's apparently on his way. He's coming dressed in his scream outfit,' Ryan says as he stares across at Kate.

I roll my eyes. He knows how that outfit freaks me out. He once jumped out of my wardrobe wearing it. I don't think I've ever really forgiven him.

'Yeah, I know, I told him you'd hate it,' he laughs.

'Actually,' I say, scanning my eyes up and down Tyler

and Ryan, 'what the hell are you supposed to be?'

They have their normal clothes on.

'Duh, we're male models.'

We all start pissing ourselves on cue. They're such dicks—bless them.

'Oh, duh, of course.' I giggle, rolling my eyes. 'How didn't we guess?'

I grab my drink from Zahra, 'I'm going to scan the party looking for...people'. I realise I nearly said his name. The guys would rib me forever if they knew I had a crush.

'Have fun,' Kate laughs, standing very close to Ryan. 'Be a good girl, or I'll have to hit you with my truncheon.'

I walk away quick enough to avoid Tyler start some bad truncheon innuendos

I'm so nervous at the prospect of seeing Zach tonight that I've decided on sneakers instead of heels. I'm glad that I can walk around feeling confident, instead of afraid of an almighty fall. Anyway, I like the sneakers. It gives the whole look a kind of preppy vibe. Like I said, not too in your face sexy.

I walk into the sitting room, and nod hello's to the people I recognise. Amelia, from my year, looks me up and down and has a little laugh to herself, flicking her long blonde locks behind her. She's also come as a cheerleader, but a far sexier version.

She has her double D's squeezed into a tiny crop top and towers over me in her skyscraper, clear-plastic hooker heels. Maybe I should have worn the heels. I look down at my small chest and pray that one day I will wake up to find a growth spurt has occurred.

She smiles sweetly, but I can see her mind working, laughing at how childish I look next to her. Way to ruin my self-confidence.

I fiddle nervously with my hair, twirling it into a thousand circles.

Heath comes in wearing his scream outfit, seemingly on his own. He walks straight over to me waving.

'Hey, you okay?' I ask still scanning the room.

No answer. Why's he playing around? He knows I hate being ignored.

'So you're doing the silence treatment on me now? What's that all about? Where's Mercedes tonight then? I ask bitchily.

He just shrugs. So annoying.

'I can't believe you wore that outfit tonight. You know how it always freaks me out. Well, look I really don't have time to chat anyway. I'm looking for someone.'

He pulls his head to the side like a confused puppy.

I sigh loudly. He's so infuriating.

'It's none of your business. Just try and enjoy the party,' I snap rudely, not having the patience for this.

He nods, but instead of leaving me alone pulls me towards the small dance floor that has formed near the dining room table. He starts dancing with me and at first I resist, annoyed that he's pulling me out of my Zach fantasy. But after a minute or two, I decide to give in. Maybe Zach won't even turn up, I mean, he didn't promise anything. It's not like he asked for my hand in marriage.

Heath's a good dancer tonight, much better than normal. I wonder whether Mercedes has been teaching him. What a whore.

He starts pulling my waist into his when the song goes a bit slower, and it suddenly occurs to me how much I've missed mucking about with my friend. Since Mercedes has been on the scene, I hardly ever see him and when I do I always overhear about all the amazing hot sex, which freaks me out and reminds me what a loser virgin I am.

Someone taps me on the shoulder. I turn round to see Erin and Kate, with another guy dressed in a scream outfit.

'Hey, who's your mate?' I ask. *Two* losers decided on this outfit?

'It's me, you doughnut,' Heath says lifting his mask to expose his face.

The blood drains from my face.

'Then who is this?' I ask turning, alarmed towards the guy with his hands still on my hips. Ugh. Who have I let touch me?

He reaches up and pulls his mask up over his head revealing beautiful eyes.

My mouth drops open. The girls giggle to each other and wander off quickly, leaving us alone. I can't stop looking at his face. The person I've been dancing with is Zach. I quickly try to think back, over what I've said and cringe as I think what a bitch I must have sounded like.

'Sorry I tricked you,' he says laughing huskily. God, he's so sexy. I feel myself literally swoon and start to feel a bit light headed.

Before I can even think about what I'm doing, I lean into him, closing the small distance, bringing my lips close to his. Can you imagine! Lean in, like some kind of nutcase. I don't purse my lips, but it must look pretty obvious that I'm leaning in hoping to get a kiss. I'm so close to his lips that I can feel his breath and notice the sound of my own heartbeat, racing like it's never done before.

I know I'm acting insane, but I don't care. I've waited too long for him, and it's clearly driven me to insanity. For a second I think he's going to lean in too, but then he turns his head to avoid me, and I almost fall over on my face from the shock. Maybe I am leaning in a bit more than I thought. The humiliation starts to take over my body like poison ivy spreading. What a bloody idiot.

He moves his whole body awkwardly away from me as if to say *'anyway'*. My stomach drops. I feel sick like I might actually vomit all over him. That would really charm him. My cheeks feel hot, and I start to worry that I'm going bright red. Dear God—don't go bright red. Just try to look casual, like you were doing something else.

I laugh nervously which comes out more like a squeal.

'I was just, um, (GIANT PAUSE WHILE I DESPERATELY TRY TO THINK OF SOMETHING), trying to...tell you something'. Well done, Savannah, you fucking idiot.

'Oh right,' he says, with a cheeky smile.

Is he laughing at me? I get the feeling he is. But at least he isn't openly taking the piss out of me. It could be worse, but then I realise it is. I'd totally forgotten about the rest of the party.

I look around, scanning the room, trying to see if everyone has seen. To my surprise, people aren't pointing and laughing in slow motion. Thank God. They seem to be just chatting normally, clearly not interested in such a boring, ordinary girl like me.

They can't have seen. If they had, they wouldn't be able to act normally. The nice girls would be giving pitying looks meaning *'poor cow'* and the mean girls would be laughing and whispering, but loud enough for me to hear. Saying things like *'poor cow actually thought she could pull him. Talk about out of your league. She's more suited to Eugene, that ugly guy in the year below'*.

Calm down, Savannah. This is not actually happening.

'Come here. I want to talk to you,' he says casually smiling.

God, his smile is to die for. Every time he looks at me it's as if his eyes are looking into my soul and my soul is telling him that I fancy the pants off him, making me blush and cringe at the same time.

God, why do I need to fancy anyone? It's really not

worth the stress it brings. Maybe I should just be an old spinster who never loses her virginity, but never has to deal with this whole embarrassing situation. It seems a fair trade. I might even be happier. But I hate cats.

'Okay,' I slur, drunk from his beauty. I follow him, mentally berating myself for what an idiot I am.

He goes towards the hallway and slowly changes his body language. I notice him put his hand on my lower back, seeming to guide me. His touch makes my skin tingle. I let him guide me, thinking that he must just be being kind before he tells me he's not interested.

He suddenly takes my hand and starts holding it. Wow, what is going on here? His hand seems so big compared to mine. It's a loose grip. Not interlinking fingers, but just sort of cupping my palm. His hands are warm and welcoming, and I start to get excited, clinging on to the tiny unrealistic hope that he likes me. Maybe he just likes giving me mixed messages. I might amuse him like a little puppy. He might be a sadistic arsehole for all I know.

He leads me into a room off the hallway and then abruptly stops, pushing himself closer against me. My breathing becomes erratic. His face is right next to mine, my neck straining a little to look up at him. My breath starts to get deeper. I hope my breath doesn't smell. My god, why did I have to eat those Doritos!

He does his cheeky little smile again, and I melt. He seems so confident, a complete contrast to my current mental state. He puts his hands on my hips and pulls me even closer. He looks down at me, his face suddenly serious before leaning in slowly, as if to kiss me.

I wonder whether I should lean in too, but I don't want to set myself up for that embarrassment again. Before I can react, he's gone all the way and locked his lips with mine.

I freeze. His warm lips are on mine, and his hands are on my face, cupping it, pulling me closer. My entire body goes floppy. Thank god he's holding my face otherwise I think I'd have just fallen to the floor in a heap.

He opens his lips, and I allow access as he slips his tongue into my mouth, caressing my tongue with his.

This is so different to the kisses I've had in the past— no mouth raping with an over-eager tongue. Just perfect.

He puts his arm around my back, wrapping me in, while the other hand puts some of my hair behind my ear. My god, I *love* him touching my hair. It seems so sweet and sexy at the same time. He pulls his lips away, and I seem to go with them, not wanting it to stop.

WOW.

I feel drained like I've just run a marathon. I realise I've been holding my breath the entire time and remind myself to breathe. But then the doubts start to creep in. Why didn't he kiss me before in the living room? Why did he embarrass me? I should just be grateful he kissed me at all. I mean look at him; he's a sex god.

'How come you backed away out there then?' I ask before I can stop myself.

What an *idiot*. Note to self: learn to stop verbal diarrhoea.

'I thought you just wanted to tell me something?' He grins, dropping his head back laughing.

Shit, he's onto me.

'Oh, so you knew the whole time. How embarrassing'.

I cross my arms annoyed and start to die slowly inside. I need to buy some Dorothy heels. *There's no place like home. There's no place like home.*

He looks me dead in the eye. I feel his power take over me.

'I knew you wanted to kiss me, but I'm not going to do it in there in front of everyone. I like some privacy. I'm not into PDA.' He puts another strand of my hair behind my ear.

PDA? What is PDA? Oh, that's right, public display of affection. Laugh quickly like you get it.

'Ok, I wasn't bothered anyway' I lie while forcing out a confident smile.

'Yeah you were, you liar,' he says as breezy as anything. 'Plus my ex is in there.'

His ex?

'Anyway, I'll call you, okay.'

'Okay,' I mutter still in his trance.

He backs out of the room, still holding my hand. I stay still and eventually my hand drops from his as he turns and walks away.

Okay, I must stay here until I compose myself. I wonder if this party will still be going on in a year. Breathe. Breathe. Regain ability in your legs. One foot in front of the other. That's it. Walk—walk into the sitting room.

But wait, what if he's gone back in there? He didn't say he was going home. It would be really awkward if I went in and he was there with his mates.

What if he's already told them like it's a joke? I mean, maybe it *was* a joke. Maybe it was all a bet or something. But then, do you really kiss someone and stick your tongue in their mouth if you're not into them? You have to be really fucked up to do that. But I don't know him. Maybe he is a sick bastard that picks on vulnerable girls.

Okay, calm down. Your friends are in there. Just head straight for them and try and act normal. To be honest, I just feel like going home, getting into bed and repeating the whole incident in my head, over and over again until I fall asleep. Yes, I should make an excuse and go home. I'm already dialling a taxi.

CHAPTER TWELVE

Monday 31st October

I worked early Sunday and then crashed when I got back from work so haven't had a chance to catch the girls up on the gossip. There's something about blow-drying a dog's hair for hours on end that just knackers your hand. The thought of even texting them was too much. And it's not like Zach has even contacted me. Am I a bad kisser?

I spend the whole of Monday hearing about the rest of the party. The girls were pretty annoyed that I'd ditched them last minute, but they got over it when I'd told them about the kiss. I was pretty graphic in my descriptions, and they were very grateful. The party apparently went on until the early hours, and I missed Erin going mental at Kevin.

'I still feel terrible,' she says. 'I mean; I *really* went mad at him.'

'I wouldn't feel bad, that guy's a waste of space,' I say feeling mean, but not caring.

How could I have missed this? Kevin annoys me more than anything, and when someone truly tells him what they think of him I'm not there! It's so unfair.

'It was pretty full on,' Zahra says with a grimace. 'I mean, you called him a retard.'

'Oh, God,' Erin says, hiding her face in her hands. 'I mean, I know I can't stand the guy, but no one deserves what I did to him. I don't even remember what I said. It's all a bit of a blur really. Just slow motion finger pointing and hatred filled words. God, I can see the look on his face now.'

'I really wouldn't worry that much,' Kate says, putting her arm around her and grimacing behind her back.

The bell rings interrupting us. Charlotte and I walk to English together.

I can't help but keep wondering if Zach will call me at all. This is the second day. I know that there's supposed to be a three-day rule and all that, but this is torture.

'Can I tell you something?' Charlotte asks,

interrupting my thoughts.

I look up and catch her lashes fluttering nervously.

'Yeah, course, what's wrong?'

She grabs a strand of her hair and starts twirling it nervously around her finger.

'Nothing's wrong, but...well...something happened to Zahra.'

'God, what now?' I say with a heavy sigh. I don't mean to sound like such a bitch, but can we ever get through one event without her causing some kind of drama?

She turns to face me, narrowing her eyes. I know she's berating me for being mean.

'Sorry,' I say trying to appear reasonable. 'Go on, what happened?'

She's twirling her hair again. Jesus, how bad can it be? She's already shagged Luke on a cliff.

'Well, nothing really *happened*. It's just that later on at the party we were outside in the garden having a fag when Luke and Robbie walked out into the garden chatting to two guys in the year above. They didn't see us and we overheard them talking about Zahra.'

'And? What did they say?' I implore, growing impatient.

'Luke said that he'd slept with her and when the other guy asked how it was he just laughed and said *'like doing an ironing board, mate'*. It was awful.'

Oh my god. Poor Zahra.

'We'd all heard but didn't know how to react. Kate asked her if she was okay and Erin just acted like she hadn't heard. Heath, Ryan, and Tyler looked totally embarrassed for her, and just kind of walked off.'

'Oh, my God.' I try to digest the information. She must have been so humiliated. 'What did she do?'

'She just said 'whatever' and left, but we could tell she wanted to die from embarrassment. We tried to leave with her, but she shouted at us to leave her alone. After walking down the whole street with her pushing us off her, we let her go.'

'You *let* her walk home alone?' I can't hide the horror from my voice.

She pouts. 'Yeah, but you didn't see her. She was furious and taking it out on us. She wouldn't let us hold her back. We physically tried, but she was so strong. I don't even know now how she got home.'

She's lucky she's alive and didn't get gang raped.

'Has she said anything to you today about it?'

'No. She's just acting as if nothing's happened. You know how stubborn she can be.'

Poor Zahra. 'God, it's awful. I mean imagine it. If that happened to me, I think I might have actually hung myself. Is anyone talking about it?'

'Well, that's kind of why I told you,' she admits. 'I keep hearing people whispering about it. Most people are saying how awful it is, but people are still talking. I had to tell you before you overheard it.'

Jesus, it just gets worse. I'm so pissed off because she's brought this all on herself.

'I mean; I don't know why I'm so shocked. This is what happens when you lose it to the biggest player in school. I still don't get how she didn't realise something like this could happen.'

'Please don't have a go at her,' she pleads, looking weary over the whole thing.

She's such a worrier. But she knows me too well.

'Of course I won't. It just sucks that she's putting herself through this, but it's done now. There's nothing she can do now'.

That right there is why I will never lose my virginity until I'm sure the guy isn't an arsehole who intends to tell the whole school. If only he'd bloody call.

#FuckMyLife

I walk into the gym hall later that day feeling like I normally feel, sick. God, I hate PE. Our school is the only one in the area that forces sixth formers still to participate. Something about an obesity epidemic or something. I say they just leave us alone, let us be obese if we choose, but oh, that's right—they want to ruin our lives.

Anyway, think positive. I wonder what sport we are doing today, the usual dark feeling of dread filling my stomach.

'Oh my god, it's trampolining!' Angela the Canadian shouts in enthusiasm.

Well, she would be excited about it; she's Canadian. Anything gets those crazy fuckers going.

Zahra looks at me with a face that after all these years I know, says 'god I just want to bunk and have a fag.' And now I feel awful. I'm the one that persuaded her to come today. We've been missing too much PE lately, and they'd sent a letter home.

Dear Mrs Franks,

We are sorry to hear that Savannah has such frequent periods meaning that she is stuck in the toilet for two hours. We are also shocked about her plain bad luck – falling down the stairs, being locked in the geography room and simply forgetting where the gym was located. If there are any issues, please do not hesitate to contact me.

Yours sincerely,

The Bitch, Butch PE teacher.

Well, something along those lines anyway. Worryingly, my Mum had actually felt the need to ask me if any of this were true, as with my luck anything was possible. She'd just laughed when she knew the truth and made me promise we'd at least go to an occasional class. Zahra had managed to intercept her letter before her Mum got to it.

Part of the reason for me insisting we attend today was so that I could try and talk to her about the whole party/embarrassment thing.

'If you could please all come around the trampoline,' the teacher instructs. 'Those of you not on the trampoline, you'll be spotting. So if someone goes flying you will have to save them.'

Yeah, right. I'm sure this group of girls are going to save me if I come hurtling towards them. I look through the crowd at their flimsy arms. I'd be safer swimming with sharks.

'Savannah, Zahra, so nice to see you both,' she says sarcastically. 'Savannah, you can be first.'

Oh, crap. How can I chat to Zahra when they expect me to bounce around like a dickhead?

I try to jump up onto it, lifting myself with my arms but fail miserably. I try a few more times, huffing and puffing, determined to get up there, but my arms just aren't strong enough. This is pathetic.

Zahra finally takes pity on me after a few minutes and grabs my legs and bum, shoving me up on it. Thank God it's a girl-only class. I'm thankful I have an ally in this class. I turn round to thank her, but she's smirking, clearly amused. I scowl at her, letting her know she's in trouble.

'Right, you need to bounce up and down and get a good height going' says PE Butch.

Bounce, bounce, bounce. Luckily my feet have healed fast so I'm no longer in agony just to walk, but it still hurts slightly jumping up and down on them. Crap, I'm really high. I can see everyone's faces looking at me, coming into view, then smaller. God, this is turning my stomach and my legs are starting to feel like they don't belong to me, the nerves clearly getting the better of me.

'No, not like that, higher!' The teacher shouts.

'I'm trying!' I shout back, out of breath, my legs now like jelly.

God, please make this end. Please just let the gym collapse and kill us all. I knew she'd pick on me for missing so many lessons.

'Right, it looks like I'm going to have to help you,' she says, walking over to the trampoline.

Unlike me, she pulls herself up on it in two seconds flat. She would with those muscly arms. What does she think she's doing? She's on the trampoline, standing next to me. I stare at her with my mouth gawping open. What is she going to do?

She grabs hold of my hand and forces our fingers to interlock. Ewww. I feel nauseated at just the thought of it. She's all gross and sweaty.

'Right, we're going to start jumping.' She grins a crazed, excited look in her eye.

Is this really happening? Or am I having an actual nightmare?

She starts to bound up and down—bouncing me higher and higher. We're so high that I worry I'll hit my head on the ceiling.

Every time we bounce up to it, I feel my body tense up and wait for the smack on the head. I'm so panic stricken that I can't even move, my whole body debilitated, flinging around like jelly.

I want so desperately to wrench my hand away from hers and shout 'get off me you fucking crazy bitch' but I can't. That's a detention for sure. I hate being so helpless. I close my eyes, praying for it to be over soon.

I wait until she finally starts to bring the jumping down to a normal pace. I start to breathe again.

'Now you can start to introduce moves to it,' she says with a smirk, clearly pleased with herself.

'I don't think so,' is all I can say, my voice barely audible.

I manage to yank my hand out of hers and stand, still in shock, trying to catch my breath. I look around, trying to get my bearings and notice the horrified faces in front of me. I can see them all: Tia, Suzie, even the Canadian, Angela, and they're all as shocked as me.

Zahra's face comes into view, and I start to feel a bit

better for seeing the friendly face, but her face doesn't have the reassurance I'm seeking. She's frowning, clearly feeling my pain and embarrassment.

I carefully crouch down and move to the edge, aware that my hands are shaking. I jump off the side onto my legs, which feel like jelly. Zahra catches me before I can hit the floor.

'Miss, she feels sick. I'm taking her to the nurse,' Zahra says, already beginning to walk me out of the hall, her hand around my waist. Heat rises in my throat.

'She seems fine Zahra, stay here,' she shouts back, hands on her hips.

'I said she's sick!' she shouts back defiantly, while she continues to walk me out of my nightmare.

The minute the doors slam behind us and we're in the corridor it gets the better of me. I give in to the choking in my throat and collapse into full on crying. Not just crying, hysterical crying. I'm not a pretty crier; some girls manage to let a few tears escape and still look graceful, but not me. I can feel my makeup streaming down my face and the snot running down my chin.

Zahra looks at me alarmed, before dragging me into the changing rooms so that no one else has the chance to see me.

She hates crying; it makes her a bit uncomfortable. I remember the day I walked round to her house after I'd had a steaming row with my Mum, a few months ago when they'd told me we had to move. I was hysterical then too, but I could still see the discomfort in her face. I'd ended up telling her how to comfort me, demanding a cuddle and for her to listen to me as I ranted. Not that I could actually tell her the truth about Mum losing all her money.

She just seems too practical for crying, much preferring light-hearted fun. She never even shed a tear during The Notebook, while the rest of us seemed to be sponsored by Kleenex. But nonetheless, she's good in an emergency. Before I can say 'I want to kill myself' she's sat me on the bench and got me a handful of tissues from the toilets.

'Did that really just happen?' I ask in disbelief, through the sobs.

'Oh yeah,' she growls, pausing for dramatic effect. 'I'm in shock myself. I can't believe that fucking bitch thinks she has the right to force you to do that. I know how scared of heights you are!' Her face is getting red with fury.

'Am I?' I ask confused. I never thought of myself

scared of heights, just scared of trampolines.

She smiles at me sympathetically, like I'm some pathetic puppy. 'Babe, you shit your pants when we got to the top of that cliff in the park a few months back, and we weren't even that high.'

Oh yeah. But I'm sure I wasn't overreacting. People looked like tiny ants up that cliff, I swear to God.

'I just don't get how she thinks that would be helping you. I mean, is she a dickhead or what? I told you we should have bunked.'

I look up realising that this is all my own fault. Why didn't I just bunk?

'But obviously you weren't to know,' she quickly adds, sensing my guilt. 'Of course you wouldn't. I mean why would you put yourself through that if you knew.' Her face drops, immediately realising she's put her foot in it.

I look at her, too weak to utter a word, with a face that I try to express as 'honestly?'

'Sorry, sorry. Don't worry we're going to get you all dressed up again and we can forget that any of this ever happened.' She promises, looking doubtful herself.

When I get home, I check my email, hoping there's

another instalment from Dylan. Luckily there is. Anything to try and get today out of my head.

DYLAN'S BLOG - AUS Update

First of all, the kayaking with dolphins was AWESOME. I cannot believe how close you actually get to them. I could almost reach out and stroke them.

Also, we walked to the lighthouse and back before we left. We saw the biggest snake so far. We heard some rustling under some dead leaves and all we saw was part of the body, but that body was about five inches thick. It was when we saw that when we decided not to hang around to see where the head was.

Got here in Noosa on Friday night. It's pretty nice here. We are staying in a 16-bed-share for the first time, which is weird as there are always people buzzing around. We do have an en-suite bathroom and shower, which is nice, but we have to share them with both boys and girls. And man, are those gals messy? They leave products all over the floor and fucking hair everywhere. It is a wonder how you girls have any hair left on your head with the amount you guys leave on the walls of the shower.

Best of all there's a bar in our hostel. BO-YA!

Today we are looking to get some work so fingers crossed, people.

Tuesday 1st November

'Hey, Sav, why don't you *bounce* on into this chair next to me,' Heath says with a wicked grin when I walk into class the next morning.

Did I imagine that bounce joke?

'Heard you had a *flying* time in PE,' he smirks.

'Who told you?' I demand, punching him on the shoulder.

I thought I could just put this thing behind me, but people are still talking about it a day later.

'Don't worry about it. I just overheard it from a few guys in the changing room.'

Great, everyone's talking about it. And guys, what guys? Probably all the popular guys laughing at how ridiculous and tragic I am. Saying 'I wouldn't bone her if you paid me.'

'Actually' he says, reading my thoughts, 'they were saying how out of order it was. Angela told them and said it was awful how she picked on you'.

228

Angela! That Canadian monster. My nostrils flare, which is never attractive. Calm down, calm down. She's saying how she the teacher picked on me. At least she wasn't bitching saying what a prat I was.

I sigh, knowing I'll just have to wait out the gossip until there's something more interesting for them to talk about. At least I've managed to take the heat off Zahra.

Oh well. I should just try to carry on like normal. I can hold my head up high and not let this embarrass me.

As the day goes on, I learn that everyone feels terribly sorry for me. Everywhere I go, I have people saying 'what a bitch that teacher is', explaining how she'd picked on them before and how they were sick of PE teachers thinking they could get us to do random sport. People that didn't normally talk to me, a lot of the very popular girls, are suddenly being nice to me.

By the end of the day I'm starting to feel better about the whole thing, but still wish people would just forget about it. I mean really, when you think about it, it is a little bit funny, and at least it has bonded all of us together in hatred for all PE teachers.

Then I hear it.

'Did you hear that reception received so many

complaints today about Miss Aldridge that they've suspended her?'

Oh, fuck. Just when I think my life can't get any worse and they throw another turd on it.

Chapter Thirteen

My phone rings when I've just finished washing up a few nights later. I look at it, seeing Zach's name flashing up. I fight desperately to rip the gloves off.

'Hello,' I stammer down the phone. It's been ages since our kiss.

'Hey. What you up to?' he asks casually, sounding a bit husky and tired.

'Just cooked dinner and washed up,' I say, boring myself at how dull my life is. He must be so bored talking to me already.

'That's what I like to hear, a woman who knows her

place,' he laughs.

'Yeah right!' I retort with a giggle. I hope he's joking and isn't really a male chauvinist.

'Anyway, you wanna do something tomorrow night? I was thinking maybe I could come round?'

He wants to come round? As in... to my shithole maisonette? I don't bloody think so!

'Tomorrow night...it may be difficult. I've got...my friend staying with me at the moment. Her parents are in Spain.'

Good lie. It sounds solid.

'That's okay, why don't you come round mine?'

'Yours?' I ask, suddenly panicking. I've never been to his house before and have no idea what to expect.

Do people do this? Not go out on cinema dates first? I suppose I just assumed he'd ask me out to the cinema or something.

'Yeah. Do you reckon you could get dropped here?'

'Well, my mum could only probably drop me really early at about six pm,' I say hoping that this will put him off.

'Okay, I'll see you then.'

Damn. Why didn't I just say I didn't want to go? What

if his parents are there? What if I need the toilet while I'm there? What if I stink out his bathroom with a sudden bout of violent shits. I'll be totally out of my comfort zone, but I know I have to be a big brave girl and get on with it.

I go up to my room and ring Charlotte.

'Don't be ridiculous' she says after I've told her of my fears.

'Ok cool', I say, trying to get my stomach butterflies to calm down at the mere thought of it.

'So, you two are getting pretty serious aren't you?' she smirks.

Is she insane? I'm going round his house. We've kissed once. Hardly the love story of the year.

'No! This is our first bloody date. My first proper thing with a guy at all.'

'It's just weird, you know,' she starts to say as if to herself.

'Why?' I ask, frowning down the phone at her. I should have face timed her.

'It's just weird because we always thought you'd end up with Heath.'

233

What is it about everyone being obsessed with some idea of Heath and me together? We are friends. Yes, we're close, but that doesn't mean anything romantic should happen between us.

Anyway, I have bigger things to worry about. My Mum's driving me to Zach's house, and my heart is beating so fast I'm scared it'll jump out of my chest and run back to the safety of my duvet.

I give mum the address that Zach texted through. All I know is that it's on the Ainsborough estate. There are two parts of the estate; one end is full of rich posh houses, but the other end is a rough council estate that I always read about in the local paper. I have to assume he's more likely to live in the rough area, which I find strangely comforting. It means I can tell him where I'm currently living. I say currently because I do not intend to end up there.

'Will you be able to pick me up later?' I ask, conscious of the possibility of having to get a taxi home from a rough area alone.

'Not until about 11 pm. I think that's too late for you on a school night anyway,' she says turning to me and frowning.

God, she's a bore. But then maybe that will work in

my favour. What if we have nothing to talk about?

'Yeah, you're probably right. Shall I get a taxi then?'

'No, your Dad's shift finishes at half nine. I'll ask him if he can swing by and get you on his way home.'

'Ok thanks,' I smile relieved.

'Here we are,' says Mum, pulling the car onto the kerb.

She looks past me. Her wide eyes make me turn my head and look at what she's staring at. Oh. I check the number again to make sure it isn't a mistake. But that's it. Number 23. It's gorgeous. It's a big cream house with a big black solid door and stones covering the drive. My stomach drops, as I suddenly feel really intimidated. Not the shit hole I was expecting.

'Have fun then,' Mum says casually, but her eyes are lit up, and I can see her already hoping I'll marry him.

I get out and walk as quickly as I can to the front door, half hoping she'll wait until the door is open. Just in case it is the wrong place. I walk on the gravelled driveway, each step making a ridiculous crunching noise. Wisteria is wound around the front door. I remember Grandad once saying that rich people have this at their houses. No shit. This must be at least a four bed. And detached! I grasp the brass knocker, my hands trembling.

I take the waiting time to inhale a calming breath. This is fine. It's all going to be fine.

The door swings open, and there stands the absolute hotness that is Zach. Shit, it *is* his house. He must be rich.

'Hey,' he says, smiling at me.

'You never mentioned you lived in a mansion!' I blurt out, almost like an accusation.

'Nah, it's not that big.

'Not that big, my arse,' I laugh, turning to wave goodbye to Mum. She gives me a cringe-worthy thumbs up. God, could she be any less cool?

He takes my cold hand in his warm one and guides me into the house. This place is amazing. All modern marble floors, and built-in lighting. I follow him through to the kitchen. I can't hide my shock at the size of it.

'It's like the ones you see on TV,' I mumble like an idiot.

The kitchen/diner is massive, and the cabinet doors are so glossy I can see my face in them. There's an enormous glass table next to it which must sit at least twelve. I have to shut my mouth as I realise I'm gawping.

'My Dad's a builder,' he says in the way of an explanation. 'He bought this house years ago when it was the smallest house on the street and then they've just built on it all around and kept going until there was nowhere left to build.'

'Oh, okay,' I say, still thinking that the size of this house is ridiculous. My whole street could live in here and still not bump into each other for weeks at a time.

'Anyway,' he says, handing over my glass of lemonade, 'let's go into the sitting room.'

I dread seeing it. Will it be bigger than this room?

The answer is yes. It's the size of our entire flat. It's so big that it has six brown lazy boy sofas in it, situated around an enormous TV on the wall. That should explain it enough. I suppose money can't buy taste. It gets worse when I see a cringeworthy black and white family canvas pictures on the wall. What kind of weirdo's am I dealing with?

'But I thought we'd go into my sitting room.' He steers me around to a door next to the stairs.

'You have your *own* sitting room?' I ask, horrified by how spoilt he is. He can *never* know how poor I am.

He shrugs and opens the door. Inside is a tiny room with only one small sofa and TV. This is more my cup of tea. I instantly feel my shoulders relax.

'You like this better then, huh?' he laughs.

'Yeah, it's cosier,' I admit, shrugging my shoulders.

I relax into the millions of cushions, wondering how I found myself here with the hottest guy in town.

'So what do you wanna do?' he asks grinning from ear to ear.

'Well...' I say, feeling put on the spot and nervous. 'We could always watch a film?'

'Netflix and chill?' he grins.

I nod back. Wait, doesn't that mean sex? Shit!

'No! I mean, no. No to Netflix and chill.'

He chuckles. 'Don't worry. I was only messing.'

There he is again with his breathtaking smile. He seems so at ease like we hang around together all of the time.

He bends down to get the remote control, and I try not to gawk at his bum openly. But my God, those buns! He sits back next to me and puts his arm round me, pulling me closer. He places my legs over his at an angle and takes my arm in his hands. He starts stroking it gently, sending tingles up and down me. Wowzers. I barely even notice him putting on some box set I've never heard of.

'What's this?' he asks, pointing to a brownish orange

mark on my arm. 'Is it a birth mark?'

Oh my god. It's a dodgy fake tan mark. How mortifying.

'No,' I admit, looking down, my face growing hot. 'It's just badly applied fake tan.'

He throws back his head and laughs. Damn Zahra for making me buy it. It's not my fault I'm not professionally qualified to apply the stuff. I should have gone to a proper salon to have it done, but of course, that would have meant me having money.

The opening credits have barely begun, and he's stroking my hair behind my ear. This is unbelievable. Am I actually dreaming this? Maybe I'm still frozen at the door, dribbling at him while I fantasise. He locks eyes with me, pulling me into him and then his heavenly lips are on mine again, kissing me passionately.

He pulls back a second later, releasing me from my dream world. How can this be really happening?

'Have you been eating melon?' he asks, a playful smirk on his lips.

I squirm. 'No, it's my lip balm.' I didn't even think of that.

'You're so cute,' he says with an easy laugh, pulling me

239

closer again.

Before long we're lying on the sofa, our hands all over each other. I can feel his toned body underneath his cotton t-shirt. He has his hands under my top and is squeezing my boobs. I just hope he doesn't squeeze too hard and cause one of the chicken fillets to jump up out of my bra. That would be pretty hard to explain.

My belly rumbling breaks us apart.

'You hungry?' he asks with a grin.

'A little. I didn't really have time to eat. Plus, I was a little nervous.'

'Nervous?' he laughs. 'Of little old me?' he mocks, with a hand on his chest.

I roll my eyes. It does seem a little ridiculous now that I'd be scared somehow of this situation. I'm feeling more at ease by the minute. He pulls a Wispa Gold bar out of his coat pocket and offers it to me.

'My hero,' I say, taking it and wolfing it down. I, of course, try to do it as politely as possible, but bits of chocolate crumble apart, staining my t-shirt. Why can't I be more ladylike?

The night continues in an easy flow. Now that we've got the whole awkward part out of the way we can laugh about the TV show. He tells me he must have watched it 50 times and it's really popular in America.

He asks me all about my brother, and I ask him about his family. I find out he has two older brothers. It makes sense for the coolness to be passed down to him somehow. The whole time we're talking, his hands don't leave me. He makes sure that he has his hand on one part of me, even if it's just my hand or him tracing a pattern on my arm, which is beyond blissful.

When the credits roll again, I glance at my phone and see that my Dad's outside waiting for me. I feel unbelievably sad to have to leave him. When will I see him again?

'I'll see you again soon, right?' he says, reading the text over my shoulder.

Is it me or does he suddenly not seem so sure of himself? Could this total stud not realise how hot he is?

'Yeah, just call me,' I say, trying to sound casual.

'And...Well...' He looks down at the floor and suddenly seems a bit bashful.

'What?' I ask confused. What the hell is he going to say?

'Well, I just wondered if you were seeing anyone else?'

He's still looking at the floor.

'Anyone else?' I repeat. Does he mean like dating someone? 'Of course not,' I laugh, shocked he could even believe that I'd be interested in anyone but him.

'Ok, well, me too,' he nods with a bashful smile. 'And... I just wondered whether you wanted to see me officially?' He looks up briefly with those big brown eyes, before looking back down again.

I'm still holding his hand, and I can feel them clamming up. He is *beyond* cute.

'Officially see you?' I ask, a little perplexed. I want him to be clear. 'Are you...asking me to be your girlfriend?'

I hope to God that's what he meant. Otherwise, a lifetime of embarrassment is on its way.

'Yeah. What do you think? You don't have to. It's up to you.' He says sheepishly.

How can he not realise how amazing he is?

'Yeah, of course I do,' I beam, touching his arm. Any excuse to feel those biceps again.

'Oh, okay cool.' He beams back at me. 'Well then...I'll call you soon.' He laughs and leans in to kiss me.

I let myself melt into it and wonder why I was nervous at all. This bitch has a hot boyfriend.

Chapter Fourteen

Thursday 3rd November

#Allergies

Heath. He was the first thing I thought about when I woke up. It should have been Zach, my bloody boyfriend, but no. He's invading my head. I still can't believe what Charlotte said last night. I haven't stop thinking about it since.

I have to walk to school today as mum had to leave for an interview. It's raining, and I have my hood up on my big duffel coat, but I can still feel the frizz forming in my hair. I walk to Zahra's house to pick her up and along the way meet Sean and Calvin. We always feel safer when we have them with us, even though I basically live in a ghetto now.

Zahra seems stressed. I suppose half the school is still talking about her.

When we get in, we're late and go straight to registration. When I take my hood off my hair is huge and frizzy, just like I'd suspected. I try to ignore the sniggers from everyone. I thank God Heath isn't in any of my classes this morning to rip the piss out of me. It's times like this I'm glad I'm thicker than him.

I can't stop thinking about him though. It makes me feel really uneasy that they're all talking about me and it's made me paranoid, thinking what else they could be talking about behind my back?

Thoughts keep creeping into my head. Could I ever see myself with Heath? Is Heath good looking? Every time they drift in, I shake my head and try to force them out, feeling embarrassed at my own thoughts.

As soon as Charlotte walks into registration, I approach her. I don't waste time with any small talk.

'What did you mean 'we always thought I'd get together with Heath'?' I ask before even saying good morning.

'God, wait until I open both eyes will you?' she snaps, putting her hands up to her face, trying to block out the morning. She, like me, is rubbish in the mornings, but today I'm too curious to be sleepy.

'Well? Are you awake now?' I say impatient, shaking her slightly.

She straightens and brushes the sleep out of her eyes, still seeming half asleep.

'Ok, what was the question?' she asks, still dazed.

'What you were saying about Heath last night. What did you mean 'we'? Who else thought we'd end up together?' I ask trying desperately to act aloof.

'Everyone,' she says with a yawn, not even having to pause and think. 'We all talk about it all of the time. It's kind of like a running joke really,' she adds, completely indifferent.

'Thanks for letting me be the punch line,' I moan, feeling a bit hurt and confused as to why everyone seemed to be thinking this.

'But *w-h-y?* I ask, dragging out the word for impact. I can't let it go so easily.

'That's what's so funny,' she says, her lips curling into a smile, 'neither of you see it. We're your closest friends, and we see you basically every day, and you're just made for each other. Even Tyler and Ryan think so.'

The guys even talk about it? How embarrassing!

'Well, it's probably just to do with us being childhood friends, you know. I mean, it's just familiarity.' I realise I'm trying to convince her.

Charlotte is confusing everything. Why did she have to tell me this? Now it will be awkward when I see him.

'Well, you don't need to worry about it anyway. He's got Mercedes, and you've got Zach,' she says as if the case has been closed.

'Yeah, I know,' I nod. 'I just wish you hadn't told me. It's fine anyway, just please don't tell the others you told me, okay? I don't want to know that everyone is watching me all the time. It kind of creeps me out how you lot have got the wrong end of the stick anyway'.

And that's what has happened. The total wrong end of the stick.

At lunch I collapse down at the lunch table across from Tyler and Zahra, exhausted from the day already. Tyler smiles and lets out a little laugh. I know it's because of the state of me, but I just ignore him and pull my sandwich out of my bag. I prod it, thinking how it really doesn't look appetising. We had no food in the house so it's just jam. Oh well, I don't have any money, so I'll just have to make do.

'Alright, frizzy?' Heath says, slumping onto the chair next to me. 'What happened?' he asks, lifting up a strand of my hair, as it to inspect it.

I slap him away with my hand and feel myself blushing. Why the hell am I blushing?

'Oh, leave me alone. It's raining, okay.' I feel tired, but also aware of how I can't look him in the eye yet.

'Okay, moody.' He laughs.

I suddenly catch Zahra and Tyler staring at us, like they're watching a show, and then quickly look away when I look back at them. God, is this happening all of the time? Are both of us oblivious?

The lunch chit chatter goes on as usual, and I try to act normal, but I find myself watching Heath. I realise that I never really look at him, not properly anyway. He's actually pretty good looking. Well, I'd think that if I were another girl. I suppose he has grown up, but I didn't notice.

'So, how was Zach's last night?' Charlotte asks eagerly across the table.

'What? Since when are you going out with Zach?' Heath asks me, his forehead frowned to reveal hundreds of little wrinkles.

'Since last night,' I shrug, taking a bite of my sandwich. I really don't want him to interrogate me about him right now. It's still such early days. 'How's Mercedes?'

'We broke up,' he says with a shrug.

WHAT? I try to speak and ask what happened, but the bit of sandwich I've stuffed in my mouth was too ambitious. I try to swallow it quickly, but it tastes funny. What is that? Is that...peanuts? No, it can't be. I'm allergic to peanuts. Mum knows that. Unless she's trying to kill me, which is a possibility. Anything to get a bit more room in that flat.

I open the sandwich up, but all I can see is the usual jam. I must be imagining it.

I cough, still desperate to ask questions, but only a wheeze comes out. That's strange. Why do I feel wheezy? I try to breathe normally through my nose, but notice that I can't do that either. I try again to cough, but another wheeze comes out. Why am I struggling to breathe? It was just jam, right?

I try to speak, to ask for help, but nothing comes out. I'm having a reaction.

Ok, now I'm starting to panic. I start pointing to my throat with my mouth open. All I get back is confused faces, obviously wondering why I'm being so weird. My tongue feels itchy now and bigger than usual.

'Is she choking?' Kate asks calmly.

I roll my eyes. I shake my head like a lunatic, trying to plead with them with my eyes for their help. My chest feels itchy now and my stomach's starting to ache.

'Shit, is she having a reaction? Did she eat a peanut?' Erin asks, jumping to her feet. Everyone else seems to freeze in panic. I think a few of them even pull back a bit.

Erin's at my side in a second, trying to calm me.

'Get a teacher!' she shouts to the others.

My throat is closing up now. It's only a matter of minutes until I can't breathe.

Erin grabs my bag and turns it upside down, the contents spilling onto the table. I'm mortified when two tampons fall out. Ugh, like this isn't embarrassing enough!

I'm starting to really panic now. My throat feels sore, and I'm pretty sure I'm suffocating. Do I even have an EpiPen in that bag? It's been so long since I had a problem. I was eight years old for God's sakes.

I jump to my feet helping Erin search through the mountain of crap from my bag. All I can see are notebooks, makeup, and tissues. The ache is now moving to my chest, and I'm starting to feel a bit dizzy. I have to do something.

Before it's too late.

Before anyone has any idea what to do, I'm running. I run through the hall into the kitchen area, pushing people out of the way with all of my force. I can hear people shouting after me *'what's your problem?'* but I'm too intent trying not to die right now to care.

I'm not even sure what I'm looking for. A teacher? A phone to call an ambulance? I don't know. I just know that I don't want to die today. Especially death by peanut. It's just too mortifying.

Heath's by my side immediately. Just in time for me to feel light headed, as if my head is made of brick and forcing me down. The ache in my chest is getting worse now. Before I know it, my body's flopping down onto the floor.

Heath catches me just before my head hits the floor. He kneels down, so I'm lying in his arms. A small crowd starts forming around us. I can hear people shouting for teachers, but things are starting to go a bit hazy around the edges.

I want Heath just to hold me now. If I'm going to die, I want to die in peace, in his arms. I'm so extremely tired. He's saying something like *'come on'* over and over again.

I close my eyes and try to think of happy thoughts, to try and ignore the intense pain. The pain inflicted on me because of a fucking peanut. I am going to haunt my mother seriously for this. They'll be no calming crossing over for me.

Mrs Henderson appears out of nowhere. 'Out of the way, Heath. I have the EpiPen.'

She stabs it into my thigh. I'd flinch if I had the energy. Instead, I curl my face into Heath's warm chest.

Bit by bit the tightness around my chest starts to ease, and my throat no longer feeling like it's being strangled. I take one giant gasp of air, which sounds like Darth Vader and burns my throat. Then my body goes floppy, and my eyes roll to the back of my head. Luckily Heath is still holding me so I don't smash my head.

I open my eyes to see that I'm still on the floor and my wish of having passed out hasn't been granted. Heath and Mrs Henderson are touching my face and calling my name, but I can't hear them properly. The others are in a circle around me—their faces etched in concern.

Suddenly I can hear everything. It's very loud like the volume has been turned up full blast. I can hear Kate crying and Charlotte comforting her. I can hear Zahra asking Mrs

Henderson if I'm alright and Erin demanding that Mrs Henderson does something. Loudest of all I can hear Heath shouting my name in my face and slapping my cheeks.

'Alright,' I croak, my throat still burning. 'There's no need to shout. I can hear you.'

He smiles and looks extremely relieved, but still cautious about my fragile state.

'We need to get her to the first aid room,' Mrs Henderson says to him.

'Can you walk?' he asks me, his eyes narrowing.

'Yeah,' I say, trying to get up, but finding that the room is still spinning slightly.

'Right,' he says, tucking his arms underneath my neck and knees. He scoops me up before I can protest.

I pull my head into his chest, trying to shield myself from all of the staring faces. God, why did this have to happen to me? The feelings of mortification flood over me. I wish I'd died.

'Can we go with her, miss?' Erin asks.

'No, it's best you girls stay here. Go and tell the other teachers and try to ring her mum.'

'Sorry, Helen,' says Mr Whittaker rushing over. 'I was

over breaking up a fight in the playground. I've just heard and rushed over.'

'It's okay. She's okay now,' says nods. 'I'll get the school nurse to check her over.'

Easy for her to say.

Heath kicks the door of the first aid room open and lays me on the bed. Thankfully it isn't full of the usual year seven's faking illness to get out of double maths.

I'm suddenly aware that he's laid me over the blankets that probably every child in the school has got sick on at some point. I sit up, wanting minimum parts of my body touching it, but I have such a headache.

'You're so stubborn. Just lie down will you?' he says, clicking his tongue.

'The blanket's gross,' I whine, feeling a bit pathetic. 'I don't want my head touching it.'

He sighs loudly as if to show what a huge pain in the arse I am before taking off his blazer and putting it under my head as a pillow.

'There, you happy?' he asks, barely concealing his irritation.

'Immensely,' I answer sarcastically. Like I wanted to be in this shit situation.

A paramedic comes in with Matron to examine me. When I say examines, I mean she takes my temperature, gives me an anti-histamine and asks Heath what happened. She speaks to him like I'm too stupid even to form a sentence. It really gets under my skin.

'Well, she seems fine,' the paramedic says with a smile. 'But I think we should still take you to hospital for further monitoring.'

'No way!' I insist. 'Honestly, I feel fine now. Can't I just go home?'

She pouts, obviously mulling it over.

'I'm not sure. Is there someone who can take you home?'

'I can do that,' Heath offers, not missing a beat.

It annoys me that they think I can't look after myself. I'm bloody fine now. I just want to go home.

'Okay, but if you have any other symptoms you call 999 straight away?' I nod.

Charlotte brings in my bag and fusses all over me. I start walking towards the bus stop with Heath in a companionable silence. I'm still so humiliated.

'You can go now, I'm starting to feel better,' I say, preferring to be alone in my torment.

'Are you joking?' he snorts. 'I'm missing Philosophy & Ethics for this. Just shut up and keep looking sick, okay?'

'But I feel fine,' I weakly protest.

'I still can't believe it. How did you eat a peanut?' he asks, chuckling.

'I have no idea.'

'Only you could get a peanut allergy from a jam sandwich. Or was it just shock you went into after hearing that I'd dumped Mercedes?'

'Yeah, actually,' I mumble before thinking.

'Oh,' he says, his expression changing to serious. 'I was only joking.'

'What happened with you both?'

He shrugs. 'She just wasn't the girl for me, that's all.'

And who is I wonder? Could it really be me? Does he think that? Is that why he's being so nice to me? Have Tyler or Ryan told him what they think? Oh God, I'm so confused.

I'm glad we're leaving early, missing as many people as possible.

By the time we get to the bus station my chest is starting to hurt from earlier. My mum rings me explaining that she's just managed to charge her phone and so just got the several messages from the matron and the girls.

It takes about five minutes to calm her down fully and reassure her that I'm ok. She has no idea how peanuts got in my sandwich and vows to write a very stern letter to the makers of the jam.

There's a long queue for getting on our bus. We've got here early, and it seems we're getting the earlier bus with the other local school kids. We're the last to step on the bus, and we try to push in against the bodies so that we can get out of the rain that's starting to fall.

I hear the bus doors make a sound and before I know what's happening the doors are closing in on me. I try to jump my body out of the way quick enough, but I still manage to get my foot stuck in it.

'Aaaahh!' I moan, not particularly to anyone.

The doors open slightly and then close again on my foot, crushing it.

'Open the fucking door!' Heath shouts at the bus driver.

He tries to beat the doors back with his hands. He manages it because my foot finally comes free before they slam shut again. I look up, flustered, to see if anyone has noticed. Of course *everyone* has noticed and are giggling to themselves.

'You really can't stay out of trouble today can you?' he says looking more annoyed than playful. He pays for us and then puts his hands on my waist, helping me limp to a nearby seat.

When the bus pulls up at our stop, he helps me off. I'm still limping because my foot is killing me. It's more my ankle actually, and it's throbbing like mad. I catch him watching me with amused eyes. Does he think this is funny?

'I'm fine to walk the rest of the way,' I say stubbornly, arms crossed against my chest. I don't want his pity.

'Really? Do you reckon you'll be able to get home by yourself?' He's so annoying. He's only asking because the paramedic told him to walk me home. Crapstone is still a fifteen-minute walk. 'You can sort of walk, can't you?'

'Yeah course,' I blag. I don't want his pity anymore. Especially if I'm just annoying him.

'Now,' he says, looking at me seriously, like a father talking to a child. 'Do you think you can manage to walk home without jumping in front of a car?'

I'm so angry I don't even respond. My lip curls up in pure anger. I turn and walk away, trying desperately not to limp on my now excruciatingly painful ankle.

When I get home, I flop down onto the bed, glad I have another blog update from Dylan to cheer me up.

DYLAN'S BLOG - AUSTRALIA ZOO MOTHER FUCKERS

We went to an Australian zoo. It was sooo good. In one day we had a picnic with a kangaroo, stroked a crocodile, saw a dragon (who knew they were even real!), fed an elephant, stroked a koala and saw the famous crocodile show (without Steve Irwin, which is a shame).

The crocodile show was cool, but they are literally untrainable. They just have to use the crocs hunting instincts to get them to do what they want. But once you've seen one crocodile, you've seen them all. I don't need to walk around for an hour seeing all the different types.

We also found the massive snake we saw in Byron. Let's just say we were right to run away.

The next day I started work.

Have you ever walked out of work for lunch in 36-degree heat, walked into the food court and thought mmm, I really want a curry? Well, where I work supplies exactly that. It is crazy. I am the only person there who really *speaks English. My job is basically to wash up and I am the taste tester (I haven't told them that I don't really know anything about curry, I just look at them and try and gauge what they want me to say). I'm on $15 an hour, and I get two full meals in a five-hour shift.*

Adrianna is currently cutting people's hair at the hostel and is actually really busy. Yesterday she cut six people's hair.

The main problem with working in a curry house is that I am spending all my wages on shower gel and am spending an hour in the shower every night to try and get the smell of curry off me. It really is quite an experience.

Speak soon xxx

Nan burst into my bedroom, her forehead puckered. 'Oh, sweetheart, I just heard the news! How are you?' She grabs me and forces me into her cleavage before I get a chance to reply.

'I'm fine, Nan,' I mumble into her chest.

'And to think it was all my fault. I just feel awful!'

I frown. 'All your fault. What do you mean?'

'Oh sweetheart, I made your sandwich. I completely forgot about your peanut allergy and thought I'd jazz it up a bit. Gave you jam with peanut butter. The Americans love it. Call it peanut butter and jelly, they do. I just can't believe I forgot! I must have the start of Alzheimer's. Will you ever forgive me?'

I'm honestly too exhausted to care.

'I forgive you.' I smile, not wanting her to worry herself to an early grave. Although how you forget your only granddaughter has a nut allergy I don't know.

'Thanks, sweetheart. And I'm sure it wasn't too bad, right?'

I stare at her, no expression on my face. 'You're right,' I nod sarcastically. 'Not that bad at all.'

Chapter Fifteen

Saturday 5th November

#NansGoneWild

I wake on Saturday night with an anxious start, kicking my legs like I've fallen. Sweat covers my forehead, and I try to catch my breath. My legs kick the cover off me as I try to cool down and remember the nightmare, but I can't. I sit up and try to calm myself down.

I walk to the toilet and am surprised when I hear laughing and talking coming from the kitchen. My eyes dart to the clock. 2 am. What the hell are they doing up at this time?

I wander down the hall to the warming reassurance of my Mum's dirty laugh. I open the kitchen door and shield my eyes from the bright lights.

'Hello, darling,' Nan slurs.

My eyes readjust to the light as I try to look around to see who's here. There's Nan, Grandad, Mum, Dad and two ladies I don't know. They have pearls round their necks with matching twin cardigans. They look a bit too posh to be socialising with my family.

'Hi,' I say cautiously, eyeing them suspiciously.

'Tell Savannah I love her, tell Savannah I need her,' my Grandad starts singing, clearly very drunk. You can always tell, as he'll sing happily, ridding himself of his normal moody persona.

'These are my friends,' Nan starts, probably seeing the confusion on my face and deciding to ignore him. 'They're over from the South of France, visiting family, and I bumped into them at the pub. This is Nancy,' she says, gesturing to the grey haired lady.

She waves back, a bit like the Queen. I smile politely and am suddenly aware of my beehive hair and dribble stained face.

'And this is Felicity,' she says, smiling at the blonde haired lady, who seems a bit friendlier. She beams over a drunken smile. I warm to her instantly.

'We knew your Nan from school. She used to get us into all sorts of trouble!' Felicity says, throwing her head back laughing.

'I can imagine,' I laugh, smiling at my Nan as she tops up everyone's wine. She's still a bad influence.

'Come and sit with us,' Mum says, jumping up from her chair and offering it to me.

Why not? I slump down on the seat, feeling very underdressed in my Mickey Mouse nightdress and watch Nan pour me a glass of red wine.

'Nan! It's 2 am, and I've got work tomorrow. I'm not going to drink with you. I have to be up in a few hours.' She hands me the glass anyway.

'Oh, stop worrying, my little caterpillar. Just sip it.'

I sip, thinking it'll be easier to follow instruction than to argue with her.

'Anyway, where was I?' Nan asks, looking round at the women. 'That's right! I was telling you about Bridget from school. Well, she's never found a nice man and she seems quite bitter about it all.'

'It's so sad, she's always been so lovely,' my Mum adds, a sad smile on her face.

'I say she should buck up her ideas,' Nan declares.

Nancy and Felicity burst into high-pitched squealing. Even their laugh is posh.

'Nan! She's probably very lonely,' I say, feeling sorry for Bridget. She's always brought me a present whenever she's come to visit.

'There's no need to be lonely when there are all of these vibrators out there.'

My mouth falls open. Just when you think she can't shock you anymore, she goes and does it. Knowing my Nan even knows what a vibrator is, makes me feel queasy enough, but actually hearing her say it. Gross.

'Mum!' Mum gasps, turning beetroot. I'm glad someone seems as embarrassed as me.

'I'm sorry, but while there are vibrators, there is really no need for men. But I suppose they wouldn't be so handy at a dinner and dance.' She starts laughing, finding herself hilarious. 'I doubt they'd look very good in a dickie bow sitting next to you.' She collapses into hysterics.

Everyone starts laughing so hard that I'm worried soon I'll be swimming through old lady piss.

'Well on that note...I'm going back to bed.' I get up, disgusted.

I walk out of the room, looking back at the insane

people that I call my family. My Grandad is singing another song, my Mum swaying along to it. My Nan gets another bottle of wine out, being the perfect hostess, and my Dad's already asleep in the corner armchair, snoring loudly.

'Remember I've got work in the morning, so you'll need to be up early,' I remind Mum, always feeling the parent.

'Oh well, I might be hungover, so you might have to sort yourself out. That's ok, right?' Mum slurs back, her eyes red and tired looking.

'Of course.' I turn round to leave. 'I always do,' I whisper under my breath.

Monday 7th November
#BitchesBeCrazy

I walk into English class with Charlotte on Monday, really not wanting to learn anything. Although I've tried to keep a low profile today, people have still been shouting '*she's alive!*' dramatically like I'm Frankenstein. Luckily it seems that no one is genuinely being horrible, just jesting.

I feel like I have so much on my mind, but I don't even know what. My head feels clouded.

I leave her to sit in my usual spot next to Joe. I love Joe. He's always in a good mood and loves a chuckle over anything. I say a quick hello, and we start chatting about random stuff.

He's still talking to me when Mrs Phillips starts her lesson, and I tell him to shush.

'I'm so sorry, Miss Franks,' Mrs Phillips taunts, glaring at me. 'I didn't realise that your conversation was marginally more interesting than my lesson,' she adds sarcastically. 'Please, share with the class what is so fascinating?' Her eyes widen—she looks like a woman possessed.

Why do teachers always feel the need to do this? As if I'm going to turn round and tell her the truth. Yeah, Miss, we were just talking about that new TV show where they're all naked. As if.

'Sorry, Miss,' I mumble, my cheeks flushing with heat. The faces of the entire class look back at me. I catch Charlotte's pained expression, feeling sorry for me. At least someone's on my side.

'Well,' she says, 'seeing as you are *so* keen to talk, you can read the first page of this textbook.' She hands them out to everyone, practically throwing my copy at me. 'Page

106,' she snarls, smiling, clearly enjoying my discomfort.

Why do teachers find it amusing to ruin my life?

I take a deep breath and start reading. I hate reading aloud in class. No one likes the sound of their own voice and especially not me. Sometimes, I think I sound like a robot. Plus, I'm always terrified that I'll get a word wrong or start stuttering.

I'm getting along just fine with it when I hear Amelia, the girl in front of me, whispering to her table partner John.

'Her voice is so hilarious,' I overhear. I swallow hard, attempting to read on as normal.

I carry on reading, but can still hear her. Now she's doing impressions of me speaking, and John is laughing along as if it's the funniest thing he's ever heard. My throat chokes up a bit, raw emotion rising through. Don't let them get to you—just carry on.

I look round the class to see if Mrs Phillips can hear or see them, but she seems oblivious. Just when I need her. Typical.

Joe leans forward and tells them to knock it off. Amanda just turns, looks at me with a smirk and laughs, before turning back to the front.

Thankfully, my page is finished, and I curl my head

267

into my chest attempting to hide behind my hair. Hopefully, she'll pick on another poor sap.

Why do I feel so upset? I must be due on or something. I squeeze my eyes shut, fighting back the tears. I can feel them building in my eyes. How can one girl be so mean? What is her problem?

Joe turns to face me. 'Don't worry about her,' he whispers. 'She's just pissed off that you're with her ex now.'

'Her ex?' I ask, scrunching my face up in confusion. 'Who's her ex?'

'Zach,' he says slowly as if I'm stupid. 'You guys *are* together, right? I mean, that's what I heard.'

Wow. He heard that. People know. How the hell do they know?

'Um, yeah,' I nod. 'I just didn't realise she was his ex.'

It does make sense though. She must have been the blonde he was shagging at my Nan's flat. The idea of them being so intimate makes my stomach flip. It also reminds me that he's way more experienced than I am.

'Yep. Jealousy is an evil thing.' He squeezes my hand in solidarity.

He's so wise for his age. He's been brought up mostly by his Grandad as his Dad died when he was a baby and his mum works full time in the City. I often think that's why he can hold down an intellectual conversation, unlike most guys I know.

Amelia continues to turn round and glare at me throughout the rest of the lesson. I try my best not to catch her gaze and pay attention to Mrs Phillips, but I can *feel* her watching me. I can feel the hatred penetrating towards me like a laser beam. Why have I brought this on myself? She's never even noticed me before now.

When the bell rings, I'm extremely grateful. I almost run over to Charlotte and drag her towards the toilet. I'm bursting for the loo anyway. We run for the cubicles and start chatting over them.

'What the hell is her problem?' she shouts over.

'It's because I'm dating Zach. Did you know they went out?'

'No way! I never knew that. Oh well, don't even let it worry you, hun. There's plenty of bitches out there, much bigger and scarier than her.' She laughs as we both flush the loo.

We walk out laughing to find Amelia leaning against the wall by the sinks, her arms crossed over her chest. Shit. My stomach nearly hits the floor.

How has she snuck in here without us hearing her? She's scowling at me, shooting invisible daggers with her eyes. If looks could kill, I'd already be buried.

'You bitches better watch your backs,' she says calmly, a cruel smile gracing her lips.

But I can tell that she's anything but calm. Underneath the surface, I can tell she's enraged, boiling over. Her eyes are bloodshot as if she can't physically keep the rage in. At any minute I'm expecting her to tear off her clothes and turn into the incredible hulk.

We both freeze in fear. There's no one else in the toilets to hear us if she attacks us and I'm suddenly aware that if we don't turn up at our next lesson the teacher will just assume we've bunked. There will be no frenzied search party. Damn bad reputation.

'Please,' she suddenly says sarcastically, indicating for us to go to the sinks and wash our hands. To go about our business as normal. As if I can. I'm shaking like a bloody leaf.

I start to walk slowly over to the sink, scared enough to follow her orders. I trip on something and land awkwardly on my left foot. The same foot that had just about healed from trapping in in the bus door.

I turn to see what I've tripped on and realise that it's Amelia's leg. She's poised like a graceful ballerina. She wants me to know it was deliberate. I look up into her deranged face. She must be furious. Losing Zach to little old average me. Charlotte's behind her, clearly trying to think about what to do.

She sneers at me and leans into my face, close enough for me to feel her hot breath on my cheek.

'Like I said,' she whispers, raising the hairs on the back of my neck. 'Watch your back.'

She smiles again, now sweetly, which I think is more alarming. She turns on her heel and walks out with a joyful skip.

I steady myself on the sink, my head overwhelmed. Charlotte calls Zahra on her mobile and tells her to get the others to meet us in the library.

Charlotte helps me limp there. Thankfully it isn't too far from the toilets. Zahra, Erin, and Kate are already there, pretending to look for books.

'What happened?' Erin asks, watching me limp towards them.

'Where do I even start?' I sigh, feeling worn out.

We take a few random books and settle ourselves onto

271

a study table. The librarian is almost seventy and has refused to retire. This means she falls asleep every so often, and we're lucky that now is one of those moments.

Charlotte and me whisper to the girls what happened.

'She actually said that? Watch your back?' Zahra asks, clicking her knuckles as if she's preparing to fight.

I nod, shuddering at the memory.

'She must be much more pissed than we first thought,' Kate says absentmindedly.

I frown in confusion. 'What? Did you just say than you *first t*hought?'

What the hell is she talking about?

Kate goes bright red and starts stuttering something. I'm not paying too much attention to her. I'm looking straight at Zahra and Erin, demanding answers with my eyes. They're looking at each other like they're trying to communicate with each other. They know something I don't. Kate looks like she might have a heart attack any minute, her nervous rash up on her neck.

Charlotte looks just as confused and curious as me. I thank God that I'm not the only one in the dark.

'Well...' Zahra starts. I catch Erin give her a warning look. It's like she's trying to tell her not to tell me everything.

'Just fucking tell me!' I shout, losing my cool.

The librarian snorts and we hunch down, scared to wake her.

'Okay,' Erin whispers, taking control. 'We just assumed you knew Amelia and Zach went out before you got together. Anyway, we were in Maths the other day, and we heard her talking to her mates.'

She pauses a moment as she lets me digest this. 'Right.... And?'

'Well,' Zahra continues. 'It sounds like she's pissed off that you're now going out with him. She was saying all this crap like you hadn't even spoken to her about it, and that you were disrespecting her. Apparently, she only found out over the weekend when she saw him. Anyway, it kind of sounds like she wants him and can't have him... because of you.'

She sits back, nervously awaiting my reaction. All I feel is exhaustion, my limbs so heavy I can barely move my arms. Why does my life have so much drama in it? Just when I think I've got myself a nice boyfriend, it has to cause someone to hate me.

'Well?' Erin asks, raising her eyebrows. 'Are you

okay?'

'I don't even care,' I say with a sigh, feeling beaten by the whole day. 'Just let her hate me. I'm sure she'll get over it eventually.' I don't even believe myself, but what else can I say?

The rest of the day drags, but the girls' promise to take me to McDonald's on the way home gets me through. I just keep imagining that burger and the worries drift away.

We meet at the school gate as normal.

'Cool, let's go,' Zahra says, applying neon pink lip gloss. 'We're going to McDonald's on the way home if you guys are up for it?' she says, turning to the boys.

'Hell, yeah,' seems to be the joint response.

It makes me laugh how such a simple thing can make us all so happy. Fried food. Thank God it was invented. Everyone starts to walk, but I hang back.

'What's up?' Erin asks, looking at me strangely. 'Didn't you hear us? Greasy burgers are waiting to be eaten.' She laughs at her own joke.

'I don't think I can walk on my ankle,' I admit, looking at the floor and feeling ridiculous.

It still hurts like a motherfucker.

'Why? Is it still hurting?' Kate asks, bending over to inspect it.

'Why, what happened?' Heath asks, cutting in on my response.

'Long story,' Kate and Charlotte chime at the same time, making us laugh.

'Do you want a piggy back?' Tyler asks, raising his eyebrows.

'You may just be joking, but I'm serious. Can I have one?' I ask scrunching up my nose. I hate having to act like a pathetic girl and ask for help, but I'm too weak to care at this point.

He answers by flinging me roughly onto his back. The relief I feel when the pressure is off my foot is amazing. I clasp my hands round his neck and cling on like a monkey.

'So what happened then?' Heath asks as if he's dying of curiosity.

I ignore him for a little while. I can't be bothered to talk

'Is it something to do with Amelia?' he asks, grabbing my attention.

Shit. He knows too? I can't help but feel seriously betrayed. Have they all just been keeping this from me?

HEATH, CLIFF & WANDERING *Hearts*

They should have warned me to be on my guard.

'Why?' I ask. 'What did you hear?'

He glances at Tyler. It's annoying that I can't see Tyler's expression.

'Just that she was pretty pissed off with you. She thinks you stole him off her.'

'Yeah, that's what everyone keeps telling me,' I say rolling my eyes.

I tell him and Tyler the whole story on the way to McDonald's. They don't seem shocked at all, which makes me think that they've actually played down the truth.

It seems like forever until I see the golden arches of joy in the distance. A blonde figure is standing outside. I think it's Zach, but I can't see him clearly enough. Maybe my mum is right, and I do need to get my eyes tested.

As we get closer, I realise it is Zach, only in his Leamington school uniform. He looks so different and bloody gorgeous in his blue blazer and tie. Visions of me, pulling it off him rush through my mind.

He catches sight of me too and waves—confused wrinkles on his forehead. There's a group of girls surrounding him. The jealousy that overcomes me is ridiculous. Look at all of the attention he's attracting. Back away, bitches. He's my man!

'There's your lover boy,' Heath says, but not in his usual cheeky tone. He sounds a bit irritated, which is weird. What would he be annoyed at?

The girls are in front of me. They all look back at me with concerned eyes. Why do they look so worried?

'Don't worry, babe—we'll just go straight in ok?' Erin says as if trying to calm me.

Why the hell are they so worried? I look at Zach again, but, this time, I notice that one girl in particular has wrapped herself around him, flirting shamelessly away. That girl is Amelia.

'Shit,' is all I can say.

I'm finding it hard to breathe, my heart pounding away rapidly in my chest like it'll escape any minute. I feel sick to my stomach as we approach them, closer and closer. I don't even have any control, being on Tyler's back.

Now I'm even closer I can see that Amelia's friends are giving all of us evil eyes. Luckily my girls are doing the same back, seemingly not intimidated, which I've no doubt they are.

Amelia has her arm wrapped around his shoulders, playing with his hair, while she talks to him. Looking at him like he's a prize that she's intent on winning.

I notice that when she isn't scowling at me, she's actually gorgeous. Totally bloody gorgeous. She's got long blonde hair and sparkling blue eyes with big boobs that are peering out of her undone top button. She's a much better version of myself really. Same basic colourings, but where my face is squidgy and cute, hers is sculptured and sexy. Her skin is totally clear, which I think I envy the most. It doesn't seem to matter what spot wash I use; I still suffer from breakouts.

Zach stares back at me, seeming confused again. Why the hell is *he* confused? I should be the one pissed off with him letting her paw all over him. He's staring so intently that Amelia's gaze from his face is forced to go towards me on Tyler's back. Her face instantly turns malicious, the beast I knew from earlier today coming to the surface.

'Hey,' he says, smiling but looking up at me with...is that a hint of jealousy in his eyes?

'What's going on? You get tired of walking or something?' he asks, looking at Tyler accusingly.

'I had an accident,' I explain, catching Amelia's eye for a second and then looking away quickly. 'It's flared my ankle up again, so I couldn't walk, and Tyler offered his back.' I slowly realise that it perhaps looks a bit intimate for someone who doesn't understand our friendship.

'Oh right,' he nods, still not relaxing completely. 'Well, thanks, Tyler,' he says, seeming fake, 'but I'll take it from here.'

He moves towards me to help me down, forcing Amelia's hand to move away from his neck. All of his attention is on me now, and I wonder whether he even remembers he was talking to her. I can't help but feel smug.

Amelia doesn't stop staring at him as if willing him to turn again.

'Well, I'll see you later then, Zach,' she says, smiling sweetly, while at the same time managing to catch my eye, in a way that says *he'll always be mine.*

How long has she known him anyway? Was it a long-term thing? I really need to ask him.

'Yeah, bye,' he says, not even looking up. He seems to be completely unaware of the drama unfolding around him. Guys can be so dumb.

Slowly Amelia starts to walk off, backwards at first, while still glaring at me. She eventually turns—her friends following behind her. Erin, Zahra, and Kate finally relax their stances and breathe a big breath of relief before

279

heading on into McDonald's.

Heath gets to me before Zach, his hands on my waist, helping me down.

'No, I've got it,' Zach argues, pushing him out of the way.

Heath looks like he might spit with rage. What is up with him?

'You ok?' he asks me, tucking a bit of hair behind my ears. 'Were you planning on eating too?'

Does he know me at *all?*

'Yeah,' I nod, answering both questions. I've got my own question burning inside me much more.

'What does she mean, she'll *see you later?*' I ask, sounding like the jealous girlfriend I now clearly am.

'It's just a figure of speech,' he shrugs. His arm wraps around my waist so he can help hoist me into McDonalds. God, how I wish I weren't so disabled.

'Don't you look cute in your uniform,' he grins, lowering me into the booth everyone is at.

'Yeah, well cute,' I deadpan, rolling my eyes.

'So, what do you want? My treat.' The guys roll their eyes at this. When did they suddenly hate him so much? I thought they were all friends?

I have to think about my response. Should I order a ladylike portion—just a normal meal? Or should I get my usual? I think about the stressful day I've had and decide I'll treat myself.

'Ok, well as long as you're sure. Can I please have a big Mac meal without cheese, with a small portion of chicken nuggets, chips and a strawberry milkshake?'

He seems taken aback. I watch as he glimpses down at my slim line legs, obviously concerned about where all this fat is going to go.

'And remember,' Heath warns him, 'no cheese on the big Mac. It's too fattening.' He bursts out laughing at his own joke.

Zach nods and goes up to the counter to order, followed by Kate, Ryan, and Charlotte who are getting the rest of our meals.

As soon as they're away, the tension eases and the chatter starts.

'Can you believe the cheek of her? Standing there all over him! Right in front of you,' Erin blasts, obviously disgusted by Amelia's behaviour.

'Yeah, but who can blame her. I mean he is gorgeous. Look at him in his uniform,' Zahra grins, looking over at

281

him appreciatively.

She stops when she realises we're all staring at her with raised eyebrows.

'Sorry!' she exclaims, laughing wickedly. 'I just know a good thing when I can see it.'

We laugh too. Trust Zahra to find someone sexy in the middle of a drama. I'm surprised she didn't go after him herself.

'I think he's got some cheek,' Heath says out of nowhere.

'What?' I ask, completely startled by his sudden hostile reaction.

He frowns. 'Being all arsey with Tyler over him giving you a piggyback. I mean, it's his fault that you got injured anyway. Maybe if he didn't lead her on like that, she wouldn't be so crazy.'

'Lead her on?' I attempt to shout in anger, but it comes out more like a pathetic whimper.

'Yeah,' he retorts, obviously unaware at what a dick he's being. 'He let her have her hands all over him. If I had a girlfriend, then I wouldn't be acting like that.' He's getting more annoyed by the second.

'Well, you don't anymore because you dumped the

lovely Mercedes.'

He sneers back at me. God, he's annoying. I turn to Zahra and Erin for some support, but they're not looking at me. As if they're deliberately avoiding my gaze

'Well, do *you* think that?' I ask them.

'No, don't be silly,' they say quickly. Too quickly for my liking. I can tell they're just trying to spare my feelings. Do they think Zach's being a douche?

They all come back to the table, and you can cut the tension with a knife. Heath and Tyler are radiating some kind of pissed off vibe towards Zach, although he luckily seems completely unaware.

'So...' Zach begins, turning to face me, 'what happened to make your foot play up again?'

'Oh, nothing,' I say, putting my hand over my mouth so he can't see the burger and chicken nugget that I have rolling around it. 'I just tripped.'

'Ha!' Heath sneers. I turn around quickly to shoot him a '*shut up*' look.

'What?' Zach asks, not missing this. 'What's funny?'

It's obvious he doesn't like being left out, but I don't want to tell him and stress him out.

'I just think it's funny that Savannah feels the need to

lie to you,' Heath says slyly. I kick him underneath the table.

'Ouch!' Zahra yelps. Whoops, wrong leg.

'Savannah, what's he saying?' Zach asks, squeezing his eyes at me as if trying to work it out himself.

'It's just...just....' I stutter, not sure how to put it.

'It's just that your ex-girlfriend Amelia did this to her because of you,' Heath says for me, his face contorting in disgust. Why is he so pissed?

'What?' he gasps, seeming shocked and completely unaware of any conflict. Can he really be that dumb?

'It's no big deal,' I shrug. 'She just apparently blames me for you breaking up.'

'Yeah, you need to have a word with her,' Heath almost spits at him. 'Before something worse happens.'

'Yeah, of course, I will,' he says, looking at Heath furiously. 'I think I know how to look after my own girlfriend, but thanks for your concern,' he says sarcastically.

They glare at each other, the room almost bursting with awkwardness. I quickly scan the room, desperately looking for some kind of diversion. Where the hell is Ronald Macdonald when you need him? Then I spot my brother's friend Shane.

'Shane!' I shout, a lot more loudly than I had planned to. Everyone seems to jump at the sound of my voice.

Shane looks up and smiles. He starts walking over, and I thank God for the diversion from the conversation.

'Hey, Savannah, how are you?' he asks, his voice warm and friendly as normal.

'Yeah, great thanks,' I smile cheerily. 'These are my friends.' I gesture around to everyone.

He looks around and smiles.

'Yeah, I remember a few of you from Dylan's leaving party.' He nods at Zahra and Erin.

Zahra's already pouting and discretely re-arranging her cleavage. She's always fancied Shane. One of the perks of having an older brother is that his friends are always in the house.

'Shane is my older brother's best friend,' I explain to Zach to hopefully stop him looking at me with such suspicion.

'So, what have you got there?' I ask looking at the posters he's holding in his hand.

'Oh yeah, you guys should take one. My band is doing a gig at the Flag and Firken this weekend. They're not really strict on ID so you guys should be ok. You should definitely come along.' He flicks his long black hippy hair over his shoulder.

'Yeah, well...we'll be there,' I say, excited at the idea of going to a gig.

He smiles warmly again. 'Good to see you, Sav. I miss seeing you these days since Dylan's been travelling.'

'Ah, don't make me cry,' I pout sarcastically, my eyes smiling.

Seeing him makes me miss my brother all the more. I miss the mayhem they used to cause and even them waking me up at two in the morning begging for me to make them cheese on toast after a heavy session.

He turns and walks away. I see Zach's chest relax. Has he been tense the whole time?

'He is *so* hot,' Zahra breathes out, fanning her face with her hand.

'You are such a slut.' Kate laughs.

'So, we gonna go?' I ask looking around, glad for a change in subject.

'Yeah, it'll be fun,' the girls say.

'What about you?' I ask Zach.

'Nah' he says, recoiling his face. 'Not really my scene.'

'Why not?'

'I'm just not into rock music.'

Me neither, but it sounds fun.

'Well,' Heath interrupts, 'I'm not into rock music, but I'll be there. It should be a laugh.'

'Yeah, me too,' Tyler and Ryan chime in.

Oh god. Why are they all acting like dicks? Why don't they just all drop their trousers and see who's got the bigger cock?

'Yeah actually,' Zach nods, looking at the guys rather than me. 'Count me in'.

Chapter Sixteen

My Mum got the job she interviewed for so now she and Dad work all hours with their different work patterns. With Nan and Grandad always out and about I seem to spend a lot of time on my own, but I can't be annoyed. They're paying the bills after all. I do try to do my bit and turn off the lights when I leave rooms. Not that there's many of them.

I do my homework and am just settling down to watch some mindless soap when the phone rings. It's Erin.

'Hey, hun, you ok?' she asks.

'Yeah, my ankle hurts a bit, but I'm fine,' I say, suddenly remembering that I should have it raised.

'Okay, good.'

'Sooooooo, did you just call for a chat or what?' I ask

confused at the silence.

There's another long pause.

'Okay, I feel I need to tell you this, but please don't worry, ok?'

'Okay,' I lie, already feeling sick. What the hell now?

'Well, I was on Facebook, and I saw that Amelia had written as her status *'that bitch is going down.'*

I gulp down the bile. 'You're friends with her?'

'Babe, I'm friends with the whole year, hence the whole idea of Facebook. But aren't you more worried about her status?' she asks confused.

I feel strangely calm about the whole thing. Almost numb.

'No. I just think if she's gonna kill me she's gonna kill me.'

'Oh, okay. Well, I just thought I'd tell you anyway. I still can't get over you still not having a Facebook account,' she laughs. 'It's so pre-historic.'

'Yeah, well this is one of the reasons I don't. I hate all the trouble it can cause. I'm glad I stay away from it.' I actually feel a bit smug.

For once she doesn't argue back. I'm always being bullied by the others for not having set up an account. I just think Instagram and Snapchat are enough. If people want to contact me, they can still ring or text me.

'Ok, well, you're not annoyed that I told you right?'

'Of course not,' I lie. I'd rather not know how much trouble I'm in, but I'm glad that they're not hiding anything from me anymore.

I go back to my soap and get interrupted again by a text message. I sigh before opening it up to see that it's Zach.

Hey, hope you're ok and not in too much
pain. I will speak to Amelia. Do you
want me to walk you home tomorrow after
school? I could meet you at McDonald's
and walk you back? xxx

I text back immediately.

Hiya, please don't say anything to
Amelia. I can handle it. Ok, will see
you tomorrow at McDonald's xxx

I feel it'll be better if he doesn't say anything to her. It'll only make her worse.

Tuesday 8th November

The next day at school isn't as bad as I thought it would be. I barely see Amelia. The only time I see her is at lunch when she sits two tables away from me. I can hear her talking loudly that I'm a 'no good bitch', but I just pretend I can't hear her and try to stay out of her way. Luckily it seems that her friends are the only people paying her much attention. I just try to look forward to meeting Zach after school.

The guys walk me to McDonald's and drop me off with Zach, who's already waiting for me, leaning against the wall, like a model.

'Hey.' He kisses me quickly on the lips.

We head off towards home. He leads me, and I follow. After a while, he offers to give me a piggyback as he can see I'm struggling to walk. I wonder if he also feels he has to compete with Tyler.

'So what happened with Amelia then?' he asks once I'm on his back. Is he asking now that I can't read his face?

'She just told me to watch my back and then she tripped me over,' I say matter of fact. I don't want to sound like a huge drama queen.

'Are you sure she meant to trip you?' he asks.

I flinch from the suspicion in his voice. He doubts

291

me? He actually doubts me?

'What? Of course she meant to,' I snap. I'm beyond hurt. Why the hell would he doubt me?

'It's just that the Amelia I know wouldn't do something like that. I mean, she was mouthy, but I didn't think she would do anything like that.'

He is. He's actually taking her side over mine. I can't bloody believe this.

'So you're saying I'm a liar then?' I ask, hurt radiating from my voice.

'No, no, of course not. It's just that when I spoke to her about it last night, she said that you just tripped over yourself and—'

'What?' I gasp, slipping down off his back. I don't want to be touching him when he's accusing me of something. 'You saw her last night? You said you weren't seeing her last night!' I scream, sudden rage filling my veins. I scare myself at how insane I'm reacting, but I can't help it.

'I didn't see her last night,' he says turning to me. 'I rang her and—'

'When I told you not to?' I interrupt. 'Why would you do that to me?'

He puts his hands up in a surrender pose 'Okay, I'm sorry. Please, just calm down. I didn't mean to upset you. It's just that...'

'It's just that you believe her over me,' I state, putting words into his mouth.

'No,' he protests, but I've already started to walk off in the opposite direction. I say walk—I mean more of a hobble.

He runs up to me, catching up in barely a stride. He takes hold of my arms, which are crossed in front of me and shakes me so that he can get my attention.

'Listen' he says, suddenly looking worried. 'I didn't mean to hurt you. Trust me, that's the last thing I want to do. That's why I rang her. After the way your friends reacted last night I needed to tell her to back off. Anyway, she said that you had tripped, but that she did want me back.'

I look away, disgusted that he would even talk to her.

'But I told her, I'm with you now. I made it clear that I wasn't interested in her. She was pretty upset, but said she understood and we should still be friends.'

How dumb can he be? She's not going to give up that easily!

'That's the thing, I don't even want you to be friends with her!'

Shit, I sound crazy.

'Okay, okay, I won't be friends with her then. I just don't want to upset you.' He tries to look me in my eyes, while I look at anything but him.

I take a deep breath and try to calm myself down. Why am I being so angry? If anything, it's just because he's too nice for his own good.

'Okay, I'm sorry,' I say with a sigh. 'I don't want to act mad—it's just that she's crazy'.

'Let's not think about her,' he says, before pulling me close and kissing me hard on the lips.

But I can't forget about her. That bitch is out to get me, and he just doesn't get it.

'Okay, but I think I'm going to go home. I have a banging headache.' I clutch my temple as if to prove it.

'Okay, I'll drop you home.'

Uh-oh. I don't want him seeing the hovel I live in. Especially after I've seen his mansion.

'You don't have to do that. I'll be fine on my own.'

'Don't be silly,' he laughs. 'You can't even walk. Just tell me where you live, and I'll drop you off.'

Shit. I'm not getting out of this one.

'Munden Road,' I blurt before I can talk myself out of it.

It's my old address and the only one I know off by heart. He throws me onto his back, and we start walking towards it.

It's easy to forget all about that bitch Amelia when you're panicking because you're making your boyfriend bring you two miles out of your way so you don't die of shame.

'This is me,' I smile, pointing to my old door. I release myself off his back.

He looks at the Astra on the drive. 'I'd like to meet your Mum and Dad.'

My eyes nearly bulge to twice their size. What kind of teenage boyfriend wants to meet the parents?

'You know,' he wiggles his eyebrows. 'So they can see I'm not going to lead you astray.'

I smile coyly. 'I have a feeling that's exactly what you intend to do.'

He winks at me, causing butterflies almost to escape out of my stomach. But quickly, I have to think of a reason for him not to come in.

'But seriously...my parents are really strict. They don't want me dating anyone.'

'Shit, so I'm your dirty little secret?' he grins.

I grimace apologetically. 'Kind of.'

'Okay, fine, but I'll watch you go in.'

Jesus, this guy and his manners are going to fuck up my lie. Why can't he just fuck off?

I start backing away from him. 'You don't have to do that. This is a safe street.' Unlike where I actually live...

He smiles back and waits for me to get to the front door. Oh, sweet Jesus. What am I going to do? I can't just knock on this stranger's door, can I?

I smile back as confidently as I can and rummage around in my bag for an entirety, searching for a key. I get one out and fumble around with it like I'm going to put it in the lock. Why is he still here?

'Bye!' I wave, turning back to the door again.

I can feel him standing still and watching me. Dear God. He really won't leave until I get in the door. I'm going to have to knock on this stranger's door.

I turn back around. 'Forgot my key,' I laugh, shrugging like I'm such a buffoon. 'You should really go. I don't want to get in trouble.'

He nods but doesn't move. Fuck my life!

I'm going to have to do it. Knock on the stranger's door. I knock—sweat beginning to trickle down my spine. Why won't he just leave?

A man in his forties with salt and pepper hair opens the door. Shit. I have to follow through now.

'Hi!' I shriek, pushing past him so violently I almost knock him down.

'Sorry? Who the hell are you?' he asks as he thankfully shuts the door.

'I'm sorry, but I have to just stay here for a minute.'

He puts his hands on his hips. 'Why on earth should I let you stay?'

'Because...because...' Shit Savannah, think of something! 'I think I'm being followed.'

'As in a potential attacker?' he asks, eyes wide with horror.

'Err...potentially?'

'Well, then we should call the police.'

'No!' I wave my hands wildly around. 'I'm sure if we just hide here for a minute he'll be gone.'

He puts his hands on his hips again. 'Is this a trick? Is a friend of yours attempting to break in around the back

297

while you distract me?'

'No! Of course not!'

'Because I watch Rip Off Britain and I'm not being taken for a fool.' He grabs my shoulders and guides me towards the door. 'Go on—get out of here. We don't want riff-raff like you around here.'

'No! I'm not riff-raff. I used to live here!'

'Whatever, scammer.' He opens the door and pushes me out. Luckily Zach is nowhere to be seen, thank God. Now I just have to hobble two miles out of my way to get home. Yay.

Chapter Seventeen

Tuesday 8th November

#Don'tBeLate

That night I lay in bed wishing my life were different. Why can't I still be living in that house? I only had a quick chance to glance around while I was there, but I saw that he'd painted it a god awful Moroccan orange colour. If only I could win the lottery and buy it back, all of my problems would be over.

The phone rings, pulling me out of my daydream. I race to the phone, pathetically hoping it's Zach. I'm surprised when I see it's Zahra. We don't often talk on the phone. She's more of a texter.

'Hey, Zahra.'

'Hey,' she says as she breathes out what sounds like cigarette smoke.

'What's up?' I ask, curious.

'I just hate my life, that's all,' she says between puffs.

'Why, hun, what's happened?' I ask trying to sound like I don't have a clue. It's pretty obvious it has something to do with Luke.

'One of the girls must have told you what happened on Saturday.'

'No...Well, I...'

'You don't have to bother lying. Even if they hadn't you must have heard the whispers around school.'

'Ok, I've heard,' I admit. 'I'm so sorry, babe. I can't believe what a dick he's being.' My previous annoyance at her behaviour disappears. When it all boils down to it, she's my friend, and I'll protect her no matter what.

'That's the thing. Out of all the people, you knew what a dick he was. You knew he was capable of this kind of embarrassment, but I refused to listen to you. I just got swept away by anyone who would give me a second glance. I just feel like such a stupid, reckless slut.' She breaks into a bit of a sob. She never cries.

'Don't be stupid. I understand how you must have

felt. I'm sorry if I was mean to you about it. I don't mean to be a judging bitch—it's just in my nature.'

She laughs, making me feel better.

'Thanks for making me feel better, but I don't deserve it. Anyway, it's over and done with now. Everyone will be talking about something else in a few days. Then you can just move on and forget this ever happened.' I doubt it will be over that quickly, but I have to give her something.

'That's just the thing,' she says sobbing into the phone. 'I can't just forget about it.'

'Why not?'

'Because...oh God I don't even think I can tell you.' Why does she sound so hysterical?

'Yes, just tell me,' I say, a trace of frustration coming across.

'I...I...My Mum washed my jeans with the morning after pill in it. So...I never took it,' she says quickly.

My own silence is deafening.

'And now my period's late.'

Shit.

Wednesday 9th November

We'd decided to meet at her house in the morning and get the bus into town to get a pregnancy test. Zahra had taken about 10 minutes to calm down. At least that means she's taking this seriously.

We walk down the high street and go into Boots. We'd ideally have liked to buy loads of things so that the test could be nestled in between them discreetly, but with limited funds between us, it looks like we can only buy that. Especially when we see the price of them!

We casually walk past the family planning aisle, trying to crane our necks to find them. The first few times we only see condoms. A bit too late for them I think. The third time we spot them and Zahra grabs the first one she sees, panicking. The lady stacking shelves starts to look at us with raised eyebrows, clearly judging us.

I look over at Zahra and wink, signalling to play along.

'The thing is,' I say, changing my accent to a common one, 'even if I am preggers, I just don't know who the dad could be.'

The lady's ears prick up, and the shock shows on her pink face.

'Wasn't it Greg? Or was it Tim? Or it could always be Charlotte's dad?' Zahra teases.

The lady is looking over now, averting her gaze when we catch hers.

'I just don't know.' I pretend to chew gum loudly. 'Either way, I might just have it anyway. I've always fancied a baby. I mean you can get loads of benefits and a flat and stuff can't you.' It's hard to keep a straight face.

'Yeah,' Zahra nods, but now I can see her expression changing and she's getting back to her current situation and worrying.

I grab hold of her hand and give it a reassuring squeeze. 'Don't worry. It'll be fine.'

She smiles meekly. We pay for it, double checking that no one we know is in the shop. We have to pay in coins and just about have enough. How embarrassing. We can't afford the bus home now, but at least we'll know.

We walk straight to the nearest McDonald's and head for the toilets. She decides she wants to go into the cubicle by herself and I'm secretly glad. My head is still spinning from all of it. Everything is running through my mind. What if she is pregnant? Will she want to have an abortion? Will she want to keep it? Either one will have an enormous impact on her life. And her strict Azerbaijani parents! They'll have a fucking shit fit.

How will I feel if she wants an abortion? I've always been against them, but now it's one of my friends I can totally understand why people make that decision.

I hear her pee and do a little prayer. Come on God—help us out here.

My phone rings and I nearly jump out of my skin. I reach for my bag, hoping it isn't my mum bollocking me for bunking school again, but the name that flashes up is Zach!

'Hi. How are you?'

Zahra starts screaming. 'It's negative. It's negative! I'm not pregnant! Thank god!' She jumps out of the cubicle, completely forgetting I'm on the phone.

I wave my hands in the air trying to remind her I'm on the phone.

She mouths *'shit'* and calms herself down.

I reach the phone back to my ear to hear him say 'did someone just say pregnant?'

I laugh nervously. 'Of course not,' I snort, laughing hysterically. 'I'm just in McDonald's at the moment, and there's a crowd of girls in here gossiping.'

'Oh yeah, bunking school are we?' he asks, teasing me.

'Well, it's a long story. Anyway, do you want to do something this week?'

I'm not normally this forward, but I'll do anything just to get him off the phone at this point. My stomach is doing somersaults, and I need to talk to Zahra.

'Yeah, what about tonight?' he asks, catching me off guard.

'Tonight?' I repeat. 'Will your mum let you out on a Tuesday?'

He laughs. 'Yeah, I'm a big boy now. I even dress myself and everything. Will your parents be ok with it?'

'Oh, um...I just remembered you can't come around mine. My parents have friends around.'

'Oh, well, then why don't you come round mine?' he asks in a cheeky tone.

Damn. Why did I tell him that?

'Yeah, but my Nan will probably want me home at a reasonable time,' I add quickly. 'Well, I have to go. So should I come round about seven-thirty, yeah?'

'See you then.'

'Bye.'

I'm already having a panic attack. Is he going to expect sex tonight? Or if not tonight, then very soon? I don't know if I'm ready for that. I haven't even told him I'm still a virgin. I wonder how that's going to go down.

It's Zahra's turn to comfort me, as I nearly hyperventilate. I have no time to get everything done. I have to wash my hair, shave my legs, find something to wear, decide on what we can talk about. God, the pressure is crushing my chest and making my head spin.

When I've calmed myself down, I help Zahra jump around McDonald's toilet in joy that there is no bastard baby in her tummy. Thank God for that. I don't think I'd have been able to cope, let alone Zahra.

We walk back towards home, which thanks to having no bus money takes the best part of an hour, but in that time we make a plan. I'll get in the shower as soon as I get back. By then Zahra would have text through an outfit suggestion. I kiss her goodbye—so glad we don't have to welcome a baby into our group.

When I get out of the shower, I get changed into a matching bra and knickers set and moisturise my body from head to toe. If we do end up getting naked tonight, I want to look good.

I apply fake tan as well as I can and then get changed into Zahra's strangely sensible outfit choice. I'm in jeans and cute sneakers, but with a nice white off the shoulder t-shirt that clings in all the right places. It seems to make my boobs look big (well bigger than they are anyway) and you can see the faint line of the stripy pattern on my purple and pink bra. It's enticing enough while at the same time being simple.

I blow dry my hair to within an inch of its life, almost burning it in the process, and then straighten it. I do my makeup like my outfit. Flirty and playful, but not full on glamour. Zahra wears eye shadow even to school, but I can't seem to wear it without looking like a drag queen. I just put on some bronzer and blusher. Then lashings of mascara and a pale pink melon-flavoured lip balm.

By the time I finish I'm horrified to realise it's already seven. I beg Nan to drop me round and make it just in time.

He greets me at the door, his dazzling smile almost making me pass out. He guides me into his cosy sitting room. I'm just starting to relax when his front door bangs. I freeze.

'It's just my mum. She's been dying to meet you,' he says, practically beaming.

He's been talking about me?

'Oh, ok,' I nod, feeling nervous. I was expecting to discuss my virginity and maybe get a bit naked—not meet his bloody mother.

'She'll love you, don't worry.' How can he read my thoughts like that? He gives me a little squeeze round the waist.

'Hiiiii,' she says, opening the door.

I quickly straighten my clothes and check my nails are clean. I must look so rough and common compared to his previous girlfriends. I bet Amelia is from a rich family. Bitch.

'Hi Mum, this is Savannah,' he says, presenting me proudly.

I look up and smile at her, but not for long. Staring back at me with the same horrified expression is the lady from Boots today. The lady that Zahra and I acted like idiots around. The woman I had pretended I might be pregnant around. Oh God, I pretended I didn't know who the father was. Just in case I'm the smallest bit unsure it's her, I can see her Boots uniform underneath her coat.

Kill me. Kill me now.

'Hi,' I attempt weakly, desperately trying to pull myself together.

'Hi,' she says, reserved. 'Very nice to meet you' she adds coldly.

I can see Zach look a bit confused by her reaction, but he ignores it.

'Mum, can you have a quick look at Savannah's ankle? She had an accident the other day, and it's still quite swollen.'

Oh god, why did he have to bring that up? The last thing I want to do is show this woman my ankle. And it's not even still swollen, is it? Does he think I have fat ankles?

'Ok,' she sighs begrudgingly. 'Let me see it.'

I pull my foot out of my sneaker and show it to her, while at the same time trying to plead with her in my eyes not to say anything to Zach.

She holds my foot in her cold, perfectly manicured hands. She rotates it around slightly, and I wince when it causes pain to shoot up my leg.

'Are you able to walk on it?' she asks, still looking at the foot and not at me.

'Yes,' I say, trying to sound polite. The fact that she's still trying to rotate my foot is making me want to kick her in the face.

'Yes, it looks sprained. I'll go and get you a foot bandage.'

She returns a little while later with the bandage and to

my surprise puts it on me. It makes me feel so uncomfortable for her to be putting it on me like this. The tension in the air can be cut with a knife, but Zach seems oblivious to it. Typical guy.

'Keep it raised and ice it when you go home,' she says, before quickly leaving.

'There, all better,' Zach says giving me a wink.

He leans in to give me a quick kiss, but I hold onto him and kiss him back forcibly. I remind myself to make the most of this beautiful person. For all I know his mum is about to tell him about the Boots incident. He'll be put off me forever.

Chapter Eighteen

Friday 11th November

#Metal

After meeting his Mum, I didn't feel comfortable bringing up my virginity with Zach, but luckily he seemed content with just cuddling up and watching TV. Tonight is Shane's gig, and we're all excited to see them play.

'We don't have to go in if you don't fancy it,' Zach says, holding my hand.

Why is he being moody?

'No. I'm looking forward to it,' I reply, ignoring his gloomy expression and looking ahead at the pub, a thrill of excitement running through my spine.

'Yeah, come on, Zach, it will be fun,' Zahra says,

skipping in front, her boobs bouncing in her black satin Basque.

'£5 entry,' the tattooed bald man says at the door, pointing to a sign stating the same.

We hand over our money while trying not to attract any attention to ourselves. He stamps our hands with a black star and waves us in without asking our age.

We easily get served at the bar and settle in to listen to the first band. I wouldn't really call it a band or even music really. It's more just a noise; just a lot of screaming and jumping up and down.

I keep glancing at Zach's glum face, annoyed that he can't just even pretend he's having fun. Everyone else is chatting and smiling while he just looks awkward. His body is rigid, but he'll smile when I look at him, a smile that doesn't reach his eyes. What's going on with him?

'Just try and have fun,' I beg him, squeezing his hand.

He dazzles me with his smile, and I can see him trying, but it annoys me that I even have to ask.

By the time Shane's band, No Smoking Fireworks, comes on, I'm drunk. I grab hold of Zahra and Kate and run them down to the front of the crowd. Shane waves at us as they start singing something about *'partying like it was 1999.'* I find it easy to sway along to.

We start to get into the spirit and dance around like maniacs, even head banging to the rockier tunes, swishing our hair back and forward in time to the music. The guys join in with us too. All apart from Zach.

I look around and love the mix of people here tonight. There's a girl with blue hair and tattoos covering all of her arms and next to her is a girl with three piercings on her face. They're dancing and singing along, not caring what they look like. When they catch my eye, they smile and nod, unlike most bitches who would scowl at you.

I love the atmosphere; everyone is only interested in the music, not what they look like. Everyone except Zach. Where is he?

I jump up and down to see over the crowd, only seeming to encourage everyone to do the same. I try to jump higher and spot him still at the bar, looking miserable.

I dance on over to him, concerned that he may be ill.

'Hey, what's wrong?' I ask.

'Nothing,' he shrugs, not meeting my eyes. 'It's just that rock music really isn't my thing.'

'I know, but I thought you'd still *try* and have fun.

Loads of us aren't into rock, but this music is okay, don't you think?'

'I suppose,' he shrugs, with a face like a spoilt brat.

'Can't you just get pissed and have a dance around anyway?' I point towards the dance floor at the others. I spot Heath jumping up and down like a loon and Erin head banging with a stranger who now seems to be her new best friend. I smile at how carefree they can be.

'I've tried, but I can't. I'm sorry, but I'm gonna go. I'll call you soon though, yeah?' he says with a fake smile on his face. He's clearly only humouring me.

'Yeah, of course,' I mumble, letting him kiss me on the cheek. Why is he being such a killjoy?

Once he leaves, I really let my hair down. Now I don't have to babysit my boyfriend, I can just enjoy the night. I carry on dancing with the others and meet Erin's new friend Sebastian. He's got long brown, typical metal hair, but when he speaks, I'm shocked to hear that he's incredibly posh and well-spoken.

'Would you guys like some shots?' he asks, heading towards the bar.

'Yeah!' they all squeal in unison.

'Not for me thanks,' I say shaking my head. The

memory from last New Year's Eve is too fresh in my mind. I'd done one shot and ended up pole dancing on a lamppost. Not my finest hour.

'Oh, don't be a misery, Sav,' Tyler laughs.

'Yeah, you don't want to be like your boyfriend, do you?' Heath asks, smiling sarcastically.

I don't like how he's having a go about Zach, but realise that I had thought the exact same thing a mere ten minutes ago.

'Oh, shut up.' I dig him in the ribs.

Sebastian returns from the bar with different flavoured vodka shots.

I choose one called pear drop but pause with it in my hand. I watch the others do theirs without hesitation. They all chug them back without a care in the world. Even Kate seems to be able to do it.

'Come on, Sav, you lightweight,' Erin teases.

I look at the tiny shot in my hand. What real damage can this tiny thing really do? I try not to think logically and throw it back. The taste is disgusting, but it's drowned out by the cheers from everyone. I hold the glass over my head victoriously.

'To tonight!'

Saturday 12th November

I open my eyes, feeling as if they've only been shut for a second, to see that I'm in a bed. I look around and try to work out where I am. I notice the green curtains and the familiar smell, but can't place it.

I sit upright and wish I hadn't. My head is banging. I lay back down again, closing my eyes to try and block out the spinning room.

I open my eyes again and see enough to realise that I'm definitely in Heath's bedroom. I feel down my body and see that I'm fully clothed, thank God. But where the hell is Heath? And why am I here?

The door creaks open and Heath appears with two cups of tea. My hero.

'Hey, sleepyhead. How you feeling?' he says smiling smugly, like he knew exactly how bad I'd be feeling.

'Terrible,' I answer. I sound so moody as if I'm blaming him. 'Why am I here? What happened?' I croak. My throat feels raw, and I have a funny taste in my mouth.

'You don't remember then? Damn, I owe Tyler a fiver,' he chuckles.

I think for a moment, trying to scan back a memory. I remember doing the pear drop shot. I push the thought to the back of my mind as the memory of the smell is making my stomach churn. I remember having a drink with Shane and the gang.

'Zahra getting off with Shane. I remember that and then it all goes black,' I admit, still desperately trying to remember something after this.

He laughs arrogantly. God, why does he have to be so pompous at a time like this?

'Well, you were pretty wasted. So I guess you don't remember jumping up on stage dancing and trying to do a stage dive.' He laughs at the memory.

'No, I didn't, you liar! Tell me the truth.'

But I have a terrible feeling this is the truth. My whole body kind of aches a little bit.

He laughs and hands me his phone to show a picture of me dancing on stage. Oh god, the horror.

'So once we'd picked you up, which was a mission on its own as everyone was 'moshing', you proceeded to get sick: on the dance floor, in the toilets, in the taxi coming home. You just couldn't stop. The taxi guy threw us out three streets away, and we had to walk the rest.'

'Oh no.' I recoil at the slight hazy memory that's coming through. I put my hands up to my face trying to block out the memory.

I run my hands through my hair and notice that a bit of it is clumped together. I pull it closer to see it's dried sick. *Gross*. Thank God Zach went home.

'We knew that we couldn't take you back home as your mum would go mad, so we decided to bring you back here while you recovered, as my Mum and Steve were out at a menu tasting thing for the wedding.'

'Thanks.' My stomach churns and vomit rises in my throat.

'I actually still feel a bit sick now,' I admit, feeling shaky.

Yes, it's coming. I run to the toilet and make it just in time to hit the toilet bowl. I don't have time to shut the door, and Heath is behind me, pulling my hair out of the way before I can stop him.

This is the last thing I need—him seeing me vomit.

'Please just go away,' I plead in between spewing. 'I don't want you to see me like this.'

'Just shut up and be sick will you,' he snaps, sounding irritated but still holding my hair for me.

318

I'm too weak to fight back. My whole body is being thrown around from the alcohol that is rejecting itself from my body. I'm so sick that I wonder if my actual stomach lining will come up soon. Even though I hate getting sick, I hope that it'll stop the banging in my head. If not, I think I'd actually prefer death.

After a while, I eventually stop. I still hold myself over the toilet bowl as I don't trust myself to leave it.

'Have you stopped now?' he asks, still collecting loose strands of my hair and bringing it back to the ponytail he's created with his other hand.

'I think so,' I croak, my body still shaking violently.

'Do you wanna go back to my room for a sleep?' he asks, looking seriously at my face, which I've no doubt is as white as a sheet.

'I don't think I can leave this bathroom,' I admit, my head still leaning over the bowl. 'I'm scared I'll get sick again.'

'I could get a bowl for you or something?' He turns me round to face him and releases my hair.

'No, I honestly don't think I can leave here.' I feel like I want to collapse. 'I might just lay here for a while.' I stretch out onto the cool tiles. They feel nice against my

319

hot, sweaty body.

'Okay, do you want me to get you anything?' he asks, starting to get up.

I grab hold of his arm a little too desperately. 'Please don't leave me,' I beg, sounding like a child. I don't care; I'm scared. I've never felt this ill in my life, and I'm a little bit scared that I may be dying. I don't think that's dramatic at all.

'Okay,' he nods. He stands up, and for a second I worry that he's already breaking his promise and will leave me here to die. I reach out for him again with a pathetic groan.

'Don't panic,' he says quickly, seeing the look on my face.

He grabs two towels and comes back to me on the floor. One he folds and puts under my head as a cushion and the other he throws over us as a blanket.

He lies down next to me, pulling my hair off my face and feeling my forehead. I have my eyes already closed, trying to block out the spinning and trying to think calming thoughts. I feel him wrap his free arm around me as I start to drift off into a dreamless sleep.

###

'Heath?' I hear someone call.

I open my eyes to see Heath's mum Karen standing at the door of the bathroom with a confused look on her face. I'm still on the floor with Heath wrapped around me and the towel over us.

I'm suddenly aware that I have vomit in my hair and close my eyes tight, trying to pretend this isn't happening.

Heath stirs and jumps when he opens his eyes and sees his Mum.

'Oh, Mum...hi,' he smiles, getting up and pulling the towel off me in the process.

'What the hell is going on?' she asks, more puzzled than angry.

'What time is it?' he asks, ignoring the question and letting a yawn escape.

'It's 4 pm,' she says, getting a little irritated now.

'Wow,' I gasp, before thinking. I sit up to realise that I no longer feel the room spinning. My stomach is still unsettled, and my head is still fuzzy, but I'm better.

'Hi, Karen.' I look more at the floor than her.

'Hi, Savannah. Are you ill?' she asks, scanning me from head to toe.

Ah, she's obviously noticed that I'm in the same clothes as the night before and that they have vomit stains all over them.

'A little bit,' I admit. The understatement of the year.

'Yeah, she must have got her drink spiked or something,' Heath attempts, trying to lie for me.

'There's no need to lie, kids,' Karen snaps. 'I can see from Savannah's ashamed expression that this is her own doing.'

'I'm sorry,' I say again, feeling like a massive inconvenience.

'Don't be silly,' she says, suddenly warming up. 'Me and your mum have got in far worse states.'

Her being nice to me makes a sudden heat build up in my throat and tears burn my eyes. A few tears escape, and I wonder why I'm crying. It's like her being nice to me is too much to bear.

'What's wrong?' she asks, kneeling down to me on the floor and wrapping me into a cuddle.

'I'm sorry. I'm just so embarrassed, and I still feel so ill. Please don't be angry with Heath. He just didn't want to upset my mum.'

I look over to him and see that he's totally

uncomfortable with this situation. He looks like he's debating whether or not to leave the room.

'I'm not angry with him,' she says smiling, 'and your mum won't be angry with you either. We were young once too you know.' I just sniff in response. 'Come on. I'll call your mum and tell her I'm dropping you off. Go and get your things.'

I stand up and walk with Heath to his room. I search around for my shoes and handbag with no idea as to where they could be. Heath gets them from the back of his door and hands them to me. I put my shoes on as Heath pulls some tracksuit bottoms on over his boxers.

I can hear Karen on the phone to my mum, telling her that I'm safe and sharing idle neighbourhood gossip.

I lie down on the bed, sure that they'll be on the phone for a while. Heath lies down next to me, and I wrap my arms round him. He pulls me closer until we're completely chest-to-chest. I want to say thank you for looking after me, but I'm too exhausted for words. I don't worry anyway as it's like he knows. He doesn't interject with a joke—we just lie there.

His mum eventually drives me home.

'Send my love to your mum won't you?' she says as she

pulls up outside my house.

Heath and me look at each other, both thinking that they've already done that with the thirty-minute phone call. I smile at him, and he responds by smacking my thigh playfully.

I go in the house to face the wrath of my mum. Before she has a chance to find me I run into my bedroom and open up my email. A blog update from Dylan pops up.

DYLAN'S BLOG - FRASIER ISLAND...just...WOW

So since the last update, I went to the beach and got horrifically sunburnt. Scorched would probably be a better word. I was literally untouchable—even my lips got scorched. Since then I think I've lost about two stone in weight from peeling skin. So I was a bit miserable for a few days, that and someone stole 200 bucks out of my wallet while I was asleep.

For Halloween, we went to the local bar. They had a live covers band and people actually dressed up really well.

Then we travelled to Rainbow beach for the Frasier Island trip we won a few weeks ago. Fuck me, how they got the name Rainbow beach, I don't know. It was like the scene in Euro trip when the get man trucker drops them off in the middle of that shitty town. It was grey, run down and tiny, and in the middle of nowhere. We looked down what they were cheeky enough to call the 'main strip'. It had (exact list) a travel agent, a hostel, a bottle shop, a cafe, a supermarket (corner shop) and a surf shop. That's it.

The hostel we were staying at, well, it was somewhere between a shed and a barn. I didn't do a very good job at making friends when we sat down to watch a film with some people.

'What film are you guys watching?'

'Marley and me.'

'Oh, isn't that the one where the dog dies in the end, and they end up crying for twenty minutes?'

'Well, I've never seen it before but thanks for telling us the end.'

'Oh, sorry.'

Also, I fell out with a French bastard who rudely told Adrianna to SHHHHH!!! I nearly walked over to him to tell him to shut the fuck up.

The next day we set off to Frasier Island. I cannot explain how awesome this trip was. It is basically a sand island uninhabited by humans with wild dogs everywhere. We drove down the beach with nothing but the horizon in front of us and swam in lakes with water that was soooo clear you were actually allowed to drink it. We walked down a river through the rainforest, looking up at the rainforest from the lake and looking down at the fish swimming between your feet. Then we walked to a place with loads of catfish and stuff. If you stay still for a bit, little fish come up and eat the dead skin off you. And with how much I was peeling they had a bloody buffet. We went camping and every so often a wild dog (dingo) would wander over to see what you were up to.

Anyway, running out of time right now so gotta go. We are heading back to Noosa tomorrow for work and stuff.

Speak soon xxx

Chapter Nineteen

Monday 14th November - Ski Trip

#AustriaSkiTrip2016

I can't believe the ski trip has come around so quickly, but I have to admit that I'm looking forward to the break. What I won't admit so easily is that I can't wait to spend the week with Heath and not Zach. How terrible am I? I have this hot boyfriend who's really into me, and I'm totally taking him for granted just because Charlotte put some stupid idea into my head.

I'm barely on the coach when Heath pushes Erin playfully out of the way and sits himself down next to me.

'Hey, Sav, you stoked for skiing or what?'

'Ooh, yeah, *stoked*,' I joke back sarcastically.

He grins. 'Still got your hangover, have you?'

'Sssh!' I hiss through my teeth. 'Don't be telling anyone about that. It was embarrassing enough without the entire school knowing what a total lightweight I am.'

'Don't worry,' he smiles, his eyes lighting his whole face up. 'Your secret's safe with me.'

I look around for Erin and see that she's sat across from us with Zahra.

'Are you seriously planning on sitting next to me for the next twenty or so hours?' I ask Heath. I don't think my stomach can handle the pressure.

'Yeah, why? Is it because you're scared you'll annoy me?' He grabs my head and ruffles my hair into a mess. 'Silly, Savvy! You won't annoy me.'

'Yeah,' I deadpan. 'That's exactly what I'm worried about. Me annoying *you*.'

'So did your Mum go mad when you went back home looking like Casper the friendly ghost?'

'Hardly,' I snort. 'They all thought it was hilarious. Couldn't stop laughing and then Nan insisted on taking pictures of me and uploading them to Facebook with a *first hangover* tag line.'

Heath bursts out laughing.

'Nan's should not be allowed on Facebook.'

'I bloody love that woman,' he chuckles.

'But seriously,' I admit shyly, 'thanks for looking after me. No doubt with my luck I'd have choked on my own vomit if left alone.'

'No doubt,' he grins.

It's going to be one hell of a long coach ride.

Austria is bloody amazing! The twenty-four-hour coach trip however, not so much. Although I can't lie and say, I didn't enjoy my time with Heath. It was great to have him all to myself like that. It feels forever since it's just been the two of us.

Regardless of any fake feelings I have for him at the moment, it's nice to have my friend back. But...well I did fall asleep on his shoulder at one point. I vaguely remember stirring awake and seeing him stroking my hair. Just like I used to make him do when he was younger. Only now he's not doing it because I'm threatening to flush his action man down the toilet. He's doing it because he wants to. And yes, when I woke up, and he was still sleeping, I did take some time to gaze at him and take full advantage of being so close. I still can't believe he got so beautiful before my very eyes and I just seemed to miss it.

The hotel we're staying at looks like it's stuck in the eighties. It definitely needs a refurbish, but I suppose it's fine. As my Mum would say, it's clean at least. The rooms have between two and five people so us girls are lucky enough to have a room to ourselves with our own bathroom. But that still means one bathroom for five girls. Yeah, it can get a bit stressful in the mornings.

Yesterday was our first proper full day so we hit the slopes. I'm surprisingly better at skiing than I thought I would be. Although, I'm obviously on the beginner slopes, and it helps that our instructor is hot.

The scariest thing is those bloody chairlift things that you have to throw yourself onto in the hope that you catch it in time. Then you're just left bloody dangling over cliffs, hanging on for dear life while you pray to god it doesn't break down.

I'm knackered. I thought it would be more me sitting in a ski lodge sipping on hot chocolate, but apparently, that's frowned upon. The actual skiing part is one-part terrifying and one-part exhilarating! Feeling the cold wind whip past your face as the sun beams down on you so brightly you feel you could touch it...well it's really something else!

Today we've all gone ice-skating in town. I don't know how to skate either so I'm left holding onto the sides like a bloody idiot while everyone else whizzes past me shouting loser. Happy bastards. I don't expect to be good at everything, but I mean, come on! At least *something*.

I've managed to avoid Amelia until today. She keeps skating round and glaring at me, but she also has a strange smirk on her face. Like she knows something I don't. It's really unnerving.

What the hell could she have on me apart from thinking Zach is going to dump me? I spoke to him briefly on Facetime last night, and he seemed fine.

Heath and the girls skate over to me. Heath smirks like he finds me hilarious.

'You okay, bambi?'

'Oh, shut up,' I snap. I know I must look like a fool, but he's not helping.

'Come on,' Erin laughs, grabbing my arm. 'We're gonna teach you.'

Kate grabs my other arm off the side, giggling like she's finding me hilarious.

The girls and Heath surround me from the front and back shouting encouragement, drawing attention from everyone. How humiliating. I'm actually shaking from nerves.

'Told you you'd get it soon, Sav,' Heath smiles, practically beaming with pride.

Ice is suddenly sprayed over me. I look up to see that Amelia has skidded to a stop in front of us and is standing in our way, hand on her hip, glaring at me.

'Excuse me,' Erin says loudly.

'Savannah,' Amelia snarls. 'I'm so sorry to hear about your circumstances.'

Circumstances? What the hell is she talking about?

'Sorry?'

'About your house.' She pouts her lips, faking sympathy.

Oh no. Please tell me she doesn't know where I live now. Not her. Not in front of the girls.

'What's she going on about?' Zahra asks, pushing herself forward.

'No idea,' I shrug. 'Come on, let's just ignore her.'

I attempt to move, but no one moves with me.

'Oh no.' She places her fingers over her mouth in mock

332

shock. 'Don't tell me your friends don't know?'

'Don't know what?' Charlotte asks.

'Nothing,' I insist, attempting to look as confident as possible.

'That she no longer lives in Munden Road.'

There's a huge collective gasp.

She decides to carry on—happy she's getting the reaction she wanted. 'That her parents are now poor, making her poor. She now lives in Crapstone.'

'Crapstone?' Kate repeats in horror. She turns to me. 'What the hell is she talking about, Sav?'

I gulp down the bile threatening to escape from my throat.

'Err...I don't know.'

'I think it's time to tell them now,' Heath says, placing his hand on my shoulder.

'You mean *you* knew about this?' Zahra gasps in disbelief. 'Who else bloody knew this?'

'How could you keep this from us?' Charlotte asks, hurt radiating from her voice.

'Yeah,' Kate nods, frowning at me. 'I thought we were friends, and now I find out you've been lying to us this whole time. What the fuck, Savannah?'

333

'I'm...I'm sorry,' I mumble, looking down at the floor.

'Sorry to be the bearer of bad news,' Amelia says, turning and skating away.

Yeah, I'm sure you are, you snidey bitch.

'This is bullshit!' Zahra explodes. 'What the fuck is wrong with you, Sav? Why on earth would you do that? Don't you trust us?'

'I do! I'm sorry.'

'I can't even look at you right now,' she snaps back. Charlotte folds her arms across her chest.

This is it. I've lost them. Lost them because I was too ashamed to admit I'm poor now. I have to get out of here. Away from their judging stares.

I turn and exit the ice, attempting to run further away. Only I forgot to remove my skates so I have to do a sort of hop/run thing. I'm sure I must look like a constipated giraffe. That is until I feel my ankle twist to the right before my leg has time to react. Searing pain rockets up my leg from my ankle. Fuck! I go down like a tonne of bricks.

But I don't want their sympathy. I jump up and use the adrenaline coursing through my body push myself on.

I don't stop limping until I'm back at the coach.

'Sav! Wait up!'

I turn to see Heath running after me. Bless him; he does care.

'Are you okay?' His liquid chocolate eyes bore into mine as if desperately trying to soothe away my pain.

'Of course I'm not okay!' I shout, pushing against his chest. His strong, broad chest. 'My whole life just fucking fell apart, *and* I've fucked my ankle.' I have no idea why I'm being so horrible to him.

He sighs with a crooked smile on his face. Why the hell is he smiling right now?

'I think you'll find, drama queen, that your world fell apart the day your Mum told you that you were moving. It's been you that's chosen to keep it from your mates.'

God, I hate when he's right. He can be so smug about it.

'Yeah, I know,' I shrug, my throat clogging up with emotion. 'It's all my fault. I'm a shit person.'

I am. Not only have I lied to my friends, I've lied to my boyfriend. Who I've also failed to mention to, that I might be developing feelings for my best friend.

I look up at him, struggling to keep my emotions in check.

He rolls his eyes but takes my hand. I watch as his

fingers close around mine, the connection restored between us.

'You're not a shit person, Sav. You just fucked up. They'll all forgive you.'

I nod, feeling the warmth in his voice settle over my frayed nerves.

'Will they, though? I'm not sure I'd forgive me.'

'Seriously, Sav, take a breath.' He takes hold of my upper arms. 'You're fine. It's all going to be fine.' He squeezes my shoulders. It's over in a second, but the spark leaves a tingling sensation all the way down my arms.

'I just...I'm so embarrassed,' I admit on a sob, a big fat tear trickling down my cheek. 'Why am I such a dick?'

He grabs me and forces me into a hug. 'You're not a dick.' I close my eyes and drink it in, his smell, his warmth. He kisses the top of my head while I let it all out. I need a good sob. 'You're just a bit of a div.'

I laugh, despite the tears. 'Thanks,' I snarl sarcastically, with a smile.

'Come on. We'll wait on the bus.'

What would I do without him?

'I can't face them. I just can't.' Just thinking of their disappointed faces.

336

'Don't worry. We'll hide at the back. Erin's probably calming them down anyway.'

He helps me onto the bus and wraps me in his arms, knowing I need the comfort. It's the first time we've been this cuddly in what feels like years. I've missed it. It feels nice, really nice. His scent envelops me. There's no strength left in me to resist it—no willpower to pull away from this highly inappropriate behaviour for a girl with a boyfriend. Instead, I allow myself to melt into it completely, moulding against his body.

Who knew something disastrous could turn out to be okay because it's brought me closer to Heath? I've always known he was caring but what I haven't admitted to myself before is how attracted to him I am. And I am. I feel drawn to him like a magnet as if I have no control of it myself at all.

The others start to infiltrate back onto the bus. I'm lucky that I don't see them.

'You can come back to our room when we get back. Build up some courage before you face them.'

I look into his deep brown eyes. There's so much sincerity there. 'Thanks.'

Heath was true to his word. He took me to his room, and the boys cheered me up. Tyler told me he'd still talk to me even though I'm poor now, which did make me laugh. That's what I love about guys. They're so easy. They understood why I didn't tell them and they were over it. My ankle has swollen up to twice its size so they've got ice from the bar and fussed over me.

They cheered me up enough to go and speak to the girls. They all waved me off dramatically making me laugh. I go down the long hallway and knock at the door because Erin had the key.

Kate answers the door. Her expression relaxes when she spots me. 'Thank God, I've been worried sick!'

She grabs me into a cuddle. I'm so shocked I can't even react. I just let her hug me. She pulls back, and it's then I see the others sat on the bunk beds.

'I'm so sorry,' I admit despondently. 'I only didn't tell you because I was ashamed.'

'We understand,' Charlotte admits on a sigh. 'I'm just upset you thought we'd judge you. As if.'

'I can't believe that bitch was the one who told us,' Zahra growls. 'She's such a nasty twat.'

338

'I hate her, but it was my fault. I shouldn't have let her have that over me.'

Erin nods. 'Let's just forget it now and carry on enjoying ourselves, yeah? Us being fine will just annoy her even more.'

CHAPTER TWENTY

#PartyHard

They always say things look better in the morning and today they truly do. Last night they took us bowling and although people kept coming up to me asking if it was true—if I really was living in Crapstone—it actually wasn't that bad. Most people were sympathetic, and I managed to laugh about what a nightmare my life is. Every time I managed to tell someone the truth I saw Amelia get more pissed off.

Today I've lived the dream and rested my foot in the ski lodge cafe. The fire was roaring next to me, warming me through, and I had a hot chocolate with marshmallows in my hand. You'd think I would have been lonely on my own with the others skiing, but it was actually nice to just be alone with my thoughts.

Zach tried to call me last night, but I let it go to voicemail. I know Amelia would have got to him by now and I can't bear facing him being pissed off at me. I've decided I'm going to deal with it when I get home.

Tonight we're at a crappy disco they've put on for us. The foreign DJ has been playing a lot of Abba and nothing that has been released in the last two years.

Us lot have already agreed we're heading back to the boys' room afterwards for our own party. The legal age for drinking over here is fifteen, so we managed to club together and buy a bottle of vodka.

The lights finally turn on, and we go up to the boys' room. Heath gets the bottle out of the wardrobe, and we fill up the plastic cups we stole from downstairs.

'Finally, a party we can relax at,' I say with a sigh, leaning back on Jesse's bunk bed.

The next few hours are filled with gossip, giggles, and fun. I'd love to live with this lot full time. There's so much less drama than with my whole family trying to squeeze into one bathroom every morning.

I'm quite drunk when I decide to climb up onto the top

bunk bed, knowing full well it's where Heath sleeps. It's three in the morning, and I'm finding it hard to keep my eyes open. But I know if I press my face into his pillow I might get a whiff of him. That's sure to wake me up. As I inhale, I realise I'm right. I get his delicious scent teasing my nostrils.

'What you doing up here?'

I turn round, mid sniff, to find Heath has climbed the steps and his brown eyes are staring at me questionably. Oops.

'Err...just...so tired,' I say, faking a yawn. How cringe.

'Yeah, me too. Move over, you lightweight.'

I budge over, lying on my side so that I can face him. He's changed from his jeans and shirt into his boxers and a t-shirt. God, his legs are all muscley and hairy. All that football is paying off.

'I'm not even that drunk,' I say with a smile. I let out a giggle. Damn it, way to sound sober.

'Yeah, okay,' he grins with an eye roll. It's nice up here, the chatter of the others falling into the background. 'So anyway, does Zach know where you live now?'

Wow, change of subject or what.

'No. Although I'm sure the chatty Amelia will have

probably filled him in by now. I still have no idea how she even found out. She must have followed me home or something.'

'Do you think he'll dump you when he realises you're poor?' He smiles and someone that hadn't known him all his life would probably think he's joking, but not me. I can see that there's a lot of truth behind the question. His eyes probe intensely into mine.

'You mean because he lives in a massive house? You just assume he's a heartless arsehole?'

'No,' he says, slightly offended. I raise my eyebrows, challenging him. 'Okay, a little bit.'

I look over his shoulder as I consider it.

'To be honest, I really don't know how he's going to react. The truth is that I don't know him that well. I suppose I've been so desperate to get serious enough with a boyfriend to have sex with him, that I haven't really stopped to get to know him much at all.'

Shit, I *am* drunk. Why am I confessing all this shit to him? And Heath of all bloody people!

'Shit, Sav,' he whispers in disbelief. 'I didn't realise you were trying to get rid of it that quickly. Please tell me you haven't had sex yet?'

I look away from his scrutinising stare.

'Not yet,' I admit on a whisper, an involuntary shiver dancing down my spine. How is it just a look from him can have me feeling hot and bothered?

He takes hold of my chin and forces me to look at him again. His eyes bore into mine, so much unsaid.

'I'm glad,' he admits on a whisper. He seems embarrassed like he's just admitted to something excruciating. 'You shouldn't rush. It should be special.' He licks his lips, drawing my attention to how beautiful and plump they are. 'It should be with someone who knows you inside and out.'

Does he mean him? My chest is suddenly rising and falling so quickly and loudly I'm scared he'll notice. Only...well now I look, his is going pretty fast too. I can't stop looking between his lips, and his eyes.

He moves his face a fraction towards me. It's such a small movement I wonder if I've imagined it. I swallow, my mouth suddenly dry. I really, really want to lean forward too, but I'm scared. What if I'm imagining it all? And what about my boyfriend back home? Have I completely lost my mind as soon as I've had a bit of vodka?

But...oh God, I want to lean in so badly it's like I can

feel my body pulled towards him like a magnetic force.

'What are you guys doing up here?'

I jump so fully that I actually feel myself leave the bed. I turn, my heart in my throat to see Tyler grinning up at us innocently. Then he burps and falls about laughing.

Well, that's a moment truly ruined. I can't even bear to turn back and look at Heath to see his reaction.

'Nothing much,' I say as brightly as I can, shifting to the end of the bed and climbing down the ladder.

'I'm tired, guys,' I say to everyone. 'I'm gonna head to bed.' Where I'll replay this whole scene in my head over and over wondering what might have happened.

'Us too,' Erin smiles sleepily. 'Let's go.'

'Night,' I call to everyone.

'Night,' they call back. I look up to the top bunk, and there's no movement. No movement at all.

We're just in the corridor when I hear the teachers.

'Shit, they're coming back,' Zahra says, her eyes wide with panic.

'Quick!' Erin screams, grabbing my arm. 'We have to get back before they see us. They'll kill us for being out of our rooms at this time.'

We run up the long corridor, all the time hearing their

345

jovial voices getting closer and closer. We round the corner to our room.

'Who has the key?' Kate asks, already rocking back and forth with panic.

They all turn to look at me. 'What?'

'Sav, you had the key,' Erin snaps. 'Where the fuck is it?'

Shit, did I?

I search my bag, but it's not in there. 'I don't know. I think, maybe it must have fallen out of my bag in the boys' room.'

'For fuck's sake, Savannah!' Erin snaps.

The laughter from the teachers is coming closer by the second. They're going to murder us.

The door next to ours opens, and Rochelle Evans sticks her head out, her hair like a bird's nest.

'What's with all the noise?'

'Rochelle!' I turn and knock her out of the way. The girls follow me in, just as the teachers sound like they're rounding the corner. We slam the door behind us.

'What the hell is going on?' Rochelle asks, backing away from us like we're mad.

I grab her and wrap my hand around her mouth to

silence her. She struggles so I have to trap her arms down with my other arm wrapped round her.

We wait silently for them to pass and when we finally can't hear them anymore I release her.

'Really sorry about that,' I grimace. 'Kind of a long story.'

Chapter Twenty One

Friday 18th November

#DramaDramaEverywhere

The teachers have given the okay for us sixth formers to go to a club tonight. It's really close and not exactly huge so they've told us as long as we keep a low profile and take two teachers with us it should be fine.

Even with the legal age being fifteen I'm sure I'll still be refused entry. I look like a child compared to the others, but I'm still looking forward to it.

I try to get out of the taxi as confidently as I can, so as not to show that I'm nervous. I'm nervous about *everything* tonight. Not just trying to sneak into a club, which I'm sure that I will be refused entry of, but what if

Amelia is out tonight? What if I fall over in my heels? What if there is a crazed killer on the loose? There are so many possibilities. We don't even know this country.

I try to think rationally and take a deep breath to try and calm my jittery stomach. Most people say they get butterflies when they're nervous. I've always hated that expression. When I'm nervous, it feels more like I have ten puppies in my stomach, jumping up and down barking.

Dammit, I need a wee again. I've already been five times before we left. I'll soon be in the club and can go straight to the toilet then. Just calm down, Savannah.

The girls and I walk over towards the brightly lit up club. It looks more like a strip club than a regular club with its pink neon flashing sign.

I'm sure everyone on the small snowy high street is staring at us. They know we're under age and if they know, the bouncer will definitely know.

'Savannah, what did I tell you? Try and act mature,' Erin barks at me, the nerves clearly taking her over. She can get so snappy when she's worried.

'Alright, I'm only walking,' I snap. I know it's what she does, but sometimes it hurts when she overreacts, and I'm the punching bag.

'Just don't draw attention to yourself, okay?'

'Fine! I won't even breathe,' I growl, catching Charlotte's gaze and rolling my eyes.

'Hey, bitches,' Tyler says, grinning from ear to ear as he gets out from another taxi. 'Savannah, you've dressed like a girl again! You really are making a habit out of this aren't you?' he says sarcastically.

I glare at him in response. Zahra forced me to wear one of her bright pink bodycon dresses. I feel like I can't breathe without looking fat in it. It's so uncomfortable.

'Okay, so the plan?' Zahra says, looking at Erin.

'The plan,' Mr Rafferty interrupts, 'is for you all to stay out of trouble. We meet back here at midnight. If you're not here, we go without you.'

We all know he's serious. I'll be keeping a close eye on my watch. He nods and walks off towards the club.

'Right,' Erin says, gathering us all round in a circle, 'the plan is that Savannah is going to walk in with Charlotte and Tyler. The rest of us will go in ahead.'

'Sorry, but why are we going separately?' Charlotte asks, puzzled.

Zahra and Erin exchange cautious faces.

'Well, the thing is...well, to give us more chance of

getting in...'

'Basically, I look like a twelve-year-old,' I interrupt. They're so easy to read. 'So there's more chance of me getting in with big tits McGee and big burly Tyler, right?'

'Well...kind of,' Zahra admits with a grimace. 'I'm sorry. It's just that there's more chance of us getting in that way.'

I roll my eyes even though I know they're right. 'Don't worry. I'm not bothered. I just hope I don't stop Charlotte and Tyler getting in.' I look at them, already apologetic.

We join the queue. I smile nervously at the few other small groups from our school year. It'll be even more humiliating if everyone gets in apart from me. But I haven't seen Amelia yet—so silver linings and all that.

The line goes down quite quickly and so far, no one has been turned away.

The others go first—my stomach doing summersaults. The brawny man in the leather jacket waves them in quickly, barely giving them a second glance. This looks good. Kate turns round and smiles at me hopefully.

I walk up to the bouncer slowly, conscious not to fall over in the snow. His small beady eyes look us over from head to toe. Just my luck. He starts giving a shit when it's my turn.

I hold my breath, trying to look relaxed and confident. He waves us through. Wow. We're in!

The inside of the club is not as glamorous as I'd imagined. If anything I think it looks a bit grotty, but I can't really tell much from the dark. Just that it has peeling wallpaper and sticky carpet.

The smell of smoke is overpowering, invading my sensitive lungs. How can it when the smoking ban has been around for years? Do they not have it in Austria? I'll have to ask Erin. She knows this shit.

We head to the bar, chatting excitedly.

Heath places a drink in my hand before I've even had a chance to decide between vodka or wine. I sip the vodka, lime and soda, glad that he made the right choice for me.

That's the thing with Heath, he knows me so well. Probably better than I know myself.

I smile gratefully at him. It's the first time we've had any direct contact since last night. I've avoided him all day, totally humiliated.

Did I just imagine the whole thing? Maybe there are no feelings at all on his side.

Charlotte gives me a funny look, narrowing her eyes

and smiling. I look back at her puzzled.

'I swear Heath's suddenly into you,' she shouts into my ear over the music.

A big smile breaks across my face at the ridiculous thought. I quickly bite my tongue to stop it from showing.

'You're crazy,' I shout back, still smiling wildly. Why can't I stop smiling!

I look over at him and catch him staring at me. He quickly looks away, seeming embarrassed at being caught out. Is he? And why am I hoping that he is? I have a boyfriend.

When everyone has got their drinks, we head for the tacky flashing dance floor. I'm very aware of how close Heath is to me—as if I can feel the air shift every time he moves.

I smile to myself, watching him dance awkwardly. This really isn't his scene, and it isn't mine either. I'm glad to have someone else as anti-social as me.

A group of guys, who seem way too old to be with us, wander over and start dancing. The dark haired one tries to talk in my ear over the music. I can't hear a thing that he's saying, so spend the whole time with my hands in the air and forcing my face to look as puzzled as possible. He takes this to mean that he can start dancing with me.

Oh, well this is awkward. He wraps his arm around my waist and the dancing quickly turns into grinding. Ewww. He's sweating all over me.

I look around at the girls for support, but they all seem happy enough to be grinding up against their men, with Kate and Ryan kissing in the corner.

I look around for Tyler, thinking maybe I can pretend he's my boyfriend, but he's dancing with a random girl I don't recognise. Heath is the only one free.

I walk over to him, but the guy still follows me. I put my arm around Heath, and I pray that he'll catch on quickly. Thankfully Heath gets the message and kisses me on the cheek before hugging me tightly into his chest. God, it feels amazing, even if we are just pretending. And this close he smells *amazing*. All fresh, cool, and fruity.

'He's gone,' he shouts into my ear.

'Thanks.' Things quickly move back to being awkward. He removes his arm from around me, and I stand beside him, chugging my drink.

'I'm just going to the toilet,' I shout over the music, embarrassed by our close embrace only a second ago.

I go to the loo by myself. I need some time alone.

Living with this lot all day was great at first, but I'm starting to feel suffocated. It's hard having someone around watching you constantly. Especially when I feel so conflicted.

I waste some time washing my hands and spraying on some of the complimentary perfume. I'm starting to wish I'd never come tonight. This isn't my scene.

I know that the girls will want to stay here for hours and I can't exactly leave on my own, so I'm stuck here.

I sigh heavily and go out to face the mayhem. I walk out of the door into the dark corridor that separates the toilets from the main club, the music vibrating through the walls.

'Hey sexy,' an Austrian-accented voice says from behind me.

My head darts round to the unfamiliar voice. My body tenses when I realise it's the guy from the dance floor. He walks quickly over to me, a big grin on his face, as I consider my options.

Can I tell him to leave me alone and run? No, that would be rude. Before I can even think about running for it, he pushes me up against the wall, pushing his lips against mine and attempting to stick his tongue down my throat.

I try to push him off, repulsed by his Jack Daniel's breath.

'Woah, I have a boyfriend,' I say as his kisses move down my neck.

I assumed this would stop him immediately.

'I won't tell. I know you're a bad girl.' He crushes his lips against mine again.

Shit. This guy's a nutter. I try to push him off, but fuck, he's strong. It takes all my body strength to get his lips off mine.

'No!' I attempt to shout. It comes out more like a whimper, terror pulsing through my veins.

He takes this to mean that I want him. Of course he does, he's fucking insane. He puts his hand up my dress, grabbing my bum with his sweaty hands. Oh my god. Please tell me this is not happening.

Fear and adrenaline surge through me, suddenly giving me the strength to scream.

'GET OFF ME!' I scream at the top of my lungs, hitting my hands as hard as I can against his chest and face. My nail catches his face, scratching it. He winces, releasing a hand to hold it. I'm glad I hurt him.

I take this split second to try and run for it, but it's as if I'm moving in slow motion, my limbs heavy. Am I in shock?

He grabs hold of my wrists, throwing my body against the wall, hitting my head hard. I wince from the pain. It makes me weak for a moment, clouding my vision. He's at my knickers now, trying to pull them down.

How is this happening??

I scream at the top of my lungs, not quite believing that no one is around to witness this. Does no one need a piss in this club? How can this be happening?

I try to knee him in the balls, but the position he has me in means I can't. He begins undoing his jeans. My eyes cloud with the hysterical tears streaming down my face. He's going to rape me, and there's nothing I can do about it.

'Please, I'm a virgin,' I whimper. I close my eyes, not wanting to see his face anymore.

He doesn't stop. This is horrendous.

His body weight is suddenly off me. I open my eyes to see that he's no longer even in front of me. I look down to see Heath on top of him, punching him on the floor, so ferociously that I worry he'll kill him.

The guy seems so shocked by his attack that he isn't even really fighting back, just trying to defend himself. He's twice the size of Heath, but Heath's like a tiny Rottweiler, not stopping until he's torn off flesh.

I want to scream for him to stop before he kills him, but no sound will come out of my mouth. I'm frozen, my body trembling so hard I have to focus to breathe. I just watch, feeling helpless and responsible.

The doors fly open, and two bouncers come running in. About bloody time. The bouncer tries to pull Heath off him, but he isn't planning on letting go. It eventually takes both the bouncers to drag Heath off and restrain him against the wall.

I look towards the floor at the damage Heath has done to my attacker. His nose is bleeding heavily, spilling into his mouth and his entire head is red and already beginning to swell. His eyes are almost closed. Is it wrong that I regret Heath didn't get a chance to kill him?

'He started it. He attacked her!' Heath screams, pointing at me.

The bouncer looks at my tear stained face, as I pull up my knickers, which are almost down to my ankles. I've never felt so ashamed in all of my life. He nods, releasing

Heath. They pick the bastard up from the floor roughly and drag him off on his unsteady legs.

'Don't worry. We'll look after him,' the darker bouncer says menacingly. I don't care what they do to him. I'm just glad he's being taken away from me.

Heath watches him go before turning towards me, still seeming furious.

'Are you okay?' he asks, still panting from the fight.

'Yeah.... I suppose.' I try to make my voice sound even, but the tone of it's all over the place. I still can't believe that happened. If it wasn't for Heath coming to look for me...well, I shudder to think what could have happened.

'That fucking arsehole! He screams, punching the wall. 'Ah, fuck! My hand!' he says, wincing from the pain and clutching it close to him.

I've never seen him so angry in all of my life, and it scares me rather than reassures. His nostrils are flaring, and a vein is popping out of his neck.

'That's why I was worried when you were dancing with him. It leads guys like that on.' He pulls me into his chest. I notice he's also shaking heavily.

'Sorry?' I ask confused, pulling myself away from him.

'Are you saying that I led him on? That this is my fault?'

Is he serious?

He frowns, grounding his jaw. 'No, but guys like that take any small sign as a yes and – '

'What? So it's okay to *rape* me?' I scream, escaping from his arms, which he's still trying to wrap around me.

'No. I didn't mean it like that,' he shouts back. Frustrated, he starts to scowl, attempting to clutch at my hands.

'Well, what the fuck *did* you mean then?' I shrill back, shocking myself at how loud my voice pitch reaches. Who knew it could even go that loud?

'I didn't mean that!' he sighs. 'Will you just listen and stop being a stubborn little bitch!' he snaps furiously, his eyes wide with anger and his lips curling back with rage.

I cannot believe what a dick he's being. Stubborn little bitch? Where the hell has this come from?

'What is your fucking problem, you twat?' I wail, so upset now that my voice breaks slightly at the end of it. I try to blink back the tears, not wanting him to see me any weaker than I am now. Two minutes ago I wouldn't have said it was possible.

'I'm sorry!' he shouts, a little louder than I think he

meant to. He attempts to take a deep breath, but I can tell from the strange expression on his face that he's still hostile, furious.

'No, you're not.' Tears are falling down my cheeks again, but now for a very different reason.

How can he be treating me like this when I just almost got raped? Doesn't he think I need comfort and reassurance now? Not to be shouted at and blamed.

He grabs my jaw aggressively, and for a second I think he's going to throw me against the wall, like my attacker. I close my eyes protectively, expecting the thud of the wall behind me. I'm shocked beyond words when I feel his lips kiss me roughly. I freeze, my eyes widening to check I'm not imagining this. I look again. What the hell is he doing?

I push him off, furious that he's put me in this position.

'What the fuck are you doing?' I ask, totally confused and teary.

'I'm sorry,' he says, all aggression gone. He looks at the floor, seemingly mortified.

'I don't get it. One minute you're screaming at me, and the next you're trying to kiss me? I have a boyfriend, remember.'

The thought of Zach finding out makes me feel sick. He's been nothing but good to me, and here I've been fantasising about my best friend. Who, I now realise is insane.

'How could I forget,' he snaps sarcastically, a blank, scary expression on his face.

He reaches for my handbag, which has been thrown across the hallway in the struggle and picks up a few things, which have escaped onto the floor. Thankfully nothing embarrassing like tampons.

I'm still reeling, my heart hammering against my ribcage.

He gives me a hard look before storming away. I run after him, more from fear of being left alone. He turns as if he's remembered me and grabs my arm. He drags me through the club, squeezing my arm so hard it hurts.

When he stops by the group, I shrug his arm off roughly and hit him in the chest as hard as I can. He doesn't even seem to wince. I hate him so much I think I might burst into flames of rage, but instead, I just seem to cry harder.

Heath seems to signal to the others that something bad has happened and we have to leave, but it's hard to make out in the dark with the flashing lights. Concerned faces greet me, but I can't look anyone in the eye. Not yet. The girl's arms wrap around me, guiding me out onto the street within minutes.

'Are you okay, hun?' Kate asks, her forehead puckered.

'Yeah, I'm fine,' I nod, feeling the exact opposite. I wipe away the tears with the back of my hand.

I look over at Heath who's chatting and laughing as if nothing has happened. How can he act like this? I have no idea who this person is right now.

'What happened?' Zahra asks, putting her hand on my shoulder.

'Nothing,' I snap, shrugging it off. I'm trying so hard to forget it I couldn't bear repeat it out loud. It would make it a lot more real. 'I'm just homesick.'

The girls exchange perplexed expressions. We find some benches where we've agreed to meet the teachers.

'Are you sure you're okay?' Erin whispers. The look on her face tells me she already knows the answer.

I just nod, exhausted from all of the drama. I just want tonight over so I can forget about it.

Tyler sits down next to me and instinctively wraps his

363

arm around me. He must know I need the comfort. I relax back into his chest and appreciate that he isn't joining in with all of the questions.

My breathing starts to ease back to a regular pattern as his familiar Jean Paul Gautier aftershave soothes me.

I remind myself that I'm safe with him. I calm so much that I almost fall asleep, but I'm jolted awake when I hear some commotion.

'Woooooo!' Zahra and Ryan yell.

I look up and follow their gaze to see what's so funny. Charlotte's getting off with someone. I smile, pleased that she's found someone, but confused as to who it could be.

They turn slightly, and I crane my neck eagerly to see if I recognise him. Maybe someone in our year.

My stomach drops when I see that it's Heath.

I do a double take, sure that I must be mistaken, but it's clear to see. They have their hands all over each other. I react as if I've been punched in the stomach. I feel winded, and nausea creeps from my stomach up my throat until it feels like someone is strangling me.

Wasn't this the same Charlotte that only tonight told me she thought that Heath was into me? Some friend she is. I know I do have a boyfriend and have no right to feel any of these emotions, but it doesn't stop me feeling them.

Maybe I'm just possessive of him, the years of friendship making me feel like I own him. Something tells me that Charlotte did know, probably better than the others, that there was something between Heath and me. Something that no one, including myself, can understand right now, but enough for her to know not to get off with him in front of me. I feel so betrayed.

They finish kissing, each looking up smiling, embarrassed from the attention. Heath catches my eye, and for a split second, I swear he glares at me vindictively. Is he doing this just to piss me off?

The ride home is pretty intense. Charlotte has the cheek to get in my taxi when it pulls up. I can't even bear to look at her. It must be quite clear as once we get back, Erin corners me away from the others.

'Well, what happened tonight then?'

'What do you mean?' I ask vaguely, staring out of the window.

'Something must have happened with Charlotte. You could cut the atmosphere with a knife.'

I try to ignore the question.

'She just did something out of character, that's all,' I

shrug, attempting to look unbothered.

'You mean getting off with Heath?'

Dammit, she's good. I forget she's known me since primary school.

'Whatever,' I shrug. 'It's nothing to do with me.'

She stares at me knowingly, studying my face. 'You don't have to suffer in silence you know. I know how confused you are at the moment and it's nothing to be ashamed of.'

My mouth falls open. Does she really know what this is about? Does she know I have feelings for Heath? I don't even know about my feelings right now so how can she?

'Isn't it?' I ask just in case, recoiling from the mere thought of the situation.

'No, it's not.' She shakes her head. 'We're only seventeen. We're not supposed to have it all figured out right now. Come on, everything always looks better in the morning.

Chapter Twenty Two

#BusWankers

The next morning, I do feel better. I was completely overreacting last night. Charlotte was well within her rights to get off with anyone she liked, and I shouldn't care about it. I have a boyfriend. Any feelings I think I have for Heath are just something I worked up in my head because Charlotte put them there in the first place.

I've tried to act normally around the girls. It's hard when I've had to explain why I have bruises on my wrists from where my attacker restrained me. I came up with some lame excuse about me having a nightmare and doing it myself. To my surprise, they've let it drop. Maybe Heath's already told them.

Today we're travelling back home, and I cannot wait to get back to my shitty maisonette. The thought of being able to have a warm bath and not have to fight the girls for a shitty shower seems heaven right now. Especially when we're on this sweaty bus.

I've avoided Heath and Charlotte as much as I could and made sure Erin was sitting next to me on the bus. I also fought for the window seat, so I can stare out and try to ignore the others.

'I'm going to queue for the loo,' Erin says as she gets up, stretching her legs like an Olympic athlete.

I nod sadly. I was considering napping on her shoulder. Now I'll have to wait. I turn to look back out of the window when I feel her sit down again.

'Queue too long?' I ask, turning my head.

I nearly jump in shock when I see it's Charlotte. Shit. What's she doing sitting next to me?

I tuck my hair behind my ear—conscious she has her eyes on me. She smiles at me apprehensively. I try to remind myself that I have nothing to be embarrassed about, but I can't seem to relax my body. I start fidgeting.

'Hey,' she says, smiling weakly.

'Hi,' I say coldly back, avoiding her gaze and choosing

to look back out of the window.

'I'm so sorry about last night,' she whispers, low enough that no one else can hear.

'What do you mean?' I ask, trying to play it cool. I don't want to give her the satisfaction of being upset.

'About Heath and me. I'm sorry. I don't know what came over me—I don't even like him. I just...'

'What?' I snap, interrupting her, a sudden irrational anger overtaking me. 'You just thought fuck it, why not? So what if I told Savannah earlier, he was into her. It's only her feelings.'

'That's not it at all.' She grimaces. 'I was drunk, and my stupid idea was that I'd make you jealous. Jealous enough to react and confront your own feelings for him.'

'I don't have any feelings for him!' I growl. 'When are you going to get that into your head?'

'Then why are you upset?' she challenges with raised eyebrows.

She's got me there. I sigh heavily. 'You can do what you want.'

'I've already talked to him, and we've agreed that it was a silly one-off. He seems more mortified than me. We're still friends.'

'Why are you telling me this? Why should I even be bothered?' I say feeling very bothered indeed.

Her eyes are wickedly amused. 'You don't have to lie to me. I know you're into him.'

'No, I'm not,' I say quickly and defensively. Too quickly in hindsight. 'I have a boyfriend remember.' I *have* to keep reminding myself of that. I try to picture his gorgeous face. His gorgeous, understanding face. It's probably just being away from him for a week. Out of sight, out of mind and all that.

'I'm very aware of your current situation,' she says leaning more into me so that no one has a chance to overhear. 'I'm probably more aware of it than you are.'

What the hell is she talking about? Why is she talking in riddles?

'What does that mean?' I shoot back.

'I'm just saying that whatever you decide, you don't have to worry about mine or the girls' reactions. We're with you whatever.' She takes my hand in hers and gives it a little squeeze.

All the girls know this? They can't do, can they? I sigh, frustrated, but then squeeze her hand gratefully.

'Thanks'. It does mean a lot to know they wouldn't

turn on me no matter what.

I look up to find Kate and Erin staring at both of us. They quickly look away. Was this whole conversation planned? Either way, I smile at the reassurance that they will love me no matter what. I know some people wait their whole lifetime for that kind of acceptance.

Sunday 20th November

We finally arrive home early Sunday morning. I'm barely home and running a bath when my phone goes. It's a text from Zach. Dread finds its way into my stomach. Uh-oh.

```
Hey, hope you had a great trip.  Can
you come round later? x
```

Does he actually know I'm poor and lied to him? I mean, maybe he really is still in the dark. Or maybe he's inviting me round to dump me. Either way, I should get to him as soon as possible. Get it all out of the way.

'Sure, what about around 6 pm tonight at yours? x'

His text back is almost immediate.

'Cool, see you then.'

That gives me almost a full day to bathe, nap, and start

to think of what the hell I'm going to say to him.

I have to admit that it's bloody good to see him when he opens the door. His blonde hair is messed up just how I like it, and his hazel eyes are warm. He's pleased to see me too from the big grin on his face. This can't be too bad.

'Hi,' I say shyly, fidgeting with the edge of my hooded cardigan.

He smiles endearingly as if he finds me adorable and grabs me, pulling me into him. His lips meet mine in the most romantic, patient kiss I've ever experienced. He pulls back, leaving me staring up at him in drunken wonder.

'I missed you,' he smiles. 'Come on.'

He helps me into his sitting room, and we start watching a random film on Netflix. He fusses over me and asks all about the trip. I give him an edited version. I can't help but like the attention. He *has* missed me. And still no mention of me being poor.

'So...' I say, clapping my hands together like a teacher. 'Have you...heard from Amelia while we've been away?'

He smiles sweetly, tucking a bit of hair behind my ear. 'You mean did she tell me that you don't live at the house you said you did?'

Shit. He *does* know.

I grimace. 'Err...yeah. I'm sorry for lying, but I was just mortified that I now live in Crapstone. Especially when I saw this mansion!'

He narrows his eyebrows, his eyes sad. 'Do you really think I'm that shallow?'

'No. It's not that. It was more my hang up. I'm sorry.'

He shakes his head. 'Well, I know now. And I couldn't care less.'

He places a soft kiss on my lips. God, how did I end up with this guy again?

I hear his mum come in and walk towards the kitchen. I really need to speak to her about the whole Boots fiasco. Let her know I'm not a slut.

'I'm just going to ask your mum for something,' I say, getting up.

'Oh, okay,' he nods, a strange look on his face. He seems pleased that I'm making an effort with her. If only he knew the truth.

I walk nervously into the kitchen. I forgot how big the house was and only realise as it takes me ages to get around.

She's standing by the sink waiting for me. She

obviously heard me approaching and is ready to see what I want.

I take a deep breath and smile at her.

'Hiya, I just came in to get a drink,' I lie.

'Help yourself,' she says, still seeming no friendlier. She smiles wearily.

'Well, anyway, I actually wanted to explain something to you.' I try to brace myself.

'Yes?' she asks, a knowing face staring back at me.

'That day when you saw me in Boots with my friend. Well, what I said...it was just a joke. It wasn't really for me. I was just being stupid and messing around.' I look up from the floor to see her reaction.

'I know,' she says with that knowing smile again.

'You know? How?' I ask, staring at her aghast.

'Well, for starters, you put on a common accent, and you sound completely different. That and Zach told me you were a virgin,' she adds casually as if she'd just asked me if I wanted a cup of tea.

'Sorry?' is all I blurt out.

He told her I was a virgin? How could he do that? I haven't even told him I'm a virgin. Is it that obvious?

'He didn't mean to talk about you behind your back,

but I voiced my concerns that you might be leading him astray. He explained there was nothing to worry about as you were still a virgin.'

'Yes, but...I haven't even told him that yet. How could he know?' I wish I could stop myself from talking. This is getting more humiliating by the second.

'I don't know,' she shrugs. 'I assumed that you had told him. He must just know. Either way, I approve. You seem like a nice enough girl.'

Nice *'enough'* girl. I wonder if she's Team Amelia.

'Thanks,' I smile, but I'm already worrying.

Yeah, it's good his mum likes me now, but everyone knows I'm a big fat virgin. I might as well be walking around with a big virgin sandwich board.

I walk back into his sitting room and look at his gorgeous face. How can he be both so understanding and gorgeous? I thought you had to choose between one and the other. He's been so patient with me, not rushing me into anything. Meanwhile, I'm over here having stupid fantasies about Heath. I don't deserve him.

'Zach, I'm going out,' his Mum calls from the hallway.

This is my chance. I'm going to have to be bold and his Mum leaving is a bloody sign.

'Can I see your bedroom?' I ask shyly, twirling my hooded cardigan around my fingers.

His eyes almost bulge out of their sockets. He quickly recovers himself with a confident smile.

'Yeah, course.'

I'll show him who the big fat virgin is. I'll prove to him I'm not a baby.

I follow him up the stairs, steadying myself on the bannister. This is it. My first sexual encounter. I shouldn't be nervous. He's great. The best thing to ever happen to me.

I walk into his bedroom, my mouth falling open in shock from the size of it. It's decorated in black and white with a massive telly, and a wall, which seems full of all the games consoles in the world. When I peer further inside, I see he has his own walk-in wardrobe and en-suite bathroom. His bedroom is bigger than my whole maisonette.

I sit down next to him on the bed, suddenly at war with myself. My heart is thundering, and I feel a bit dizzy. Where's the brave bitch from a minute ago? Pull yourself together. You can do this.

He leans in and kisses me. I hungrily kiss him back.

This is what I've needed. I've needed to see and feel him, remind myself I'm lucky enough to be with.

I lean back onto his bed, indicating for him to come with me. He does, pressing his strong chest against me. My pulse quickens. I push off my hooded cardigan. He takes this as encouragement, reaching up underneath my top and unhooking my bra. Shit. This is getting real quickly.

How's he going to react when he feels my boobs and realises that they're not as big as my padded bra would have him believe. That they're not much at all.

He slips his other hand underneath my jean zipper and starts to tug it down slowly. He breaks his lips from mine while he unbuttons it and tries to yank them down. I take the break to take a discreet deep breath. My stomach is churning from fretfulness.

I raise my hips so that he can pull them down to my knees. He takes my sneaker-clad feet and quickly throws them off so he can remove the jeans fully. I'm left in just my socks and top. Sexy. Not.

He kisses my neck tenderly, his fingers trailing over my knickers. Thank god I wore silky black ones today and not big white granny pants. His finger hooks into the side of my knickers. My breath halts in anticipation. He's going to see my vagina. This is a big fucking deal. He yanks them down without any hesitation.

A wave of nervousness washes over me. I wince my eyes shut. He's looking at my vagina. Gah! This is mortifying! Try to remain calm. Don't be a big fat baby.

He grasps hold of my boob at the same time as his fingers prod at my folds. That's what it feels like—like he's just prodding me. Is it supposed to feel like this?

'Just relax,' he whispers into my ear.

Yeah, like it's just that easy. I take another deep breath. You can do this, Savannah. Just get it over and done with.

He tries again, a bit more forcefully and I wince from the pain. Uneasy pain. He stops kissing me, and I realise it's because I'm openly grimacing. Sexy. *Real* sexy.

'Sorry, am I hurting you?' he asks, trying to study my face.

'A little bit,' I admit, my cheeks on fire. Turns out I am a big fat virgin.

He sits upright. 'Look, don't worry about it. We don't have to do this now. I can tell you're nervous, and we've only been together a few weeks. It's no big deal,' he says reassuringly, brushing a bit of hair behind my ear.

'Are you sure?' I ask, hating myself. 'I feel so pathetic.'

'I'm sure. It's only normal for your first time to be a worry.'

'Okay.' I bend down to grab my knickers and frantically try to put them on. 'Plus...I need to tell you something.'

'What?' he asks with a smile. He pulls me close and turns on the TV.

How can he make me feel so good when I'm still acting like a five-year-old? He seems so much more mature and experienced than I am. It makes me uneasy.

His body tenses for a second. 'It's not because...no, don't worry,' he says out of nowhere.

'No, what? Ask me, it's fine,' I say, wanting to know why he's had a sudden change of mood.

'Well...it's nothing to do with you not being into me, is it? You're not interested in someone else are you?'

I straighten myself up and turn to look at him properly.

'What?' I ask, totally confused and hurt. 'Of course not. Why would you say that?'

More importantly what the hell has he heard?

'It's just that someone told me you and your friend

Tyler are really close, and some people didn't know whether you got together sometimes.' His eyes scrunch up as he looks at me insecurely.

There's only one person who would have told him that. Amelia, of course. How often is he bloody talking to her? Anger rises in my throat. I give him a hard look.

'And by *someone*, you mean your bitch ex, Amelia, don't you?' I snarl accusingly.

He's silent. He doesn't need to answer. I already know the truth. That bitch is filling his head with poison, turning him against me.

'I'm sorry. It's just that she told me that, and then I see you having a piggy back from him, and I got a bit insecure. Can you forgive me?' he asks, giving me his puppy dog eyes.

I try to swallow my fury towards her and remember that I'm looking at him. I get swallowed up by his big hazel eyes and nod.

'As long as you don't believe anything else she says,' I warn.

'Of course,' he agrees, pulling me in for another gentle kiss.

But I have a bad feeling that this isn't going to be the

last I hear of Amelia.

Chapter Twenty Three

DYLAN'S BLOG - BACK AT NOOSA

So we got a place to live here for now. We now live in a little suburban road with views of the beach. The street is a weird mix of tiny bungalows and massive luxury homes. We are living in one of the tiny bungalows with a hippy lady. I mean proper hippy. I mean her job is selling handmade shoes and jackets out of second-hand sheets. A hippy. Like all hippies here she thinks that supermarkets are a conspiracy to make us all look the same, but still drives EVERYWHERE in her battered old campervan that takes loads of petrol. She has a gorgeous little staffy which we are helping her look after.

The only problem is that it is now getting really hot here. So all the crazy bugs are starting to come out. We have found (in the house) a huntsman spider (literally the size of my hand) and something that looked like a massive cockroach, but then it started flying. We are trying to find ways of killing all the bugs without insulting the hippy that owns the house.

I was still working in the curry house (this time in the guy's restaurant) as a kitchen hand. One day, one of the waitresses called in sick, and he asked me if I could cover. I have done this sort of stuff before in the pub, but kinda sucked at it. It's been a while though, and it turns out, I fucking rule at waiting. It was a bit like going back to school with the level of confidence that you have now. Since he has given me as many days on the floor waiting as he can. I am now working six nights a week.

Yesterday, to celebrating my new shifts I decided to spoil Adrianna for the day. We went to the cinema, which only showed old films. It is an awesome cinema, one of the really small but nice ones with only about 30 seats per screen. Then we went to a bar for a few hours and then got a pizza on the way home.

BTW, RED is AMAZING!!! It is such a fun film. It portrays everything that comics are. Fun, stupid, and clever with awesome characters. It's like somewhere between Kickass and Taken.

Saturday 26th November
#MrandMrsBanks

'Ready?' Tyler asks, grabbing my hand.

I think he's more nervous than me and is using me as an excuse for some reassurance. No one could be more nervous than me. I've managed to avoid seeing Heath this week at school, which is some feat. I can only imagine he's avoiding me too.

'Yeah, let's go for it.'

We both take a deep breath and walk into the imposing hotel. The reception area is just as grand as I'd imagined. It's all marble and dark mahogany wood. There's a posh looking woman behind the counter who stares at us the moment we arrive. Obviously wondering why such riff-raff think it's okay to approach her hotel. We walk over, her staring so intently it makes the walk feel longer.

'You must be here for the wedding reception,' she says, her chin high in the air.

A bit presumptuous. We could be rich for all she knows. We are looking amazing tonight. Tyler has on a black suit, which looks more Armani than Asda, (even though it is) and I have on a short, cream chiffon dress. It's just the right amount of sexy while at the same time managing to remain elegant. It took Erin and me three hours walking around the shopping centre before we found it.

'No, actually,' Tyler says coolly. I quickly dread what he's going to say. 'We're actually here to get a room. You hire them by the hour right?' He wraps his arm around me and gives me a little squeeze and a wink.

I laugh loudly to myself, mortified. He's such a baboon. I quickly shrug his arm off.

'Yes, we're here for the reception,' I say, ignoring him.

I'm a bit scared of this woman. She's now looking at us like she might call security to get us escorted off the premises.

'Great,' she says insincerely. 'Walk down this

corridor, and it's the first door on the right.'

'Ok, thanks.' I usher Tyler away before he can make more of a fool of us.

'Have a great night,' she says smugly. God, I really hate her.

We walk down the long corridor and find the door. Tyler clasps my hand again and takes a deep breath. Then he opens the door for me, and we walk in.

Wow. It's amazing. The big hall is covered in fairy lights and has deep purple ribbons entwined into them. Most people are up already, dancing to the Beatles tribute band that's playing on stage. Men dressed in suits are walking around handing out glasses of Champagne. It's everything I'd imagined for my own wedding. Not that I've thought about it. Much.

I spot the bride, looking stunning in her tight, white fishtail dress. Then I spot the bride's son. Heath looks gorgeous. He sees us both and walks over. He's obviously already started to let his hair down, as his jacket is off and his cravat pulled down, with his top button open.

'Hey, guys,' he says when he gets to us. 'Thank god you've arrived. I was starting to worry. And my Auntie Sylvie was just starting to bore me with how many times my uncle's been sick this year.'

'No worries,' I say with a shy smile. I stare around the room in awe. 'The place looks amazing.'

'You don't look so bad yourself,' he says with a cheeky grin.

I actually feel myself blush at the compliment. He must be quite tipsy if he's throwing compliments around.

'Yeah, I really can't believe how smart the three of us look. We need to make sure that we take loads of pictures tonight.'

The night goes fantastically. We all have a bit of a dance, with Tyler and Heath taking turns to spin me around the dance floor. We drink loads of free champagne, even though the bubbles go up my nose.

At about 11.30 pm we order a taxi back to Heath's house. His Mum and Stepdad are staying at the hotel tonight and then going straight to the airport tomorrow morning so we'll have the place to ourselves.

Once we get back, we relax and kick off our shoes. Heath brings some cold beers out from the kitchen, and we put on South Park. The beer tastes much better than the champagne.

I'm sat on the smaller couch, with Tyler on the larger

three-seater, so I'm surprised when Heath chooses to sit next to me. He puts his feet up next to mine on the poof so close we're almost touching.

We start chatting and laughing about the night's events. Heath's uncle got terribly drunk and threw up on the dance floor. His Auntie Sylvie had jumped up on the stage and tried to sing along to the Beatles songs and his new stepdad had flashed us from underneath his traditional kilt. I swear I will never look at him the same again. Let's just say, no wonder she wanted to seal the deal after all these years.

Tyler calls a taxi at around 12.30 am and offers to share it so that he can drop me home.

'Actually, I'm supposed to be going back to Zach's tonight,' I admit feeling a bit embarrassed. We'd agreed that I would stay over tonight what with the wedding and stuff. Mum will be too pissed to notice, and he's promised that we'll just cuddle up and sleep. I think it was his way of knowing I wasn't going home with Tyler. I know he says he's fine with him, but he's still a man and is obviously worried in case something might happen. Little does he know he's worrying about the wrong male friend.

'Oooh! Get you, you little minx!' Tyler says with a

chuckle.

Heath looks devastated, his big puppy dog eyes boring into mine, hurt radiating from them.

'Well, you can carry on to his after you drop me off,' Tyler says completely unaware of Heath's reaction. He even adds a yawn.

'Okay.' I'm pleased that I don't have to get a taxi on my own this late.

But I find myself staring at Heath's face in the dark. Every now and again the glare from the television hits his face, and I can make out his features clouded in sadness.

I try to do it when he's not looking, but always seem to get caught out. He really seems to be having a growth spurt at the moment. Every time I see him he seems a little bit taller, a little bit broader and his cheekbones seem more defined. Is it him changing, or me changing how I perceive him?

Tyler stands up and looks out of the window. 'Taxi's here.'

Why is it I don't want to leave anymore? It's like there's a magnetic force pulling and keeping me here.

'Why don't you stay over?' Heath asks out of nowhere.

He wants me to stay the night? Here? Alone with

him?

'I'm not sure,' I say stiffly, but I'm smiling back at him.

I already know I want to stay, but I'm supposed to be going round to my boyfriend's house, not staying here, drunk, with someone I also have feelings for.

'Come on. Why don't you just forget about Zach and stay here?' Heath says in the same whiny but encouraging voice he uses whenever he talks me into doing something. Like when I drank that Sambuca and ended up vomiting on his carpet.

I think about it for a moment. There should be no question in my mind. I should be gagging to get over to Zach's house. I shouldn't even be considering this. But I am. Something about the way he's looking at me stirs something inside me. His eyes are boring into mine, something like lust glowing from them.

I swallow the lump in my throat. I feel nervous, and I never normally feel nervous around him.

'Oh, okay,' I grin, giving in to him with a roll of my eyes.

Tyler says his goodbyes, none the wiser to the current atmosphere and is gone. I pull out my phone and text Zach.

`Hi, crashing at Heath's tonight. Will`

c u 2mo x.

I quickly turn my phone off afterwards in case he texts me back. I don't want a reply. I want to deal with the repercussions tomorrow and just live for tonight. Even if I know I'm being a horrible human being.

'Do you want to get changed into something more comfortable?' he asks, pointing towards the stairs.

All I can think about is how he wants to go upstairs with me. To his bedroom. I take a discreet deep breath, but smelling his mandarin scent instead drives me mad with lust.

'Yeah, that would be good.'

I follow him up the stairs and into his bedroom. There's a weird new tension in the air. I don't know why. I've been in his room hundreds of times before, but, this time, I have butterflies in my stomach and a sense of anticipation. My palms are even tingling.

It's like sexual tension; well, for me anyway. I know deep down in my heart that I have to stay tonight to try and figure out if Heath has feelings for me, and if I have feelings for him. Or if it's just a stupid idea that's been put into my head by Charlotte.

His eyes are gloriously intense. 'You can have the bed,

of course. I'll take the floor.' Even his voice is smouldering like never before.

'Okay, whatever.' I smile, a thrill going through me at just the idea of sleeping in his bed. If I admit it to myself, I want something to happen. Calm down, Savannah. Just see where things go. You big slut, your boyfriend is at home.

But the truth is that I'm forgetting all about Zach every time Heath sends me a shy smile.

'So...have you got something I can wear?' I ask suddenly feeling very overdressed for his bedroom.

'Oh yeah.' He shakes his head as if forcing himself to concentrate. He goes into his chest of drawers and throws me out one of his t-shirts. 'Don't worry, I'll turn around,' he adds cheekily.

He turns and so do I. Facing the bed, I slip off my dress. Thank god I'm wearing nice matching underwear. I pull on the t-shirt and wonder if he's caught a peep of me. When I turn round to face him, he's still looking the other way, but now he's only in his boxers and a t-shirt. We were probably both partly naked at the same time.

'Finished,' I announce a little breathless.

When he turns to face me, he looks a little red in the

face, kind of flushed. He avoids my gaze. I smile, wondering if he did sneak a peep. I'd like to think that my body could do that to someone, even if the reality is that he has just been getting changed too close to his radiator.

I lay on the bed, trying to pull the t-shirt down a little. It's still very short, just skimming the top of my thighs. Thankfully they're bronzed and shaved. I made sure they looked good for the wedding. I'm glad that they're the only bit of my body exposed, as they're my best assets. If it had been reversed and my itty-bitty titties were on show, I definitely know I wouldn't feel so confident.

'Why don't we watch some TV before we sleep?' I suggest, desperate for the night not to be prolonged. I pat the spare side of the bed to him, smiling as seductively as I can.

'You okay?' he asks, with a quizzical look. 'You got a stomach ache or something?'

Okay. So I obviously failed if I look gassy.

I shake my head quickly and look away, hoping he doesn't notice my cheeks pinking up.

I lie down so he has to climb over me to lie closest to the wall. He does it so slowly, deliberately not touching me. He's obviously also cautious of us being alone in a confined space. Something is definitely different in the air between us. Normally he'd have made some comment about my thunder thighs or called me fatty, but there are no jokes whatsoever. All that hangs in the air is the sexual tension between us.

He leans forward and turns the small TV on. A scary movie is on, some big-breasted girl running from the room screaming. A scary movie could be a good way to snuggle up close to him.

'Let's watch this,' I suggest quickly.

Not that I've ever been good with them, but I don't think I could manage to watch a romance with him right now. I might just implode. His eyes widen, but he just shrugs it off.

He lies back down next to me with his arm propping his head up. This leaves a perfect little nook by his armpit that I have visions of cuddling into. He smells *so* good. I shut my eyes and drink it in.

The film takes ages to build up to its next scary scene, but when it does, I freak the fuck out. It's seriously horrific with blood everywhere. I'm not following it completely, too aware of Heath's proximity, but there's a nutter in a mask with a chainsaw. I turn my face into his chest to escape the horror, and okay, get a better sniff of him. He responds by wrapping his free arm loosely around me. I lean into his embrace. Something inside me fires, setting my heart racing.

I move my legs closer towards his until our warm bodies are pressed together. I just can't help it. It's like my last shred of resistance is melting.

I look up at his perfect face. He's still watching the film, seemingly unaware of how I'm radiating towards him. If I were a dog, I'd be humping his leg. He turns his head, noticing me watching him. He frowns. Oh God, I'm making a fool of myself.

He swivels his head to face me properly. I say nothing. I just look into his eyes and see the same need in them that I expect I have in mine. Against my better judgement, I feel a shiver of excitement. His brow creases, but his eyes continue probing. There's no question of me looking away.

I pull my shaky hand up to his face and boldly stroke his cheekbone with my fingertips. I let them drift down his face delicately until they touch his lips. His eyes are still locked on mine. He's watching me look at his face as if I've seen it for the first time. I let one finger fall between his lips. He purses them together as if to kiss it.

I slowly move my head in closer to his—my eyes still locked on his. He unleashes the full, devastating power of his eyes on me as if trying to communicate to continue. My eyes fall to his lips. I edge my lips closer to his and close my eyes. His laboured breath is on mine, but nothing happens. Is this rejection? I open my eyes just in time to see his lips plunge onto mine.

Even though this is what I've wanted, it still shocks me—his lips electrifying my body with desire. He's just as passionate, his tongue caressing mine so delicately as if scared I'm going to break.

He wraps both of his arms around me, his hands creeping under my t-shirt to stroke my lower back. Then they move down to my hips. He pulls me further towards him until I can feel the beginnings of his erection. His pull is a little rough, but I enjoy it. I want him to stop treating me like a china doll and pull me harder towards him.

His hands drift up to my back again, searching for my bra strap. They awkwardly unhook it, one of his hands finding its way around to the front. My boob is slowly caressed, so softly that I let out a soft, wanton groan. His lips move into a smile, but I don't have time to be embarrassed. I'm too busy pushing my lips back to his hungrily.

My breath hitches as he reaches down and touches the edge of my knickers, teasing them away from my skin. Teasing me. I can't bear it so decide to take matters into my own hands. I reach down and pull them off myself. I want so badly for his hand to touch me where I'm throbbing. I'm weak with longing. Pure lust taking control of my body.

The tips of his fingers trace down my back. A shiver runs down my spine, making me arch with yearning. His hands slowly go round to the front, playing lazily with my folds. One finger plunges speedily into me. Unlike with Zach they glide through, not a problem. He's filling me with burning want. The more he moves that finger, the more I want it. I had no idea it could feel this good.

His lips move down to my neck, his kisses hungry. I absorb every touch, letting it warm my heart. He lifts up my t-shirt and kisses my stomach tenderly, causing a giggle to escape from my mouth. Then he moves down to my legs, parting them roughly, kissing the insides of my thighs. Jesus fucking Christ, this feels amazing! A small moan escapes my lips. The left thigh, then the right, getting higher and higher each time. I must be soaking wet by now.

My heart pounds in my ears, every nerve ending I possess on high alert. I can't take the teasing any longer. I need him. I grab hold of his t-shirt at the neck and pull him up to me. He smiles, his eyes locking with mine, mischief in them. He grabs hold of my face with both hands, pulling his lips onto mine, ferociously. I groan, shamelessly now. It's like I'm no longer in control of my body. It's taken over.

I grab hold of his boxer shorts and yank them down. I find his erection and grasp it with my hand, gasping at the size of it. Now I'm a bit scared. Intimidated by the size. Can that honestly fit inside me? He moans in my ear. I don't care. I need it.

I push my body up to his and cling tightly to his hair, moving my lips to his ear. I don't have any idea what I plan on saying. I just know that I need to say something.

'Please,' I moan in a desperate whisper.

He pulls back and looks at me seriously, his eyebrows narrowed.

'Are you sure?' he asks, testing the waters.

I just nod, completely entranced by him. He reaches up above me to his top drawer of the bedside cabinet, his t-shirt rising so I can appreciate his tight, bronzed stomach. He comes back down with a condom and a shy smile. It makes me want him even more.

He struggles to get it on quickly but still kisses me every spare, frantic second. I'm not worried if he's put it on properly. My mind isn't working now. It's pure animal senses guiding me towards this.

He pulls his lips off mine, and then his t-shirt is pulled off over his head. God, his body is beautiful. He's got muscles and angles in all the right places.

He places his lips against my ear. 'I'll try to be gentle,' he whispers tenderly.

I love him all the more for caring so much.

He enters me slowly. I brace slightly for the pain, for the undoubted scream of fear that I'm sure will ripple through the house. But nothing comes. It stings slightly, but the other feelings in my body are much stronger than that. Happiness, complete elated happiness. I can't get enough of him. I need him inside me to even start to satisfy my need for him.

'Are you okay?' he asks, his hands on the back of my neck, cradling my head.

I try to speak, but I can't. I nod instead.

He starts moving, relaxing into a bit of a rhythm that has me panting like one of the dogs from work. A heat like

I've never known before creeps over my body, rising up to my neck, pressure building around my ears. Oh my god, what the hell is this? Am I having a stroke? Bolts of lightning cascade through my body like electricity, making my body twitch of its own accord. Fuck!

I don't know what the fuck that was, but it was amazing. I look up to him, glowing from feeling so loved and contented.

He stills and finishes with a groan so loud I have to stop myself from giggling out loud. He slumps down beside me exhausted. For a second I feel naked. Obviously, I am, but I feel alone. Vulnerable. Like I've made a mistake, been used.

That doesn't last long as he soon pulls me into his embrace, his warm skin settling me. I can hear him catching his breath as I cling on to his chest. He moves my hair from my face and kisses me on my forehead. I've never felt so loved or cherished.

Sudden exhaustion consumes me until I'm completely and utterly bone tired. I close my eyes and fall into a heavy, blissful sleep.

Chapter Twenty Four

Sunday 27th November

#RealitysaBitch

When I wake in the morning, the first thing I see is the condom wrapper on the floor. Wow, it wasn't a dream. It was real. I stretch my aching muscles, a huge smile on my face. I turn round in the bed to face him sleeping peacefully. I can't get over how beautiful he is.

Then the guilt comes crashing in. Shit, what the hell have I done? I've cheated on Zach. Lovely, gorgeous, Zach. Zach who I have been so obsessed with keeping. Now I've just thrown all of those feelings away, and every time I think of his gorgeous face I feel a stab of guilt in my stomach. Why did I do it?

But then I remember why. I look at Heath's face again and the memories of last night come flooding back. Feelings so strong they almost choke me rise in my body and the thought of ever having to leave this house fills me with dread. I need him. It isn't a question. I need him, not want him. I haven't done this to hurt Zach. Obviously, it isn't ideal, but as long as I tell Zach the truth quickly, it will be okay. I tell myself this is logical thinking, but I know that me escaping from this unscathed is highly unlikely. I deserve everything I get. I still can't regret it though.

It takes all my strength to get out of the bed and leave him, but I know I have to. I have to speak to Zach. I find my bag and get my phone out, walk into the hallway and call a cab, so as not to wake him. I go to the toilet for a wee and notice spots of blood in it. It stings slightly too. Well, that's my virginity well and truly gone.

I tiptoe back into the room and quickly get dressed. I'm just putting my shoes on when he wakes up. He squints his eyes and stretches out—all gorgeous shaggy bed hair. He looks good enough to eat. He leans up on his arms to look at me, still with his eyes barely opened.

'Where are you going?' he asks in a deep husky morning voice.

'I'm going to break up with Zach.'

This soon wakes him up. He clears his throat and jumps up to a sitting position, his hand raking through his hair.

'Are you sure that's a good idea? I mean, don't do it because of this.'

My jaw falls open. Is he fucking serious?

'What? Don't do it because of *this*? I suppose *this* was pretty insignificant really?' I jump up to standing. Anger and betrayal choking me, numbing me from the pain that I know will later crush my heart.

Right on cue, the taxi beeps outside.

'No, it's just that...well, you know...' He puts his hands through his hair again.

Yeah, I know. It meant nothing to him. Just sex. I'm such a fucking idiot.

'Maybe you just wanted to take my virginity. It's not a fucking prize! I thought you were better than that.'

I'm not ready to listen to him try and talk his way out of this. I'm out of that room like a shot, tears already starting to stream down my face. He isn't running after me though. He's just letting me go, and that hurts way more than it should.

403

I tell the cab driver Zach's address and start to think of what I'm going to say to him. Regardless of what happened just now, I still have to break up with him. I have to tell him the truth. He deserves that at the very least.

The cab pulls up to his house quicker than I'd have liked. I pay the driver and walk up to the door. I knock twice, swallowing down the bile rising in my throat. His Mum opens the door.

'Oh, hi, Mrs Scott,' I say taken aback. 'Is Zach in?'

She looks me up and down, clearly noticing that I'm still in last night's clothes. The walk of shame. That's what my mum calls it.

'Savannah?' Zach's voice says in the background. His face suddenly appears from inside. 'It *is* you.' His beautiful face lights up. 'I didn't know you were planning on coming over?'

'No, a change of plan.' I grimace at him, his mum still staring at me.

'Come on.' He grabs my hand and runs up the stairs to his bedroom. The minute he closes the door behind him, I burst into tears.

He rushes over to comfort me, but that just makes me feel more disgusted with myself. I have no right to be comforted. I'm a bitch. A cold hearted bitch.

'What's wrong?' He looks at me, a line appearing between his brows.

'I'm an awful person,' I admit through the sobs. 'I've done something awful. I'm horrendous.'

'Don't be silly.' He pulls me into his chest and squeezes me tight. That same comfortable feeling I always get with him takes over me, and for a second I wonder if I have to do this. Can I just forget that I ever got with Heath and live happily ever after with Zach? But I know the answer. I can't do it.

'What did you do that's so bad?' he asks, still holding me tight.

I have to tell him quickly. There's no other way to say it, but I know the moment I speak those words there's no going back.

'I slept with Heath,' I blurt out. Okay, so I should have definitely worded it better.

Zach is silent. I'm still in his embrace, but his grip on me loosens like I've knocked the stuffing out of him. The silence continues for a long time. Too long.

'Did you hear me?' I ask, quieter now. I'm scared of how he's going to react.

'Yes,' is all he says. He pulls me to sit next to him on the bed.

'Do you mean you slept in the same bed?' he asks innocently, his eyes confused.

Oh god, this is awful.

'No.' I look at the floor, wanting someone to stab me for being such a horrid person. I feel like I deserve physical pain for what I've done.

'So you had *sex* with him?' he asks, still eerily calm.

I nod, my throat burning with all the self-hatred I harbour.

He pushes himself back, clearly thinking. He's still for what seems like ages. Then he pulls himself together and leans more into me.

'I forgive you.'

'W-what?' I blurt out, my mouth agape in surprise. 'You forgive me? How can you possibly bloody forgive me?'

The guy must be having some sort of breakdown.

'I just do,' he nods. 'I've thought about it, and I understand that you were really drunk and it was a mistake. Heath took advantage of you. That's it. We can just try and forget about this and move on.' He says it so finally—like the decision had been made and that's the end of it.

'But...I can't carry on seeing you. Don't you see that?'

'Why not?' he asks with a shrug. 'The way I see it, you've been honest and told me the truth.'

How the hell can he be so understanding? I don't deserve this kind of treatment.

'No.' I pull myself back. I have to be straight with him. I could quite easily go back to pretending everything is the same, but it's not and never will be again. 'I can't go on acting like normal. Things have changed. It's changed everything.'

'No it hasn't, silly,' he says with a smile. 'I'm going to let Heath know that he overstepped the mark and he'll pay for it, don't worry.'

The thought of Heath being hurt over me makes me feel sick to my stomach.

'No!' I shout, a little too loud. 'It wasn't him; it was both of us. I wanted it too. Please don't hurt him. But I can't carry on seeing you, it's not fair.'

'Look, you're confused, okay? Look at you— you're still in last night's clothes. You're probably still drunk,' he reasons with a sympathetic smile.

I shake my head and look away.

'Can you honestly say you don't still have feelings for

me?'

He looks at me with his big hazel eyes. They still make me swoon. Is he right? Am I just confused? Has Heath just confused my mind? I mean, why am I so intent on breaking up with Zach anyway? Heath told me last night had meant nothing to him and I've told Zach the truth, and he still wants to be with me. Am I crazy?

'Well, no. I still have feelings for you, but not as strong as before. I'm...confused.'

'Let me remind you.' He grabs my face and kisses me on the lips. For a few seconds, I resist, and then I let myself melt into it. It feels so nice, like a warm blanket. Can't I just be happy with this? But I know the answer. It doesn't feel like it does with Heath, even if I never get to have that again.

I pull away and stand up. 'I'm so sorry, but I don't feel the same. Please don't hate me.'

I turn and walk out of the door before I can change my mind. I run down the stairs, ignoring his calls and the sound of his footsteps behind me. Why couldn't Heath have run after me like that?

I run out of the door and out onto his road. I slow to a walk when I realise he hasn't been behind me since I left the house.

Why is it that he can chase me down the stairs and want me so much when Heath, who I still so desperately crave, just let me go so easily. Have I made a mistake? I know I have, but that I've also done the right thing. I can't lie to myself and lead Zach on like this. He deserves a girlfriend that will love him. Even if it is crazy Amelia.

I walk down another street when my feet start to throb. Last night's dancing has finally caught up with me. I can feel blisters appearing. I remove my shoes and decide to walk in my bare feet. I hope no one I know sees me, but at the same time, I don't really care anymore. I mean, my life is in tatters, so what does it matter anyway? I call a taxi anyway, but they say it will take minimum twenty minutes. I could walk it in fifteen, and I feel safer on the move, rather than having to wait on a street corner.

By the time I finally turn onto my street all I want is my bed. I walk past each neighbour's house hoping that they aren't looking out of their windows. Not that any of these skanks can judge me.

I put the key in the door and open it to hear my mum chatting away about the wedding. How beautiful it was, etc., etc. She must be on the phone.

I walk in, planning to grab a chocolate bar from the fridge before bailing for bed. I halt in my tracks when I see him. Heath. Sitting at the kitchen table with mum, acting as if nothing has happened. He looks up and smiles at me apprehensively. Too bloody right he should be nervous. The spineless dickhead.

Mum opens her mouth to speak, but I cut her off.

'I'm going to bed.'

I see the shock in her face. I turn on my heel and head for my room. I can hear her apologising to Heath for me. 'I don't know what's come over her'.

Then I hear footsteps behind me. I know it's him following me, but I don't acknowledge him. I walk in silence and let the door of my bedroom slam in his face. He catches it just before it hits the latch and comes in. He still doesn't say anything, just shuffles on his feet, as if scared.

'What do you want?' I snarl, inspecting my black feet from walking barefoot.

'I came to say sorry.'

'Well you've said it so you can go now,' I snap coldly.

'Please let me explain.' His voice is still anxious.

I just roll my eyes.

'Well, if you're not even gonna listen...' he explodes

410

out of nowhere. 'God, you're so fucking stubborn sometimes.'

'No, I'm not! How dare you treat me this way!' I scream, distress entering my voice. 'You seduce me, take my virginity, then tell me it's no big deal, and I shouldn't break up with my boyfriend in the morning. Now you're here calling me stubborn. Why don't you just get a knife and stab me in the chest?' I realise that last bit is a *tad* dramatic.

'Jeez, always with the drama...'

I stiffen, ready to launch a verbal attack on him, but he puts his hands up in surrender.

'Look, you've got it all wrong. I did want you to break up with Zach, but I didn't want you to do it because of me. I wanted you to do it because you realised your feelings for him weren't strong enough and not just because you were filled with guilt. I was trying to give you a free card. I still am. If you want just to forget that this ever happened and live happily ever after with Zach, then that's fine. I won't stand in your way.'

Well. That's thrown me off.

'Really?' I sound pathetic. 'You do kind of...like me in that way?'

411

He laughs. 'Of course I do, you idiot.'

God, I hate him sometimes.

'I already broke up with Zach, anyway. I told him the truth. He still wanted me, but I told him I couldn't do it.' I'm speaking without emotion now. I'm so drained from this all. I just need to sleep.

'Oh.' A big smile breaks on his face. 'Well, I suppose I'm gonna get beaten up tomorrow then.'

I laugh, glad that the tension has been broken. 'Probably.' I sigh heavily. 'Look, I'm so tired I really can't think about anything right now. I need time, ok?'

'Yeah, course.' He walks over to me, and I think he's going to cuddle me, but instead he lifts me up and swings me over his shoulder. I go like a rag doll.

'Put me down, you friggin idiot!' I shout. He knows I hate being upside down. 'I'll vomit all over you'.

He flings me down on the bed. 'You say the sweetest things,' he retorts.

I'm so tired I can barely keep my eyes open. He lifts my arms over my head and pulls off my dress. I hope he isn't expecting anything like that to happen. But then he shoves my pyjama top on. He lies me down and pulls the covers over me, but not before he jumps in with me. He slips his trainers off and pulls me in close to him. He smells incredible.

I nestle my head next to his chest and close my eyes. He pulls my hair away from my face and strokes the top of my forehead. This feels so right. I let the feelings of contentment wash over me as I drift into a deep sleep, knowing I'm finally with the right person. My soul mate. My Heath.

THE END

Acknowledgements

First, thanks to you the reader for downloading my book. Especially my current fans who knew it was going to be a bit different to the usual. I love your faith in me!

Thanks first to my beta readers SJ, Natalie, Megan and Julie. I love your honesty!

Huge hugs to Claire at Bare Naked Words - you are my go to editor! You put such thought and care into your work that it makes it a pleasure to work with you.

Leigh Stone, you are my formatting wizard! I know I'm a pain in the arse with all my changes, but I get there in the end!

Yummy by Design - I'm so grateful to have finally found a designer who totally gets me and also works up until midnight! I feel safe knowing my vision is so easily shared with you.

To my PA's Kaprii and Lorraine, you girls are so organised and help me get my life together!

Last but not least thank you to my crazy family and friends. Without you guys I wouldn't have the love, confidence or hilarious stories I need to keep going. Love you!

Lightning Source UK Ltd.
Milton Keynes UK
UKOW05f0052271016
286262UK00001B/3/P